The Time Remaining

The
Time
Remaining

Samuel Hazo

SYRACUSE UNIVERSITY PRESS

ISBN: 978-0-8156-1009-0

Library of Congress Cataloging-in-Publication Data
Hazo, Samuel John.
  The time remaining / Samuel Hazo. — 1st ed.
    p. cm.
  ISBN 978-0-8156-1009-0 (pbk. : alk. paper) 1. Arab-Israeli conflict—1993-—Fiction.
2. International relations—Fiction. 3. Murder—Fiction. 4. Political fiction.
I. Title.
  PS3515.A9877T56 2012
  813'.54—dc23   2012025943

Manufactured in the United States of America

For Mary Selden Evans

Inexorable étrangeté! D'une vie mal défendue,
rouler jusqu'aux dés vifs du bonheur.

How inexorably strange! In this shaky life, to
throw even the quick dice of happiness.
—Rene Char

Injustice is a wound that never sleeps.
—Greek proverb

The author of more than thirty books of poetry, fiction, essays, and plays, **Samuel Hazo** is the founder and director of the International Poetry Forum in Pittsburgh, Pennsylvania. He is also McAnulty Distinguished Professor of English Emeritus at Duquesne University. From 1950 to 1957 he served in the United States Marine Corps, completing his tour as a captain. He was graduated magna cum laude from the University of Notre Dame and received his master's degree from Duquesne University and his doctorate from the University of Pittsburgh. Some of his most recent books are *Like a Man Gone Mad* (poetry), *This Part of the World* (fiction), *The Stroke of a Pen* (essays), and *Watching Fire, Watching Rain* (drama). He has also translated essays by Denis de Rougemont and the poems of Adonis and Nadia Tueni. His book *Just Once: New and Previous Poems* received the Maurice English Poetry Award in 2003. The University of Notre Dame, from which he received the Griffin Award for Creative Writing in 2005, awarded him his tenth of his eleven honorary doctorates in 2008. A National Book Award finalist, he was chosen the first State Poet of the Commonwealth of Pennsylvania by Governor Robert Casey in 1993, and he served until 2003.

The Time Remaining

ACCORDING TO THE POLICE REPORT, *a detective named Martin Cobb, based in the District of Columbia, was shot at the wheel of a Mercedes coupe while he was waiting for a red light to change one block south of Dupont Circle. The only witness to the incident (a tourist from Maine) reported that he saw a Washington taxi pull alongside the aforementioned Mercedes, then heard three shots fired from the passenger seat of the taxi at Cobb. The first shot, which struck Cobb just behind the left ear, was probably fatal. The following two shots, one in the left cheek and the other just above the left eyebrow, were fired as Cobb was slumping to his right from the force of the first shot.*

The account of the shooting on page 5 of the "Washington Post" with an accompanying photograph of Cobb's body on a covered stretcher beside the Mercedes indicated that Cobb was driving a vehicle owned by Dodge Didier Gilchrist, a journalist of some note not only in the capital but throughout the nation and abroad. Gilchrist, when contacted, stated that he and Cobb had been discussing an incident that received wide coverage only the day before and that Gilchrist had given Cobb the use of his car after their meeting. Gilchrist then added that the bullets were probably intended for him and not for Cobb. Gilchrist did not elaborate.

I

Ahead of Time

1

HE CALLS HER HOLLY. She turns toward him and says, "My name's Janet. How would you like it if I called you George or Harry and not Dodge?" She waits for him to answer and adds, "Just how would you like that, Mr. Dodge Gilchrist?" Dodge tells her it would make no difference. When he attempts to draw her closer to him, he sees her frown, twist away, sit stiffly up in the bed, and remain that way, waiting, waiting, waiting for what he knows she expects him to say. All he does is look at her, memorizing the outline of her body in the half-dark. He surprises himself by imagining how like a seal's body her body seems, how mammalian and rounded and—he fishes for the word—slippery. Why that word? He smiles, remembering all of a sudden Plato. For years he has neither thought about nor read a word by Plato, but now he is certain that it was Plato who taught him both as an undergraduate and as a graduate that beauty was a "smooth, slippery thing." Gilchrist wonders if Plato had a woman's body in mind. Possibly, he muses. But Van Gogh thought differently. Gilchrist recalls reading in one of Van Gogh's letters to his brother Theo—Gilchrist preferred autobiographical writings above all others, and he read voraciously in the genre whether the writer was an artist, a criminal, or a politician—that a seated female model, viewed from the rear, always reminded him of a wrestler relaxing on a stool between rounds. Now as Gilchrist looks at the woman he should have called Janet (what prompted him to call her Holly when he was not even thinking of Holly, had not, as a matter of fact, thought of her for months, years?), he sees what Van Gogh was writing about—the settling collapse of breast weight and hip spread around the compressed midsection. He is busy counting the three accordioning rings of skin there when Janet turns her head slightly to the left so that he can see both her pout and particularly her profile—her best feature. When this provokes nothing but further silence from him, she edges to the side of the bed and stands. After gathering her underclothes and dress from the chair beside the bed, she holds them over her breasts and loins with the willful modesty of an offended Venus and strides into the bathroom, locking the door willfully behind her. When she emerges a few moments later, she is fully though hurriedly dressed (the dress is not quite centered), and she makes a loud point of not looking directly at him. In that instant he sees her exactly as she is—a divorcée used to living alone in Washington, organizing herself to get away from him speedily now in the name of pride if nothing else in a soap-opera departure, thinking about tomorrow, always tomorrow, to avoid thinking about today or, worse yet, yesterday. He imagines her following the same ritual in exactly the same manner every morning just before she leaves for her job as a research director in her cubicle at the Smithsonian. Momentarily, she pauses, and he senses that she might be waiting for some footnote from him to set everything right again, to give her pride all the reason it needs for her to slip into bed beside him and resume where they left off. Gilchrist still says nothing. Whether she comes back or not does not concern him now. They have gotten what they wanted from one another, he concludes, so why worry about a denouement when the climax is behind them. His various lovers always seemed to prefer postclimactic conversations, while he was invariably more interested in eating a weighty sandwich or a chilled apple and then smoking a Jamaican cigar.

Janet gives Gilchrist one last, long stare before she opens the door of the apartment, steps into the empty hall, and pulls the door shut behind her. Instead of the slam and click that he expects to hear, Gilchrist hears only the softest of jointures. He tells himself that a slam would have been an indulgence, a way of telling him that he had mattered to her, a defeat at the final moment of the only victory she had left. A soft close was her way of trivializing him. Fair enough, he thinks. No victory either way.

Gilchrist lies on the mussed sheets a little longer. The echo of her Joe Morgan perfume is still on the pillow beside him, and when he lifts the sheet to stand, he can smell the musk of her body and the residue of—again he fishes for the phrase that he suddenly coins—her sex-sweat. It is this postcoital moment that he knows he will remember longer and more distinctly than what created it. He will remember how her body reacted next to his body, but that will blur and become intermingled with the memories of other Janets he has brought to this same bed. He will not particularly remember how he teased her breasts with his hands and lips or how he stroked her inner thighs until she almost seemed to be purring. Just then he knew that he could do whatever he wanted to with her, but he wanted only to finish what he started. He will remember less vividly the final cleaving and gripping and pushing that made him think, as it always succeeded in making him think, of nothing else but what was happening at that very moment, nor will he remember the spent and easy way their separating bodies returned to themselves exactly the same way that the world returns to actors and actresses after they've left the stage and started to remove their makeup. It is not guilt that he feels now, and it is certainly not shame. It's something close to fatigue-in-the-name-of-nothing. Or else it is like the boredom he has momentarily forgotten or been briefly distracted from, as sleep might distract him from unpleasantness or tragedy before the time of sleep ends and he awakens to find one or the other unchanged and waiting for him in the morning.

Gilchrist swings out of bed as a swimmer might leave a pool—no longer a creature of that element. He crosses naked to the glistening bedroom window and glimpses the tip of the Washington Monument, and he thinks, almost by reflex, of the obelisk in the center of the Place de la Concorde and of similar obelisks in Karnak or Luxor or in Muhammad Ali's palace in the middle of Cairo. He knows that this is nothing but a confirmation of how he's trained himself to think—concentrically rather than "ahead" so that he is always looking for multiples in the apparently unique. Below his balcony he can see his gray Mercedes coupe parked in its special slot like the sleekest of yachts moored at its assigned dock. Then he faces about and stands akimbo. He reminds himself, for the seventh time in a week, that the bookcase beside his bed needs a good weeding. The books are crammed vertically and sideways, and he knows that it is worse in his study where, in addition to book stacks and clutter on shelf and floor, his computer waits in complete obedience. It is waiting for the column he cannot seem to write. He feels the blankness of the screen summoning him to fill it so that it can be added to the collection of columns he has created on this same computer (a black laptop that he refuses to abandon) and subsequently saw syndicated (twice a week when the subject and his spirit were compatible if not exactly willing) in fifty-seven newspapers in the United States and Canada.

He walks into his study and tries to think of something to do so that he will not have to confront the computer. Standing with his back to his desk, Gilchrist presses the blinking message button on his phone. There is only one message. "I am Sharif Tabry's secretary. Mr. Tabry would like you to call him at your earliest. He said you have his number. Thank you."

Even though he and Sharif Tabry have remained good friends since their student days when they roomed together at Georgetown University, Gilchrist is mildly surprised by the call. Periodically, his work had brought him and Tabry into contact, but it had invariably been serendipitous. Usually, they met by accident in restaurants or while walking on Wisconsin Avenue or M Street on their way to or from someplace. At such times they brought one another up to date on themselves and then resumed living their separate lives until the next meeting. Professionally, they had little in common except the knowledge, or rather the certitude, yes, the deep certitude, that theirs was a friendship that would survive simply because it had. This was something beyond proof for each of them, but they were as convinced of the truth of it as they were of their very names and histories.

Gilchrist rarely discussed with Tabry his work as a professor of classical Greek at Georgetown, and Tabry never discussed with Gilchrist his career as a journalist except to write him a short congratulatory note when he wrote an outstanding column or received an award. Still, Gilchrist has always been intrigued by Tabry's political side. When the occupation of his country made it impossible for him to return there after graduation, Tabry, a Palestinian, went to Cambridge on a fellowship and returned subsequently to Georgetown to teach Homer, Euripides, Solon (his favorite), and those whom he called the "remaining masters." But he simultaneously founded a quarterly with funds he raised by himself from a variety of sources. The quarterly in time was recognized throughout the world as the most scholarly and significant journal of opposition to Israeli policies and attitudes vis-à-vis the Palestinians. Gilchrist learned that the international reputation of the journal as well as Tabry's editorship of it ranked it with *Foreign Affairs* and similar publications in the estimate of most serious students of world problems. Israeli officials took the journal quite seriously as a source of intellectual opposition, referring to Tabry himself as being "dangerously articulate."

For some reason Gilchrist discovers that he knows Tabry's telephone number by heart. It is as present to him as his Social Security number or even the rifle number he can recall at will from his Marine Corps days.

"Hello, Tab," says Gilchrist. "This is Gil. How are you? I just received a message that you called."

"Good, Gil, good. Thanks for calling back. I thought you might be abroad."

"Not abroad, Tab. Just with a *broad*. At the moment I'm standing buck naked beside my computer and waiting for my column to type itself."

"That's just a temporary blockage. All you need is a little inspiration."

"My inspiration walked out on me a half hour ago. And not in a very good mood, either." When Tabry makes no comment, Gilchrist knows that the time for amenities and repartee is over. "Well," Gilchrist says in a different tone—the tone of purposes, of business, of matters of fact—"to what do I owe the pleasure of this call?"

"Dodge," says Tabry after a pause, and Gilchrist senses that Tabry is about to be serious because he has chosen to call him by his first name. "Dodge, you remember that my brother had a daughter, don't you?"

"Yes," Gilchrist answers, remembering not only the fact of the brother's daughter but also the assassination of Tabry's brother who was his senior by many years. Gilchrist recalls as well that Tabry's brother was a prominent Palestinian poet who, after numerous incarcerations and harassments, was finally pistol-whipped in exile in Lebanon and then was shot eighteen times by an Israeli hit team later reprimanded by the Israeli government for "this regrettable incident" ascribed to intoxication and a "misinterpretation of orders." The coup de grâce to the already dead body was six carefully placed shots (one for every book the poet had written) around the poet's mouth. This was a sobering and symbolic epitaph that exoneration by intoxication could not explain away. The facts came back to Gilchrist as vividly as they were when he included them in his Pulitzer series on midcentury assassinations. The Pulitzer judges pointedly singled out Gilchrist's account of the murder of Tabry's brother as an example of investigative journalism at its most "disinterested" and, therefore, its "best." The fact that the members of the hit team were released and returned to duty with nothing more than a reprimand was never mentioned. But the story had prompted Gilchrist to read some of the translations of the poetry of the murdered brother, and, even though he rarely read poetry, he found that he was stirred and at times deeply moved. "Yes, Tab, I remember the girl. Whatever happened to her?"

"After her mother died, she was taken into what the government there calls 'preventive detention.' That was a little more than a month ago. I think I told you then that I had been trying to have both the girl and her mother join me here, but the whole effort came to nothing. Well, I just learned yesterday that my niece is being released and that she's being permitted to come to the United States under my sponsorship."

"How did you swing that?"

"State Department friends, primarily. Most of my contacts at State have never been under any illusions about the Middle East situation. They've always understood the real nature of the problems in my country."

"Well, the ordinary garden-variety politicians in the country sure as hell haven't."

"Actually, they have also, many of them. But what they believe and say in private and what they say in public are not the same. In any case, I worked through State and some friends in the private sector here and in Europe, and I received a call yesterday to the effect that a deal had been worked out. They won't tell me all the facts. I think it involved some kind of swap. Anyway, it's been one hell of a struggle."

"I can imagine."

"I was informed that she should be in Washington next week. And that's the real reason for my call to you. I'd like to see you between then and now when you have time and discuss an idea I have about her, and it could involve you."

"What kind of an idea?"

"I'd rather discuss it with you in person. Are you going to be in Washington for a while?"

"Yes."

"What would be the best time for you?"

"Tomorrow or next Saturday. Both clear."

"How about Saturday here at my place? Seven o'clock."

"Okay," says Gilchrist, then adds, "By the way, what's the girl's name?"

"Raya. It was my mother's name."

2

LOOKING AT TABRY for the first time in four months, Gilchrist notices the burst of gray in his otherwise black hair—not gray at the temples in the customary pattern but a swatch of gray just to the right of the crown. Even though Tabry is only a year younger than Gilchrist, it always seemed to Gilchrist that Tabry was his senior. Shorter than Gilchrist by several inches, Tabry is broader in the shoulders but everywhere else seems lean by nature. Whereas Gilchrist is lean from tennis, handball, skiing, and saunas, Tabry's leanness has a toughness that transcends athletics, confirming Tabry's belief, as he once told Gilchrist, that bodies are not to be indulged or toned but used. Tabry seems to have squirrel muscles, and he even moves like a squirrel, deliberately and with no excess motion. His Lucite-rimmed glasses with flip-down lenses (now flipped up) for close work do not identify him as the scholar he is but make him look like an obdurate city editor whose life is a matter of deadlines. In addition, Gilchrist notices, as he has always noticed, that Tabry still retains the same inner determination that he had in his student days. Gilchrist used to tell him that there was a part of him that never slept, as if he were a soldier perpetually on post or a sentry who never wanted to be taken by surprise. On the few occasions during their undergraduate years when Gilchrist had the occasion to awaken Tabry, he recalls that Tabry was instantly awake and thinking, not slowly floating back to fact through the semistate between sleep and full consciousness.

All through the supper that Tabry has prepared for the two of them (twin sirloins, baked potatoes with sour cream, squash sections, coffee, and Dutch apple pie à la mode), Gilchrist has been waiting for Tabry to broach the subject of the girl and his "idea about her," but he has confined himself to small talk. Once when Gilchrist suggested that he was interested in knowing, no, really curious to know, what Tabry had in mind for Raya, Tabry merely smiled and said, "Hospitality before business, Gil. That's ingrained in the Arabs. You should know that about me by now."

Gilchrist takes the final sip of coffee from his cup and resets it carefully in its saucer on the coffee table beside his chair in the living room. Tabry does the same. For a protracted moment Tabry studies both cups as if he is half expecting them to lose their balance. Then he folds his arms and looks at Gilchrist. He is not smiling.

"Raya has been in detention for almost a month, Gil. She was never charged with a thing, and, as you know, people can be detained there indefinitely at the pleasure of the government, and most of them even later never find out why. The only reason they kept Raya, as far as the State Department has been able to determine, was because of what they thought she might be planning to do. How do you like that for a legal way of doing things?"

"Superb," says Gilchrist with a smile that is not a smile. "You could jail half the world on that basis." He pauses. "Correction. The whole world."

"Frankly, I think the only reason they decided to hold her was that she was her father's daughter. And, of course, they might have taken her into custody as a way of curbing me, intimidating me."

"On the surface, I'd say it was the latter."

"Perhaps. We'll never know. There's no logic to what the secret police do there except police logic."

"And the police do exactly what the government there tells them to do. That's the logic."

"Precisely," says Tabry and stands. He puts his hands in his pockets and paces the room as if he is measuring it. Gilchrist recognizes the ritual; some people, he knows, think best when they are moving, and Tabry, as Gilchrist has known for years, is one of them. "I don't know how hard they were on her," Tabry resumes. "The Red Cross has the right to visit political prisoners only after they've been in custody for fourteen days. Well, the Red Cross did visit her after the fourteen-day period almost two weeks ago. The report was that she looked drawn but that she was in perfect control of herself. Since that time there haven't been any other reports."

"How old is she?"

"Twenty-five."

"Attractive?"

"I think so. At least, she seems attractive in all the photos I've seen of her over the years. What makes you ask that?"

"I don't trust gendarmes when they have a beautiful girl in their custody. And that includes the pope's Swiss Guard."

"Well," says Tabry slowly, "I can only hope there was no abuse."

"I hope the same, but we can't forget that some instances of abuse have been cited by the Red Cross and Amnesty International. The London *Times* did quite a piece on that subject last summer. The report was never published here, but that's par for the course, even though the account in the *Times* was carefully detailed. I know the guy who wrote it." Gilchrist stops at this point, feeling that it is preferable not to tell Tabry what he read in unpublished reports or heard from his London contact regarding the treatment of certain women in Israeli custody.

"I've told you all that I know, Gil."

"When she comes, you might ask her about that. Ask her carefully." He pauses. "By the way, when will she be in the country?"

"The day after tomorrow."

Gilchrist senses that he is now approaching the real reason Tabry wanted to see him. "Enough preliminaries, Tab. What I want to know is what I can do for you. Why did you want to see me?"

Tabry returns to his chair and begins speaking in a tone that friends reserve for friends—a tone that assumes understanding in advance of whatever it is that is to be discussed and assumes ultimate assent and support as well, as between brothers. "This is a well-educated girl, Dodge. My brother and my sister-in-law saw to that. They both knew that the salvation of the young people of Palestine had to be salvation through intelligence, and that the key to a developed intelligence was education. Raya's not spoiled even though she was an only child. She knows what being a woman means in Arab culture as well as in the West. She earned a baccalaureate. She's fluent in four languages, including English. And there's no accent whatever. She sent me several letter cassettes before they took her into custody, and there was no accent whatsoever . . ."

"Accent or no accent, Tab, what are you getting at? What are you asking me to do for you?"

"I want you . . . ," Tabry begins, then stops and starts again in a slightly altered tone, "I'd appreciate it very much if you could find a way for her to work for you."

Now it is Gilchrist's turn to stand and pace the room. He can feel Tabry's eyes on him with every step. "If I can be allowed one question, Tab . . ."

"Of course."

"I'd like to know, just as a matter of curiosity, why she couldn't work for you? You have a small staff for the journal, don't you? You could just add her to that."

"Yes, I have a small staff, but adding Raya to the staff would not be suitable, believe me. I don't want her to be involved in my struggle—in my country's struggle. Working with her would bring back memories of her father and all the things she must have gone through during the past year. I actually thought of having her work on the journal, but it just wouldn't be right. You have to take my word for that."

"Then why couldn't she get a job somewhere else? You have a lot of friends at Georgetown and in DC. If she's as bright as you say she is and can speak all those languages, she shouldn't have much trouble finding something, especially here in Washington."

"In time she might just do that. In fact, she probably will. Right now there are immigration reasons that wouldn't be an easy or a legal thing to do, even if we could work something out. Jobs in Washington are not as easy to get as you think they are. That's why I'm asking you to take her on. I think it would be good for her if she had something to do with you. You would have a good influence on her."

Gilchrist stops pacing and returns to his chair. He suddenly feels that all his options and alternatives are abandoning him—as if a decision has already been made in this matter and that he has no choice but the choice of accommodation. Finally, he says, "Tab, I've been reading your political journal and statements for the past year, and I've been thinking of all the times we talked, and I don't remember your making one reference to your niece. Not one. Why didn't you tell me about her before? Maybe I could have written something, raised a fuss, gotten her out of the country sooner. Maybe you could have interested some important people in her case, and they could have had a job—the right job—waiting for her when she came. Did you ever think of that?"

"Yes, I thought of it. I thought of it a lot. But raising a fuss would have been exactly what they wanted."

"They?"

"The ones who were holding her. They would have loved it if I subordinated the journal to a personal matter. But I couldn't let myself do that. It would have completely undercut the reason I had for creating the journal in the first place." He pauses. "It wasn't an easy temptation to resist. I had to pit all I had against doing that at that moment, not just because they were holding a girl whose name happened to be Tabry, but because I wanted to keep my focus on all the injustices that have been committed against the Palestinians by every Israeli government since the beginning. I couldn't let the issue just revolve around my niece."

"You should have taken them on, Tab. You have a lot of people who would have stepped forward to help you. Save your moral scruples for the next life, if there is one . . ." Gilchrist shifts his weight in the chair and waits for the silence to settle like a punctuation mark between what he has just finished saying and what he is about to say. "Let's put you and your enemies aside for a minute. That's your fight, not mine. I'm sympathetic, but I'm going to keep my distance from both sides. Here's what I promise to do about your niece, Rena . . ."

"Raya."

"Raya. I'll interview the girl as a favor to you and see if she's a possibility for me. How's that? After all, I can't make up my mind one way or the other until I've interviewed her, can I?" Gilchrist expects Tabry to smile, but there is no change in Tabry's expression. Gilchrist keeps waiting.

Tabry rises from his chair, takes Gilchrist's cup and saucer into the kitchen, and returns with a cup filled with fresh coffee. He places the saucered cup back on the table beside Gilchrist. "Dodge," says Tabry, "there's a little more to it than that."

"Come on, Tab. I said I'd interview her. I can't promise I'll take her on before I know what she can do. I'm not going to adopt her, for God's sake!"

Tabry acts as if Gilchrist has not spoken at all. "Let me give you a little background. It's important that you understand my reasons so that you see what I have in mind. And you have to take me seriously. You're like a brother to me, so you have to take me seriously." Tabry indicates with a nod that Gilchrist should drink his coffee, and Gilchrist, obeying the nod though not ready for more coffee, does. "As long as I keep on with the work I am doing on the journal and the small foundation I've created to support it," Tabry resumes, "I'll continue to be somewhat of a problem for certain people. I think you know that. But believe me when I tell you that this work is really my life, my oxygen. My soul is in it. If you love your country, you fight for it in the best way you can. It's something you simply have to do, and you have to keep doing it. Now there are some people who have tried for a long time to make this as difficult for me as possible. They've done everything they can do to discredit me, and nothing has worked for them. In fact, it's had the very opposite effect by bringing the journal to the attention of more and more people who would otherwise never have heard of it. They've tried to get to my financial sources, and it hasn't worked. You also might be surprised to know that I get telephone calls fairly regularly at two or three in the morning even though I'm supposed to have an unlisted number. Do you know what it is to have your telephone ring in the middle of the night? My friend Edward Said at Columbia told me that he had and still has the same trouble. He gets threats regularly, and once they even set fire to his office." Tabry pauses, remembering. "They've tried to intimidate me by arresting my brother's daughter and doing God knows what to her, and it hasn't worked." He pauses again and swallows hard as if trying to swallow his growing anger. "They have only one option left, Dodge."

"They don't have the balls for that. Not in this country."

"Why not? They've already done it in Europe to men I know—men who were doing work that was similar to what I do. And besides, America is a perfect shooting gallery. You should know that better than anyone. You wrote about it and won a Pulitzer Prize for what you wrote."

Gilchrist knows that Tabry has just said something beyond refutation. He tries to change the mood by removing two cigars from his coat pocket and offering one to Tabry, who refuses with a smile and a slight single shake of his head.

"Thanks, Gil, but no."

"Still an abstainer."

"I tried a pipe, but it kept going out."

"Pipe smokers tell me that a pipe will go out when you're talking too much and not smoking."

"Maybe. I had to carry around too many matches. It got to be too much trouble, and the sparks from the tobacco kept making holes in my clothes. I gave it up three years ago." He shrugs and returns to the previous thrust of his remarks. "I don't think they're going to do anything like shooting me in cold blood or blowing me up the way that Lettelier was blown up right here in DC. And I doubt if they'll do it the way that the KGB got Markhov in London with the poison pellet in the umbrella tip. But then again they might. With these people you never know. They know all the tricks."

"You're getting to be a specialist about your own death, Tab."

"I'm just following a premise to its logical conclusion. Gil, you have to remember that they don't give a damn about resistance in the usual sense. They have special forces and weapons to handle that. That's just an annoyance to them, and they deal with that the way an elephant deals with a toad. And frankly I'm not a backer of forceful resistance because the resisters, when they eventually get the upper hand, usually become worse than the ones they resisted. All revolutions prove that. It comes back to the real meaning of the word—one full turn of the wheel."

"I never heard it put that way, but I like it. What you're saying is that you end up with what you had in the beginning."

"Exactly. That's why resistance by sheer force has no future. It just repeats the past, usually with more tragic consequences." He tracks his fingers through his hair from front to crown. Gilchrist remembers the gesture as an old student habit of Tabry's, as if he had to ease an itching in his brain induced by intense thinking. "What my enemies fear most is a philosophy of resistance, intellectual resistance, a coherent, persuasive, and attractive system of thought opposed to their own. Diametrically opposed. Why? Because it creates the possibility of choice. That's what they fear most. Choice. They want total believers, not choosers. In my country now there is no alternative to what contradicts the government's line. All there is is resistance, blind resistance. Bombs in parked cars. Riots. Suicide raids. Things like that. Troublesome, but blind really and in the end tragic for the resisters and for the victims. There's no possibility of victory in that. What I want is a real victory, a victory of intellect."

"Are you sure there's no possibility of victory in resistance by force?"

"Not the kind of victory that matters, no. If you don't believe me, think of America in the beginning. There was a revolt but no philosophy of what the revolt was supposed to produce except to defeat the British. All you had was resistance. Without Jefferson, what would have happened to the American Revolution? Jefferson made you into something."

"Made *us* into something, Tab. Remember, you're an American citizen now yourself."

"All right, then, made *us* into something . . . He made us something, made us Americans. But the point's the same. Before Jefferson, we were just what the British called us—a rabble in arms. Jefferson's declaration changed all that. He made citizenship and not soldiering the American ideal. He wasn't satisfied with resistance. The one thing he wasn't interested in was replacing one tyranny with another tyranny. And that's why my enemies in Israel and here want to provoke me to the point where they make a mere resister out of me. And they'll go on trying with all the tools at their command. And they have a lot of tools. But I can't give up in the face of all that. If I do, they will have their victory—their real victory."

"And so you want to be another Thomas Jefferson, is that the answer?"

"In a way, yes," says Tabry and jokingly strikes a Jeffersonian pose that soon becomes so Napoleonic that he smiles. "Look, Gil, all kidding aside, I know my limitations. I'm no genius. I'm certainly no Jefferson. But I've had a good education, and I'm a persistent worker if I'm anything at all. And as far as my country—correction, the country of my birth—is concerned, I know what is needed, and I think I can make a contribution to meet that need. And that's what keeps bothering a certain group of people who don't want to see that happen."

"And you think that they might get so overbothered that they just might want to silence you, trap you, knock you off?"

"No, not exactly. If they decide to get rid of me, it won't be like a contract killing. At least, I don't think it will be. Their first goal might be to try to discredit me or make my death seem like part of the passing scene. A cold-blooded murder would draw too much attention, especially to the journal, and they don't want that. That would defeat their whole purpose. Discrediting me would be their first preference. Or there could be the kind of death that would make my whole life suspect, if you know what I mean . . ."

"Overdose of illegal drugs—cocaine—something like that?"

"Something like that. That would discredit me somewhat, and that in turn would discredit the journal. And, if I survived, the incident would dry up all the money for my foundation. If they can get rid of me and discredit me at the same time, they'll have achieved what they had in mind. Or if they can't do that, they'll choose some pedestrian way that will get a two-inch notice on page 26 for one day only. No follow-up. But some kind of final solution is in the cards, Gil. It's just a matter of time."

"Are you taking any precautions?"

"What precautions can I take? In the beginning I thought of getting a license to carry a gun. I saw ambushes everywhere. And I developed the kind of mentality that goes with that, which meant that I got no work done. Now I live day to day with a kind of faith or fatalism, take your pick."

"What's that supposed to mean?"

"I take each day as it comes. If they're making plans to finish me, let them make them. I'm not going to be their accomplice in counterpreparation. I just want to do what I must do and keep everything else out of my mind. There's no other option. The danger—whatever it is and whenever it comes—only makes me want to work harder. I feel that I have only a finite period to do what I have to do, and that intensifies everything."

"How do I fit into the picture?"

"If they succeed, Gil, I want you to see that my niece is, well, protected somehow. Cared for. Overseen. That's the real reason I wanted to see you tonight. I know she can handle the job for you. Give her whatever test you choose, and she'll ace it, believe me. There's no doubt in my mind that she'll be able to be an asset to you."

"But what you're really saying is that you want me to be a godfather on top of all that. A godfather just in case . . ."

"Exactly," Tabry answers quickly and offers Gilchrist his hand. "You're the only one I would want to entrust her with. And why not? You've been a 'godbrother' to me all these years."

Gilchrist feels Tabry tighten his handclasp like a soldier shaking another soldier's hand at the frontier for the last time. "I don't know why you picked me, old buddy. My reputation with women is not something that would edify her, and I'm not thinking of changing it."

Tabry's smile is not a smile of approval or disapproval. It simply suggests that Gilchrist has just uttered a triviality he has already taken into account and dismissed as irrelevant. "You have an international view of things, Gil. You're cosmopolitan. You know your way around. You would be able to keep her away from the wrong people until she is able to strike out on her own. That's all that really concerns me, but I'm sure that she'll pull her own weight from the start."

"All this, of course, assumes that I agree . . ."

"But something tells me that you've just agreed," says Tabry with a Middle Eastern smile.

" . . . and it also assumes that you're no longer in the picture."

"Yes."

"And since that's something that will probably not happen, I'll agree just to give you peace of mind." Gilchrist lifts his cup as if he is about to propose a toast. Tabry lifts his, and the two men click cups. For several minutes there is only silence as both finish their coffee simultaneously.

"Someday," Tabry begins, "I'll have to find a way to tell you how American you are." He pauses. "I'm living on borrowed time, and I know it, but you just dismiss it. You have that kind of built-in optimism. You don't have a tragic sense of life. You have enough money to meet your real and even your imagined needs. You even create needs that you're sure will become necessities. You have a real belief in the future. And it's always your future, the future that's guaranteed for you without a doubt. In the meanwhile you enjoy yourself as you choose. You can pick your concerns and causes, or else you can ignore them. Even patriotism is a kind of option for you. That's America, Gil, and you fit the description."

"Is that supposed to make me feel good?"

"No," answers Tabry, who seems suddenly embarrassed by his own candor. "I didn't mean to offend. I didn't mean it to be that personal. I was just describing . . ."

"How else should I have taken it?"

"Sorry, Gil. It was just bad manners. Please forget I said it. I didn't mean it the way it came out."

"Tell me, Tab," Gilchrist says after a pause, trying to strike off in a new conversational direction since he can see that Tabry has embarrassed himself into silence, "why didn't you ever marry? You would have made a perfect father." He stops and looks at Tabry. "You were frank with me a minute ago, and now it's my turn to be frank with you."

"The classic story, I'm afraid. The ones who interested me couldn't share my life, and the one who could share my life didn't interest me. Year after year it was the same cycle, and all the years have just arrived at right now, so here I am. I'm not grieving about it. I still think that love is possible, but I also think that luck has a lot to do with it. I prefer to think that I was simply unlucky. That's not a tragedy. It's just a fact. But I still have my work. I have the journal. I have my students. And I have a small foundation that keeps my work on the journal alive. And all those things keep my country and its struggle alive inside of me, and that somehow pacifies and satisfies me. No, those aren't the right words." He tracks his fingers through his hair again. "I think what I mean is that my work makes everything else seem secondary to me. It's a feeling I can't describe. I don't know if you can understand what I feel sometimes when I tell myself I'm a man without a country . . ."

"You have the US of A."

"Yes, and I'm grateful for that. I'm more grateful than I can say. But it's somehow my second country the way that the American language is my second language. Do you know what I mean? My first country was taken away from me. And for years I've had to live with the sense of not having a country. And that forces you to discover your country all over inside of yourself. It may have been taken from you in the way that the world looks at things, but you know that you always have it inside of you. You rediscover it there, and it always is waiting for you there forever. And from the moment that you discover what that means, something inside of you becomes—*you* become—sacred. It's something that religious people must feel after they've received the sacrament. Unfortunately, I've never met a woman in my life who appreciates what that means. Maybe most of them wouldn't want to share their husband's affections with a country. I don't know. I suppose there's a woman somewhere who would understand what I mean by all this, but I have yet to find her. Just my bad luck, I suppose. So I never married. I mean, I never got married just to get married, if you see my point. I can't say it's not lonely because, frankly, it is. It's lonely most of the time, especially in the late evenings. But I tell myself that loneliness is better than misery." Tabry pauses and smiles at Gilchrist. "But who are you to call the kettle black? You have all the women you want, and you've had a lot of different women in your life. And you still do. But you never had a wife. You never married. Why not?"

"You know the answer to that, Tab."

3

STROLLING BACK from Tabry's house to his apartment, Gilchrist passes a Georgetown restaurant and overhears a recording of Judy Collins singing "Both Sides Now." The words bring Gilchrist to a stop—"I've looked at life from both sides now, from near and far and still somehow . . ." The words suggest a face that's part of a time that recalls everything Gilchrist has never been able to forget. He lets himself be carried along by the song and the face and the memory as he resumes his walk. He is not taking the coincidence seriously at all. Suddenly, he is somewhere else, and his whole life is waiting to readmit him into an old niche of memory he considered dead, not dormant. He resists remembering. He walks faster, but the song has imprisoned him. Second by second, he tries to understand what is happening, but he keeps failing. He feels himself falling more and more in arrears from where he is right now. And there is no way to arrest it. He tries to catch up to himself, but he has already lost.

The song has assembled Holly's face in his mind, and he sees her face as he saw it seven years and three weeks ago to the day before the wedding that never happened. He is still walking on Georgetown pavements, but he is elsewhere. He is with Holly and her parents and an Irish writer named Mattimore on the porch of her family's house overlooking the Severn just above Annapolis. The fact that Holly seems more than casually interested in Mattimore, who is almost her father's age, is something that Gilchrist misses or, rather, dismisses completely. All he is thinking of is Holly, who is wearing his engagement ring on her tanned finger, and he is memorizing how stunning and relaxed she looks. Her reddish hair is lifting softly in the breeze. She is wearing white slacks and a silk blouse whose particular flavor of blue rhymes with the blue of the slowly flowing Severn. Each time the breeze lifts her hair, it also shapes her blouse over her breasts before the blouse falls slack again. This will remain Gilchrist's most ineradicable memory of Holly for years.

The previous night after he arrived from Washington, where he was an assistant financial editor for the *Post*, he had gone to dinner with Holly in Annapolis. He did not pay much attention that she seemed preoccupied. Later, when they were alone, he asked her how she felt about becoming Mrs. Dodge Didier Gilchrist, and her only answer was a hesitant smile. He waited for her to say a word, but she said nothing. That night he slept in the family's guesthouse (Mattimore was using the spare bedroom in the main house), and he awoke shortly after midnight as he always did when he was in a strange bed. He started to make a brief inventory of his years since his graduation from Georgetown and came away satisfied that he had not touched a nickel of his inheritance to which he had become entitled on his twenty-first birthday. He had lived only on his salary, and he had earned the assistant editorship on merit alone. Things were just beginning to break for him. Just as he finished his inventory, he heard the door being opened, and there in the blue moonlight was Holly whispering, "Gil, are you asleep?"

Gilchrist eased up on one elbow. Holly was in ski pajamas. She came near the bed and stood beside him.

"What's up, Holly?" asked Gilchrist.

"Nothing," she answered, but she was breathing too quickly for the answer to sound like the truth. Gilchrist reached for her hand and drew her down so that she was sitting beside him on the bed. Her every breath still came with effort, and he knew that this was begotten either of desire or of whatever courage she was summoning to say what she came to say.

"Gil," she said, "please don't be angry with me, but I'm having second thoughts."

"About what?"

"About . . . us."

Gilchrist lay on his back and folded his arms behind his neck. His previous good feelings about how things were just beginning to break for him suddenly soured like bad news from another century, another world. He huffed audibly, wanting her to hear him, and he waited.

"Maybe I just need a little more time," Holly said. It obviously was a sentence she had been rehearsing, and she delivered it that way.

"It's almost two years, Holly. What happened all of a sudden to change your mind?"

"I don't know. Maybe . . . ," she began, and then she seemed to change completely. He could feel the change through the darkness, but he had no way to know what to expect. She reached for his right hand with her left and guided it gently under her pajama top until the underflesh of her left breast settled in his open palm. His forefingers bracketed her nipple like a button. As the nipple firmed under his touch, he could hear a sound that was almost a moan from her. Then she leaned over and kissed him, first on the chin, then full on the mouth. She parted her lips during the kiss, and he could taste the sweet musk from the inside of her mouth that became an ichor he would always identify with her. When the kiss ended, she stood. In the darkness he could see her grab her pajama top with both hands at the waist, then skin it up her flanks and over her head and drop it on the bed. Then she lifted the bedcovers and slid beside him.

"What's going on, Holly?" asked Gilchrist. "One minute you're undecided, and the next minute, this."

"Ssh . . . ," she said and hugged him so that her nude breasts compressed softly against his side in the dark.

"Come on, Holly. We're not high school kids."

"Let's be high school kids," she answered. She hugged him more tightly, and he could feel his body beginning to respond to her. Again she kissed him, first on the mouth, then on his cheeks, then on his neck. Gilchrist put his arms around her to keep her as close to him as possible.

"This feels delicious, Gil," she whispered.

"Ditto."

His hand slid down her back and skimmed over her buttocks.

"Touch me, Gil," she said and began pulling down the bottoms of her pajamas.

Gilchrist let his hand coast down her right thigh, then up the inner side of her left thigh. Her legs parted slightly, and his hand finally rested for a moment on the soft hair below her navel. Just as he was about to move his hand lower, she suddenly reached for the pajamas around her knees and pulled them up.

"No more, Gil," she managed to say. "My God, I don't know what I was thinking." She eased herself out of the bed, slipped into the pajama top as if she were putting on a sweater, and ran from the cottage but not before kissing him one last time.

"Holly," Gilchrist called after her, but there was no answer.

The next day Gilchrist was scheduled to return to Washington. Before he left, he had breakfast with Holly, her parents, and Mattimore. Each time he looked at Holly, she smiled and looked away. When he kissed her good-bye, she kissed him as if he were her brother. On the following day he left for a weeklong conference in Caracas. On his return he found a small certified package in his mailbox. It contained the engagement ring that he had given to Holly months earlier. No note. No explanation. Nothing but a return address on the package without even her name above the street number. Gilchrist telephoned immediately, but the only one he reached was Holly's mother.

"Gil," she said, "I feel terrible about all this, really. You know how much you meant to Holly's father and me, and I hope you know how much we thought of you and will always think of you. But Holly was in no mood to listen. I can't understand her. I never could. The only thing I can say now is that you should try to put everything between you and Holly behind you, Gil. The sooner, the better. It will be better that way, believe me. I tried to talk to her. So did her father. But her mind was made up. But you're still quite young, Gil. You can make a new life for yourself. You have a wonderful future. I'm not happy about what happened or the way it happened, but better now than later. We can at least wish them the best, regardless . . ."

"Them?" asked Gilchrist. "Who?"

"Holly and Julian Mattimore."

"But he's as old as her father."

There was no answer. Finally, Holly's mother's said, "Didn't she write you? She told me that you were in South America. I told her to call you and explain. I made her promise. Didn't she call? Maybe she wrote. Was there a letter waiting for you?"

"Just a package."

Later, as the facts assembled themselves, Gilchrist learned that Holly and Mattimore had eloped. They were living somewhere in the west of Ireland where Mattimore owned an estate.

For months after that Gilchrist concentrated solely on his work. He gave up dealing with his feelings simply because he was unable to without experiencing every emotion from jealousy to the kind of blood hatred that made him feel he could actually kill. His work became both a narcotic and a way to buy time. But the healing happened so slowly that he did not seem to be healing at all, and one year begot the next without any noticeable change. He became less and less proficient in dealing with his repressions and hurts until he found himself believing that "getting over Holly" might become the occupation of the rest of his life. It was two years before he became seriously interested in another woman—a co-worker at the paper—but the shell that he had molded around himself was so obvious to her in time and his attention so willed and unspontaneous that she thought that something was inherently wrong with what was developing between them, and the romance was stillborn.

Gilchrist saw Tabry frequently during that period and discussed Holly with him. After the first time, Tabry simply listened as if he knew that listening at that stage was all that was expected or needed, and he was, as Gilchrist later admitted, correct.

Finally, Tabry offered his opinion on the matter. "Gil," he said, "your reaction just proves that you had an exaggerated view of Holly and of women from the beginning, and Holly was the projection of all of your exaggerations."

"Exaggerated? How?"

"You're a romantic. For you women are either virginal brides or outright bitches. No middle ground, which is where most of us, women included, live. Right now you're crucified by the fact that you thought Holly was the virginal bride you wanted for yourself, and somebody else took her away from you at the eleventh hour. So it won't be long before you start thinking of her as a bitch. And then you'll tell yourself that she was probably a bitch from the beginning, and it won't be much longer after that before you start thinking that every woman on earth is just like her. Actually, she was just someone who committed the forgivable sin of changing her mind at the last minute for who knows what reason, and she didn't have the courage or the courtesy to tell you. Maybe she didn't love you enough to face you with that. And that should tell you something about the woman you thought you were going to marry." He paused to let the words do their work. "I don't suppose it ever occurred to you that you just might be better off without her?" He paused again. "Or maybe you just regret not having had your way with her while you had the chance. It could be as simple as that, Gil."

Tabry's candor was of some help to Gilchrist, but like all disappointed lovers, Gilchrist vowed that he would never let himself be seared that way again, not if he could help it, and he promised himself that he would keep that vow at all costs. He decided to live no longer on his newspaper salary alone (after all, he'd already proved that he could, so what was the point of proving it indefinitely?) and began to tap into his inheritance. He indulged himself in suits of the best quality, a Mont Blanc "writing instrument," the most expensive seats at the theater or the stadium, Davidoff cigars, and a Mercedes coupe in a special edition. He left the financial page and became a stalwart of the editorial page. He traveled for no reason other than to travel and found that this distracted him—for a while. One day he was asked by his editor to write his column with his own byline for syndication. In a brief time he became so skilled at whittling his thoughts to a three-hundred-word length that the syndication grew far beyond the editor's or Gilchrist's expectations. Then came the series on the midcentury assassinations, beginning with Gandhi and concluding with Robert F. Kennedy, that earned him the Pulitzer. It was subsequent to this that his attitude toward women changed (or was changed) completely. After he was awarded the Pulitzer, he noticed how many women were drawn to him like moths by the sure flame of his achievements and notoriety. Little by little he came to welcome and even expect their flattery and their admiration and soon discovered that this was usually a mask for what they really wanted, which was Gilchrist himself—not merely his attention, his company, or his conversation but himself alone in whatever form of dalliance presented itself as possible. His experience with Holly had, as Tabry predicted it would, gradually soured his idealism as well as his ethics, and he accommodated himself little by little to the attention of women he met and bedded on the basis of mutual consent and then a kind of mutual amnesia. There was one senator's wife who claimed that she was faster at forty than at twenty and proved it by climaxing the very minute he entered her. There was the Venezuelan hostess who preferred intercourse while standing because her legs were long enough to make it not only possible but enjoyable. There was the actress from France whose idea of lovemaking was that the woman should take every imaginative initiative, and there was the Smith graduate who said she was writing a critique of his work and interviewed him in his apartment and stayed for a week. And there were more, but Gilchrist had long since stopped trying to remember them by name. He eased them in passing, and they eased him, no more, no less. They wanted no promises, and he made none. When Tabry asked him on one occasion if he still believed in genuine love between a man and a woman, Gilchrist told him that he believed only in the one who happened to be his partner at the moment, and that was as far as it went. If that qualified as love, so be it. If not, not. Finally, he told Tabry that he was not interested in the past, present, and future as most people understood these terms. All he believed in was the time at hand, so that he just wanted the present to go on being the present to go on being the present to go on being the present . . .

Gilchrist is still thinking of his personal history as he enters his apartment, and for a moment he feels what a man might feel by returning to an old but familiar neighborhood. The song he heard when he passed the Georgetown restaurant still has its grip on him, and he tries to concentrate his way out of the memory of it and back into the time being. The rooms in his apartment seem somewhat smaller than they were this morning. He surveys the sleek Danish chairs and sofa that are less than a month old. The chairs seem to glide in place on either side of a glass-topped table sculpted like a boomerang. Stereo speakers and an abundance of chromium dials and banks of equalizers confront him like so many instruments on the dashboard of a 747. He smiles, recalling how the income from his inheritance bought all of it—cash on delivery, just as it bought his Mercedes coupe. It reminds him that the difference between a salary and an inheritance is the difference between time payments and a straight sale, which for Gilchrist is the difference between counting and not having to count. A salary got you a Chevrolet or a small Cadillac. An inheritance made possible a Mercedes, a Porsche, or a Rolls.

Still studying the various pieces in the room, Gilchrist quietly closes the front door behind him. He shuts his eyes and stands still. In his imagination the door he has just closed becomes another door. It is more than ten years in the past, and he is entering his student room where Tabry is lying faceup and fully clothed on his bed and staring at a target spot on the ceiling.

"Are you rehearsing for your coffin or what?" asks Gilchrist as he drops his books on his bed and sits on the bed's edge.

"No," answers Tabry, "I'm just thinking."

"Wine, women, or song?"

"Home."

Gilchrist knows how Tabry's mood and outlook change when he talks this way, and he starts to think of something else to talk about while hoping that the distraction will work. "What's wrong with wine, women, or song? Answer in twenty-five words or less."

Tabry is silent for several minutes before he says, "You know, Gil, when someone takes your country away from you, it's like taking your name from you. That's the way it makes me feel—nameless. I've been lying here for more than an hour, and I feel as if I'm just here by accident and that I'll be spending the rest of my life here or some other place just like here—just by accident. I'll be a permanent stranger no matter where I am—a kind of accidental man. It makes me feel as if I'm going to be sentenced to live as a stranger for the rest of my life."

"Try not to think about it. That's the trouble with you. You think and overthink too much about stuff like that, and all you get out of it is depression." Gilchrist lies down on his back and stares at the same target spot on the ceiling that Tabry had been staring at as if the spot has all the answers. "Why don't you just pretend that Palestine was totally destroyed by a typhoon or an earthquake or something like that? Imagine that it could never be rebuilt because of some natural catastrophe. You'd have to go someplace else then and make a new life, wouldn't you? You'd have to make out as best you could, make a new home, a new life. Why don't you think about it that way?"

"If the country had been destroyed by an earthquake, I could accept it. It would take a long time, but I could accept it. But this is different. I don't have a country today because it was taken away by human beings. It's not an impersonal matter at all. Specific people stole the country from me, from us. That makes a big difference, Gil. It's hard for me to live with the fact that somebody else from Europe or some other place is living off my father's land, and that this somebody just came back and took it as if it were his all along. They point to the Bible to prove it. But why should Christians or Muslims accept that? All we know is that we were kicked out with no compensation, no convincing explanation, not even the admission that my father owned what he and his father had owned for generations, owned it legally . . ."

"Well," says Gilchrist, "just try your best not to think about it all the time. I can see what it's doing to you. It's eating you up. When you're tempted to think about it, try to think of something else right away."

Tabry sits up in bed and swings his legs to the floor. "I should keep my thoughts to myself about this. It's worse when I talk about it. Honest to God, it's really much worse when I hear myself say out loud what's inside of me, but it comes out anyway." Tabry shakes his head in a slow but deliberate *no* for several seconds before he resumes. "When you have no country to go back to, it's as if you had no history, no real address, no flag, no identity. And then you realize that your country has become just a memory of where you know you should be. That's all. That memory is all you have, and you try to keep that memory from fading. It becomes that special place inside of you that is your country. There's that special place, and there is everywhere else. And everywhere else is the rest of the world." He pauses. "I have to keep my country alive inside of me, Gil. I have to keep it going like a fire. That's the only home I have."

"Nothing wrong with that, Tab," says Gilchrist, hoping he's heard the end of it. In the silence that follows he finds himself comparing Tabry's destiny with his own—Tabry, a Palestinian scholarship student from abroad, and he, Dodge Didier Gilchrist, the only son of the Gilchrists of King of Prussia, Pennsylvania, Anglo-Saxon with a dash of French, Protestant as far back as the Huguenots, a graduate of Groton, enrolled now at Georgetown and headed for its School of International Studies, determined not to touch his million-dollar inheritance (it would automatically and unconditionally be his the instant he reached his twenty-first birthday) so he could prove to himself and especially his father that he could "make it" on his own in what his father persistently called "that lousy world out there." As Gilchrist makes the comparison between Tabry and himself, he wonders what it would be like not to have a home to return to at Thanksgiving or Christmas or Easter and the various semester breaks and how he would survive the moist, stifling Washington summers by working in the city, as Tabry did summer after summer, instead of surfing and sailing near Cape Cod or Martha's Vineyard.

Slowly, so slowly that for an instant or two Gilchrist seems to be living in two different time periods at once, the fading memory of his student room at Georgetown blurs back into the fact of his apartment again. He walks through it in the darkening twilight, knowing that everything is just as he left it, and, except for Thursdays when he pays a Jamaican maid to clean and dust the place, will always be that way. He tells himself that most men his age would give a lot to have his life—his income, his reputation, his fame, his freedom to navigate socially and geographically as he chooses. He keeps reminding himself of that as he opens the door of the refrigerator and starts to sip chilled milk from an already opened carton. The sourness of the milk shocks him, and he spits the mouthful into the sink with more force than is necessary. Then he turns on the tap and watches the beam of water wash the clumpy milk down the drain.

4

"I AGREED in a weak moment, Ruby," says Gilchrist. "I need a secretary as much as I need a wife."

"Gil, sometimes I think you need a wife more than you realize."

"Why do you say that? You of all people?"

"Instinct . . ."

Gilchrist watches Ruby crush her cigarette into a zigzag in the ashtray beside his bed and stand. She has always appeared to him as a woman who looks exactly her age, unlike the others he has known who strive to look younger or older. If someone guessed that Ruby Levenson was thirty-two years old, he or she would be exactly right. And it is a fit thirty-two. She is slightly taller than five and a half feet, and she has the kind of taut facial skin and set jaw that come from having done a lot of things outdoors and liking it. She is still wearing Gilchrist's terry-cloth white bathrobe that she slipped on after she showered. Unbelted, the bathrobe parts as she stands and reveals the naked axis of her body from the breasts and down.

"How long have we known one another, Ruby?" Gilchrist asks.

"Three years. Three years on the fifth of July."

"And how many times have we been together like this?"

"Here or in the apartment in Saranac?"

"Altogether."

"What do you want, a tally?" Ruby pulls the bathrobe around her and belts it with a quick bow. "You always know just what to say to take the romance out of the moment, Dodge. It's a good thing I'm as cynical as you are, or I'd be hurt."

"There's no cynicism in it, Ruby. You please me, and you tell me that I'm good at pleasing you. It's an even trade, and it's based on mutual

self-interest, which means that it's based on the best of all possible founda-
tions. And there are no lingering questions, right?"

"Right," says Ruby, but she is not smiling.

"When do you head north for Saranac?"

"Later on. I still have some things to do in the city."

"Still hooked on your horses up there?"

"What do you have against horses? For pure grace there's no other
animal that can match them."

"The female nude puts them all to shame," says Gilchrist, tugging
at her bathrobe so that Ruby has no choice but to sit on her side of the
tousled bed where he is still lying on his back, naked.

"Come on, Gil. Get dressed. You're going to make me believe that
you're a subliminal nudist."

"Why subliminal?"

"All right, just a nudist. Forget the adjective."

"Are you in a rush to go somewhere?"

"You're the one who said we were going out for dinner. Did you change
your mind? Do you want to go or don't you?"

"In due time," says Gilchrist. He eases up until he is sitting beside
Ruby on the edge of the bed. He runs his hand up and down her back, up
and down, and down.

"Come on, Gil. This is one Jewish girl who happens to be hungry."

"You confirm my theory."

"What theory?"

"My theory of the world."

"What might that be?"

"We're all creatures of appetite. Appetite and consciousness are all we
have going for us. Understand those two forces, and you understand the
way things are. Camus understood that."

"Camus? Did that great insight come to you just because I said I was
hungry?"

"In part, yes."

"I was talking about dinner. What appetite are you talking about, or
should I ask?"

"Guess."

"You're impossible."

Gilchrist stands and turns slowly to the right so that he is facing her. Ruby does not look up at him even when he takes her hands in his and raises her slowly to her feet so that they are standing face-to-face. Using first his right hand, then his left, Gilchrist slips his arms under her loosening bathrobe flaps and locks his fingers at the back of her waist, which is still moist from the shower. The loose bow of the bathrobe belt slowly unties itself until the folds of the robe part completely. Drawing her closer to him, he kisses her on the forehead, then on each brow.

"Is this Act 2?" asks Ruby, still not raising her eyes to look at him.

"Look at me," says Gilchrist. It sounds like an order.

"Come on, Gil. I just took a shower. I don't want to have to take another one."

"Look at me, Ruby. I don't give a frank damn about the shower or about the dinner."

"But I do."

"What kind of horsewoman are you?"

"How did horses get back in the conversation?"

"Because I want to feel how strong your grip still is." He pauses for a moment.

"How's this?" she asks, embracing him around the neck and situating herself hard against him from the kneecaps upward.

"No, the full grip, Ruby."

"Which leg first?" She is looking directly at him now.

"The right one."

Ruby raises her right leg and locks it around his thigh.

"Did you know," says Gilchrist, "that this is the way that Josephine Baker liked to do it in her Paris days—standing up?"

"I'm not Josephine Baker, Gil. I'm Ruby Levenson, and unless you want me to lose my balance, you're going to have to do your part and help me."

Gilchrist lets his hands slide under her buttocks to make a seat sling as she lifts her left leg and interlocks her left and right ankles around the small of his back. Then she hugs him simultaneously with her arms and legs.

"It's at times like this, Ruby, that I'm grateful for your experience on horseback."

"Gil," she says, kissing him on the side of his neck, "you're shameless. Has anyone ever told you that?"

"Shall we dance?" Locked together, they make a slow circle in place.

"Stop it, Gil. I'm not as light as I was ten years ago."

"I didn't know you ten years ago."

"You've made up for it."

"We've both made up for it."

Gilchrist turns around with her and seats himself on the side of the bed. He feels her weight settle slowly into his lap so that they are able to connect easily. With his arms around her hips he tugs her closer to him, and she responds by pressing her body from the waist down against his to make the connection sure. She places her head on his shoulder and lets her arms drop to her sides so that the bathrobe slips to the floor.

"Gil?" she whispers.

"Yes."

"Would you be mad if I told you something right now?"

"Depends."

"I have to say it."

"Say it."

"You know how you make me feel?"

"How?"

"You make me feel like food."

"Why do you say that?"

"I feel I'm just here to satisfy you when you want me."

"It's reciprocal, isn't it? I thought we agreed about that before."

"No, it isn't really. I don't look at you that way. Women are different from men. Coming together is more than just . . . I don't know the right word."

"Don't make too much of that." He waits, then adds, "We're starting to lose the drama of the moment."

"Doesn't friendship mean something to you? Why does the high point have to be what we're doing right now? Why does it always have to wind up this way?"

"Friendship is one thing, and what we're doing right now is something else. Let's not confuse the two."

"That's the problem with you."

"Not my problem, Ruby. Yours. Now stop acting like you've never been kissed and just enjoy yourself."

"It's your problem, Gil, but you don't want to admit it." She tightens her arms around his neck and kisses him again on the neck, then on the mouth.

"That's better," he tells her when the kiss ends.

"Gil," says Ruby, "it bothers me that I'm not the only woman in your life."

"You're the only Ruby in my life."

"That's not the point." She pauses and loosens her grip. "How many others are there, by the way?"

"That's the wrong subject for the time at hand, Ruby."

"I know there are other women. You won't shock me if you tell me how many. I like to know what I'm up against."

Gilchrist, still holding her, stands up by the bed. He releases her legs one by one so they have to separate. He waits until she is able to get her balance.

"Let's go to dinner, Ruby."

"What happened to Act 2? I may be wrong, but I don't think we finished."

"What's true of lovemaking is also true of kissing. You can't talk and kiss at the same time. You apparently want to talk. So we'll go to dinner and talk. That's as good a time to talk as any."

"Are you upset?"

"No."

"I'll stay if you want, and I won't say another word. Besides, I don't want to go out to dinner anymore." She waits a moment and adds, "Let's stay."

"It won't be the same, Ruby. The mood's gone."

"It doesn't have to be."

"Let's go to dinner."

II

Raya's Time

5

GILCHRIST NOTICES that she seems less self-conscious now than when Tabry introduced her to him four nights earlier at his house.

"Raya," Tabry said at that time, "I'd like you to meet my oldest and best friend in Washington—Dodge Gilchrist."

She smiled at Gilchrist and looked down and then looked immediately up to see if he was still looking at her, and he was.

Now as she sits at Gilchrist's desk in his apartment while he explains what working with him will entail, she appears much more sure of herself. When Gilchrist looks at her, he notices that she does not look down but directly back at him in an attitude of complete attention.

"I do all my real work here, Miss Tabry," Gilchrist is saying. "I have a desk at the office in town, but it's really just a mailing address. I'm down there, maybe, once a week for a few hours to do a little paperwork, pick up my mail, and talk things over with my editor. But the real writing is done right here, or rather it's done right here when I'm in Washington. Otherwise, my office is where my head is, and I e-mail what I write directly to the paper."

She nods to indicate that she understands completely and will always, when things are explained to her, understand completely. He leads her to his computer and asks if she can take dictation directly. She answers yes and indicates with her eyes that she is ready. Gilchrist begins reciting the opening lines from Lincoln's address at Gettysburg and studies her as she types. In her white blouse and tan skirt she seems darker complexioned than she appeared when he first saw her. She has her hair pulled back into a tight French roll, and the blackness of her swirled hair glistens. Her eyes never lose the look of total concentration. They are blue-gray, and they are as clear as mountain brooks or polished gems. She has Tabry's facial structure, more linear than oval. Gilchrist notes that her posture at the computer is almost soldierly—shoulders back, spine absolutely straight, feet together.

When Gilchrist finishes his dictation, Raya prints out what she has typed and hands it to him. There is not an error on the entire page. The spelling, the punctuation, and the spacing are perfect.

"Very good," says Gilchrist and smiles at her.

She returns the smile but stays at the computer as if she is ready for the next assignment.

6

"SHE'S DOING A GOOD JOB, if that's what you mean," Gilchrist is saying to Tabry. They are walking in the garden of Dumbarton Oaks where Tabry asked Gilchrist to meet him. "Does she talk to you about what she is doing? Does she like it?"

"She discusses very little, says very little. That's why I wanted to talk to you like this."

"Well, she's everything you said she would be. The work on the computer is letter perfect. Her efficiency is perfect. Yesterday she handled a matter for me with the French Embassy in fifteen minutes that I've been trying to resolve for more than six months."

"But does she talk about herself, about what she might be thinking, about what happened to her, about anything . . ."

"No," says Gilchrist, remembering. "No."

"It's the same with me. I'm her uncle, her father's only brother, the last person in the family who's still alive. She treats me with respect, but I have the feeling that it's her way of keeping a distance between us and keeping her private thoughts to herself. I don't feel I'm getting to know her at all, and I don't know how to make that happen."

"Do you see any serious problems developing?"

"No."

"Then why not leave well enough alone? She'll break her silence when the time is right."

"But it's not well enough, Gil, not at all. And that's my point." He plucks a budding rose from one of the bushes beside the path. The unopened petals look like a small red knot on a leafless stem. "She's like this rose. All self-contained. Tight. Perfect. Ready to bloom but not blooming, not even trying to bloom. The real rose is all on the inside." Tabry looks intently at the closed flower as if he is looking at a human face. "She does everything for me. Meals. Laundry. Housecleaning. She makes me feel like a king. But at night I hear her crying in her room. It's been like that for the three months that she's been here. Not every night, mind you. But I hear her crying a lot, even though she does her best to stifle it. It's deep crying, and it's interior."

"Do you face her with that?"

"I almost did once, but something inside of me made me stop before I started. I just couldn't do it. And I can't do it now. Honestly, I can't. I don't know why, but I can't." Tabry clenches his hand around the rosebud. "She keeps everything inside of herself. Her father used to do the same thing. But with him it eventually found its way out in a poem. But with Raya there is no poem, no outlet. She's never said a syllable about the last month before she came to the States, the month she was detained in prison. When she comes home after her work with you, she just closes the door on the world. It's as if the work is enough for her. I've invited some of the younger faculty members over for dinner once or twice. She's cordial to them, but it's the most correct cordiality you can imagine. I've run out of ways to reach her. I don't know how to bring her out of herself."

"What are you building up to, Tab?"

"Nothing revolutionary," Tabry answers and drops the rosebud.

"Let's have it. Straight out."

"Well," says Tabry, "the fact is that she's developed quite a respect for you. I suppose you've noticed that."

"Go on."

"You know that I have all your work archived at my house—a complete file of all your columns. Well, she's read the entire file. And she's read it more than once. I think she reads it because she wants to know everything she can know about you. And every time I mention your name, I can see something in her eyes that wasn't there before."

"Well, I can assure you that she's never tipped her hand in front of me. What you're saying is all new to me."

"No, she wouldn't. She couldn't. She's been raised in a tradition that precludes that. It would go against her upbringing and her character to do something like that."

"Look, Tab, one thing I don't need right now is romance. And I mean that. It would get between me and my work, and my work is my religion, and I don't plan to change religions at this point. You know my philosophy of life: doing a good job, looking to enjoy the best that exists out there in what we call the things of this world, and checking out the females of the species. If they want to show me some hospitality, okay. But I don't want any more than that, if that. No names, no obligations, no regrets." Tabry opens the garden gate as Gilchrist finishes speaking, and together they leave as Gilchrist resumes. "Raya's everything you said she'd be, Tab. She's intelligent. She has taste. She's honest, and she's doing right by me. She is terrific with the computer, and my files are in the best order they've ever been. I'd just as soon leave it at that."

When Tabry responds, it's as if he has not listened to anything Gilchrist has been saying. "Gil, when you go to the mountains next week, I'd appreciate it if you would take Raya with you."

"Take her to Saranac?"

"Yes."

"No. Double no," says Gilchrist. "You know I have a cottage up there, and I don't think it would create the proper atmosphere, you might say, if Raya and I were staying in the same three-room cottage, do you?"

"She could stay in the inn. I stayed there once, remember? It's not far from your cottage. She could work with you during the day and stay in the inn at night. You'll need someone to help you, won't you?"

"No deal, Tab. I've done all I'm going to do. I've taken her on as a favor to you, even though the immigration laws state that she shouldn't be working at all. And I don't mind having done that. She's very good, and I'll pay her out of pocket as long as she wants to work with me. But at Saranac I like to be by myself. There's some work that I'm planning to do alone, and there may be some other things to do. Why do you want me to take her?"

"I think the change would be good for her. She might open up to you, talk a little. And I think that would be good for her. She has everything so suppressed within her that I can feel, actually feel, the tension when I'm with her. I can't let her turn herself into a nun for my sake while I just stand by and wait for the pressure to take its toll."

"Still no deal, Tab. I'm not one of your junior faculty members. I have a lot of private work to do up in Saranac on my Latin American book, and my social calendar is filled with a woman I know there who loves horses."

"Aren't there some little things that Raya could help you with up there?"

"Sure there are, but the answer is still no."

After a pause Tabry shrugs and says, "All right, Gil. I understand. I just thought I'd ask."

Even as Tabry finishes, Gilchrist realizes that his refusal is already dissipating. He tries to summon the firmness of his last *no*, but it is already gone. He is thinking of that as he continues to walk in silence beside Tabry, who already seems to be on the verge of speaking about something else. Finally, Gilchrist offers, "If you make it sound like some kind of emergency, I might change my mind. You can tell her I asked you to find out if she could spend a week at Saranac to help me over the rough spots with the Latin American book. Don't be too obvious about it, that's all."

"Thanks, Gil," says Tabry. "I knew I could count on you."

Together they start down a descending back street into the center of Georgetown.

"What the hell do I get for all my magnanimity?" asks Gilchrist with a laugh.

"I'm using the essay you gave me last week as the leading article in the anniversary issue of the journal. I'll make you more famous than you are already," Tabry answers with a wink, adapting himself to Gilchrist's change of mood so that for a few moments they are undergraduates again.

"You were going to do that anyway, you old rug trader," says Gilchrist and laughs.

Tabry gives him another wink.

7

GILCHRIST WATCHES Raya approach him down the path from the inn. As she nears him, he has the sense that she has the walk of a dancer. She seems almost weightless, and she walks without self-consciousness, as if walking is secondary to her and she is capable of more balletic movements.

"Would you like to take a quick hike through the woods?" Gilchrist asks her. "It's a good way to relax after a long day's work, and we've both done a long day's work." He remembers not only the day at hand but the three previous days since their arrival in Saranac when he dictated summaries of his notes for the Latin American book to Raya. He explained in a general way that the theme of the book would be based on hemispheric differences in attitudes toward political power—the Latin Americans equating power with oratory, constituencies of friends, personal confidence, and, for lack of a better word, stature, while the North Americans seem inextricably wedded to the equation of power with money, influence, prestige, organization, and advertising. He also explained that *machismo* to the Latins is a synonym for male weakness, indicating that the "macho male" is covering up with braggadocio and posturing what he lacks in character. Now Gilchrist is word-surfeited with the nuances that his thesis has been forcing upon him. All he wants is to get away from his desk and his papers, to smell birch and spruce, to feel mountain earth under his feet.

"Yes," says Raya in response to his invitation. "I would like that."

Gilchrist has become accustomed to her easy deference to him. Actually, it is not deference, no, not quite deference. He decides to call it agreeability, but it is agreeability as a fine art.

"Do you have a good pair of walking shoes?" he asks her.

"Yes," she answers, "but they are back in my room. I can go back and change and meet you."

Gilchrist points to a hiking trail by the lake and says, "Do you see that trial over there?"

"Yes."

"Can you meet me there?"

"Yes."

Later, when Gilchrist and Raya are together on the pine-and-birch-flanked trail, they walk briefly without speaking. Gilchrist is wondering why he hasn't called Ruby as he customarily does when in Saranac—Ruby who, after her divorce, taught Gilchrist how to ride all the horses in her stable and who was always ready to be with him whenever he called her either in Washington or in Saranac. Once she had flown overnight to Paris to spend a weekend with him because she thought he "sounded lonely" and because she had nothing better to do. Invariably, she told him that they should reserve mornings for their lovemaking because then they were rested and fresh and could shower afterward once and for all for the day ahead. She and Gilchrist had come to a working agreement, deciding that the "clock of sex" had no hands anyway, so why should they or anybody become enslaved to the idea of lovemaking at night followed by sleep?

Now, as he walks and thinks of Ruby's outspokenness as well as her almost perfect legs and the soft duet of her breasts, he finds that he feels no desire for her whatsoever. Instead he turns to the girl who is walking beside him and feels a quiet pleasure in the bond that their working together has already created between them. For Gilchrist, this feeling is entirely new. Always, throughout his entire life, he has thought of work as the one absolute in his life. He regarded it as a religion, and he practiced this religion with the fidelity of an ascetic. He kept it free of surfeits and falsities. Having shared this part of himself with Raya for only a few months has forged something between them that has gone beyond professionalism and transformed itself into a pace, a vow of sorts, a trust.

"Raya," he says. It surprises him to hear the name from his own lips since it is the first time he has not called her Miss Tabry.

"Yes."

"How do you like this kind of work?"

"Have I done something wrong?" she asks and stops as if waiting for a reprimand.

"No," says Gilchrist quickly, trying to seem as casual as possible in order to dissipate whatever implication she has drawn from the question. "No, that's not what I meant at all. Not at all."

After a pause Raya says, "I like the work very much, Mr. Gilchrist. It's an entirely new life for me."

Gilchrist waits for her to add something, but he soon realizes that there will be nothing more. It is her habit—to say exactly what she means the first time she says it. In his brief association with her, he cannot recall her having used qualifiers or disclaimers, not once. Now as he watches her step toward a lilac bush and pick two of the blooms and make them into a petite bouquet, he is impressed as a writer by how well she mints her words. They do not seem to be things that evolve for her. It's as if she has the gift of saying discreetly the very thing she is thinking of as she thinks it. Even the tone of her voice is such that it keys itself to what her spoken words mean to create in a perfect marriage of tone and sense. Gilchrist is thinking of this with mild admiration while he watches her inhale the fragrance from the bouquet of lilacs. She smiles with pleasure from the fragrance and then directs the same smile at Gilchrist.

"Are you adjusted to the United States by now?" he asks.

"It's such a wonderful country, such a great country. I'm grateful to be here with my uncle, and I'm happy to be working with you, but . . ." She pauses and looks at Gilchrist. "But this is not my country. I don't mean to be disrespectful. I love it here, but this is not my country. Do you understand?"

For a moment Gilchrist thinks it is not Raya who is talking but Tabry himself. Somewhere, sometime in the past, he must have heard Tabry say something similar. The echo lingers like smoke. Gilchrist contends with a moment of déjà vu before he says, "Your uncle's worried about you, Raya."

She nods a slow but definite yes.

"He thinks," continues Gilchrist, "that you're not letting yourself come to life here, that you're holding back, not talking, not mixing, not coming out of yourself. It has him worried sick."

Raya continues to walk beside Gilchrist, but she remains silent.

"Is this something that you want to talk about or not?" Gilchrist persists. Before she has a chance to answer, he says, "I'll change the subject if you want. It's not my business, but your uncle and I have been friends a long time. I know when something is bothering him. I won't share what you tell me with him."

"It's not something I would like to discuss, Mr. Gilchrist. What happened in the past year I would like to forget, but I can't seem to think it to sleep, as we say in my country." She pauses. "For all those weeks in detention, I had no one to talk to but the interrogators, and there was nothing I wanted to say to them. Now I just focus on my work with you. If I didn't have that, I don't know what I would do. As long as I'm working, I forget." She pauses again. "Uncle Sharif tries to introduce me to new people, and they are always nice to me, but they have no sensitivity to what is inside of me. Sometimes I want to tell you how I feel, but . . ." She continues to walk beside Gilchrist, and he begins to detect through the brief space between them something stronger than memory, something more palpable. Pain? Anger? Regret? He cannot be sure.

"Were you abused in prison?"

"Did Uncle Sharif ask you to ask me that?"

"No, but it's something that's crossed his mind. You don't have to answer unless you want to."

Raya holds the lilac bouquet with both hands against her, and her grip tightens. Her eyes widen, and she looks directly in front of her when she speaks. "There was a slogan that the guards used to say to one another in the prison where I was kept—'the only good prisoner is a broken prisoner.' Every day the guards found ways to break the prisoners—to make them 'good.'" Raya looks at Gilchrist to see if he understands. A few reluctant tears edge suddenly over the brim of her lower eyelids and then streak down the sheer slides of her cheeks. She wipes them with the top of her right wrist, first from one cheek, then from the other. "You don't know what being at their mercy is like, Mr. Gilchrist, until you face it. You have no idea." The tears start again. "In the beginning they threatened me. They said that things would be difficult for me if I didn't cooperate with them. They wanted me to sign a paper repudiating my father and his writings. I told them I was my father's daughter and that I would never sign such a thing. They said that my father was a public enemy and that he deserved to die. They said terrible things about my father. They told me over and over that he deserved what happened to him. Then they left me alone. They left me alone for days, many days. When you're left alone like that, you forget what time means. Everything is only the silence right now, right now, right now, and right now becomes more and more like a dream the longer it goes on. I couldn't eat the food they pushed through a slot at the bottom of the door. I couldn't eat it. At night I could hear screams from the other cells, and I could tell they were abusing somebody. I found out later that sometimes these were tape recordings to put fear in all of us, but at other times the screams were real. There was no way to tell the difference, and the effect was the same regardless. I kept trying to imagine what was going to happen to me, but nothing happened. Finally, a man from the Red Crescent visited me. Two soldiers came with him. The soldiers let him talk to me for five minutes. That's all. I told the man that I had no idea why I was in prison. He wrote down everything in a notebook. When he finished speaking, he stood up and told me that the right people would be informed about my case. Then the soldiers took the notebook from him and led him away."

"Did you hear from him after that?"

"No. I heard nothing. Many days passed after his visit, and still no one came to question me again. I was just fed and left to myself. Finally, I was taken to an office where I was served tea in a real cup with a real saucer under it, and a woman in civilian clothes asked me if she could be of help to me. She knew my name, my family background, everything about me, and she spoke to me in Arabic. She explained that everything would be over if I only signed a paper. I asked what was on the paper since it was written in Hebrew. Instead of answering me, she showed me a dossier. She said that there was enough evidence in the dossier to prove that my father and my uncle were enemies of the state. She said there was no way to disprove the evidence. She said I had no choice but to sign the paper to show that I agreed with the findings."

"Did she translate anything for you?"

"Only the last paragraph. It said that my father was paid to write his poems by outside powers and that my uncle was slandering the government at the command of outside powers. She said the evidence in the dossier proved this beyond doubt."

"Which outside powers?" Gilchrist asked.

"There were no names. There never are. They leave the accusations vague to make them sound worse than they are. I told the woman that my father wrote poems that came from his heart, and that my father and my uncle both loved their country—their real country—and would do nothing to shame it, ever. As soon as I said that, she pressed a button on her desk, and the two guards took me back to my cell. There were three interrogators waiting for me in my cell, and one was a woman. The chief interrogator was blond with a brown mustache. I had heard about him. His name was Gelb, but the prisoners called him Double Gelb because his hair and his mustache did not match. He was supposed to be a specialist in interrogating women. The man with him was smaller, but he imitated Gelb in every way—speech, mustache, even the way he walked and sat. The woman was tall and looked as strong as a man. She approached me and told me to take off my clothes. I refused, and I told her in Arabic that it was a disgrace for her to ask me to do that, especially in front of men. Then she grabbed my dress and pulled it from me. And she did the same with my undergarments. Then Gelb told her and the other man to leave. He showed me the dossier that the woman in the office had shown me, and I could feel his eyes on me. I kept trying to cover myself with my hands. Gelb continued to look at me and held the paper and said I had to sign it. I refused. He said he could wait. He just sat and kept looking at me. I had never been without my clothes before a man in my life, Mr. Gilchrist. In my country women regard this as the greatest shame. So I felt smaller and smaller as I stood there, and I felt more and more ashamed. Gelb asked me why I was trying to cover myself with my hands. He smiled when he said that. Then he walked over to me and just stood there, wait-ing. He told me I had just a few minutes more to reconsider signing. He said he could always call the guards back and let them see me that way, and then he would leave me alone with them. He said the guards were young and did not see women very often, and they would take a special pleasure in seeing me like that." Raya pauses and drops the lilac bouquet as if she had never been holding it in the first place.

"You don't have to go on with this, Raya," says Gilchrist. "I wasn't trying to rake up old memories." He sees her turn away from him, and he notices that her flanks are shaking in quick, deep spasms like the flanks of a runner after an excruciatingly difficult race. Most of the women Gilchrist has seen in tears have wept out of disappointment or frustration or anger or even guile, but he has never seen this kind of lonely, uncontrollable sobbing. He steps toward her and touches her shoulder as if to reassure her, but the sobbing does not stop. She keeps her face turned away from him. "Raya," he whispers calmly, but she still does not face him.

After several moments Raya straightens and wipes her cheeks and eyelids with the backs of her wrists as she did earlier. Composed, she faces Gilchrist. Her cheeks are white, and her lips almost match the color of her cheeks.

"I'm sorry, Mr. Gilchrist," she says. "I've never talked about this before. Never with anyone. It is very difficult for me." She looks away and then resumes, as if she has no choice but to finish the story. "They tried to shame me. They never gave back my clothes and left me alone for hours. I kept waiting for the soldiers to come, but they never came. I kept telling myself that my love for my father and my country was more important than my feelings about myself or my shame, and I took courage from that. I slept that night on the floor, but at the slightest sound I would wake up. It was so cold. I had no covering for myself. I had nothing for my needs, nothing at all. It was terrible. Then after three days, they brought back my clothes and told me I could leave. And just a week later I was on my way to America."

"That's enough for me," interrupts Gilchrist. "Let's go back."

"It makes me ashamed to say these things to you. You really should not hear such things."

"It's all right, Raya. I've heard worse."

"Some people told me that it is better to talk," she adds, "but it is also worse."

"That depends on what you say and who is listening," says Gilchrist. Suddenly, Gilchrist becomes aware of the scent of pine and hemlock all around them. He inhales and holds the evergreen air in his lungs as if it is the last breath he will ever take. "Take a deep breath, Raya. It will make everything else seem unimportant."

She smiles, inhales, and smiles again, but the smile is still the smile of embarrassment.

"We all have our embarrassing stories, Raya," says Gilchrist as they resume walking. "Somebody has to listen. Seven years ago I knew a man who was engaged to a girl named Holly. The wedding date was set. He really loved this girl, or at least he thought he loved her, which probably amounts to the same thing, at least from his point of view. The wedding was just a matter of weeks away, and all of a sudden this Holly goes off and marries a man twice her age. Not a word of explanation. Not a word to this day." He pauses and waits for Raya to make a comment, but she is primed only for listening. "This man told me the whole story over and over, and he had no answers. What do you make of that?"

"I think he must have been disappointed. And hurt. Deeply hurt. Anyone would be."

"He was hurt all right. He was hurt plenty."

"Perhaps," says Raya, "perhaps this Holly may have realized she loved this older man more than she loved him and couldn't face your friend with the truth of her feelings. That could have happened. She may not have had the courage. It's possible for me to understand that."

"Despite the difference in age?"

"That's not the important point, Mr. Gilchrist. Your friend is wrong if he thinks that age was even a factor. Men think more about age than women do when it comes to love. In my country this is not regarded as an essential consideration at all. All that matters is the feeling and trust and love that a man and woman feel for one another."

"But this didn't happen in Palestine, Raya. This happened right here in God bless America." With that, Gilchrist pauses and continues walking with Raya down the path until they reach the lake. "Anyway, this man kept all this to himself, and in time it really poisoned him. He started to see all women as Holly, and he kept trying to revenge himself on all of them. It's only lately that he's had the self-honesty to admit to himself that he's wasted a lot of time trying to get even with many women after being disappointed by one." He pauses. "Of course, if this man had someone he could have talked to about this before it started to poison him, he might have saved himself a lot of wasted motion. If he could have talked to someone the way you've been talking to me, maybe he could have lived a little differently over the past seven years."

"Does he have regrets now?"

"He says he doesn't."

"Do you believe him?"

"Why not?"

"But doesn't he have regrets about wasting seven years of his life?"

"I don't know," says Gilchrist as they reach the shore of the lake. Darkness has descended upon them, shadow by shadow, and the moonlight has begun to speckle the surface so that it glints like armor. "God, but it's beautiful out here, isn't it?"

"Yes. Very beautiful."

"You'll think I'm crazy if I tell you what I feel like doing," says Gilchrist. Actually, the statement is more for himself than for Raya. He starts to remove his shirt. "I feel like a good swim."

"Now?"

"Now."

"But it is dark."

"That's what makes it possible. Why don't you just relax on that bench over there for a few minutes and enjoy the evening. Then you can walk back to the inn, and I'll meet you for a nightcap or a cup of coffee."

"But you have no bathing suit."

"None needed. It's too dark to matter, and there's no one else around."

"But you are not serious, Mr. Gilchrist."

"Totally serious," says Gilchrist. "It's the best way to put your troubles behind you." He smiles and walks out of sight, but he feels like a man who has just told a bad joke to the wrong person. Once at the inlet he sheds his clothes, tests the cold lake with one foot, and makes a flat dive into the glistening water. When he surfaces, he shudders from the cold and waits for the exhilaration that he knows is bound to come. When it finally does, he strokes out from shore, turns on his back and floats. He counts the indifferent stars. After several minutes he treads water and breaststrokes slowly shoreward. He thinks he hears the sound of another splash from behind the trees, but he is not sure.

He waits to hear movement in the water, but there is none. The image of Raya swimming only a matter of yards away from him in the cold lake focuses itself in his mind. Imagining her with nothing on in the water is a thought he feels he should not be thinking. But the image does not leave him. He wonders if he really heard the splash of her dive or not. He listens. He resists the impulse to swim toward where he thinks she might be, but his imagination has already overtaken him. He feels her presence in the water as if the two of them are actually swimming side by side.

Once ashore he dries himself quickly with his undershirt, then puts on his clothes and shoes and walks slowly toward the inn.

8

GILCHRIST KNOWS IT IS RUBY. Even though the horse and rider are more than fifty yards away, he can see clearly that the woman in the saddle has blonde hair and that the horse is the color of cordovan—Ruby's favorite bay. As the bay canters across the pasture and up the bridle path to Gilchrist's cottage, Gilchrist imagines that he is watching both horse and rider in a void or in a slow-motion film without a soundtrack. He cannot hear the hooves hitting ground. When he finally does, the sound is a minisecond behind the sight of them, hitting. The old law about the speed of light outdistancing the speed of sound converts itself in the film of Gilchrist's imagination into a scene in which the sound is not quite synchronized with the movement he is observing. The entire instant of the experience mesmerizes him until Ruby rears the sweating bay less than ten yards in front of him and asks, "When did you get here? And why didn't you call me?"

"I had a lot of work to do, Ruby, and I'm still not done."

"Everybody has work to do, Gil. But there are telephones. Have you been introduced to telephones? You just pick up the receiver and dial. It's really very simple. People do it all the time."

"From the tone of that statement, I have the feeling that you've been rehearsing that line all the way up here."

"Don't play the bastard. When I'm hurt or disappointed, I get bitchy. And when I found out that you were here and didn't even call me, I was hurt and disappointed."

Gilchrist hears the screen door of his cottage being opened and closed behind him. Turning, he sees Raya on the porch. She glances at him and then at Ruby, realizes that she has interrupted something, and quickly reenters the cottage. When Gilchrist again faces Ruby, he feels the fusillade of her stare.

"Is that one part of the work you are doing?"

"She's my secretary."

"Does she have the skills for that, or does it matter?"

"She qualifies, if that's what you mean."

"I'm sure," says Ruby and smirks. She canters the bay in a small circle around Gilchrist as if she is coiling him to the spot. Gilchrist picks up the acrid order of horse as the bay brushes against him.

"Is your secretary . . . ," Ruby begins. Her tone has changed so that she no longer sounds combative. "Is she staying long, Gil?"

"It depends. We still have a few more things to finish."

"This is the first time in all the years we've known one another that you've come to Saranac and haven't called me." The combative tone is back. "Do you realize that?"

"I was busy, Ruby. There was nothing personal in my not calling you." Even as he finishes the sentence, Gilchrist feels the uneasiness of untruth in his words. He wonders in passing what it is that is beginning to change him without his willing or rather despite his willing it one way or another.

"We've missed a whole week, Gil. That's one whole week we'll never have again." Ruby smiles and sweeps her blonde hair out of her eyes as she rises in the stirrups and then eases herself slowly back on the saddle. "Right now I'd like to be settling down on something better than this saddle, something a lot more interesting and better for both of us." She smiles again. "Think about that, Gil, while you bury yourself in your, how shall I say it, work." She reins the bay's head abruptly to the right and, with a quick flex of her legs against the flanks of the horse, gallops off down the path in a clatter of hooves on the small stones.

Gilchrist watches until both horse and rider vanish behind a clump of spruce and birch. Ruby's last words remain with him for just a few seconds. Four months earlier he would have found them provocative, even enticing. Now they seem somewhat off-color and brash, and, to his surprise, he finds them embarrassing.

9

"COULD YOU PLEASE read the last passage back to me, Raya?" Gilchrist asks.

Raya prints out the page she has just typed and reads, supplying, as Gilchrist has insisted, the punctuation marks as she goes. "If a person persists in his dissent in the country in question (comma) he may be arrested as a public annoyance with the hope that a temporary incarceration will cure him of his problem (period) If (comma) upon his release (comma) he returns to his former habits (comma) he is usually remanded to a mental hospital to be treated for mental imbalance (period) If this does not result in his recanting his views publicly (comma) he is destined for internal exile or prison where he is reminded daily that he is a ward of the state that he has betrayed by his actions (period) Dissent is thus seen as heresy (period) Heresy is treason (comma) and treason is incompatible with the official view of whatever the official view happens to be (period) If this resembles the profile of more than one country in our century (comma) it is probably because it could very well be the profile of a good many (period)"

"You might delete the last sentence, Raya. I think it makes the point after the point has already been made."

Gilchrist is still thinking of how he can further refine the paragraph when Raya asks, "Are you writing about what has happened in Palestine?"

"Not specifically. What happened there has a lot of old colonial politics attached to it and a lot of power politics as well. Israel and the United States play the power game better than most, but it all comes down to strengthening the relationship between the two, and anyone who challenges that can count on being called everything in the book." He pauses. "We use Israel when it's in our interest, and they return the favor. It's called the game of nations."

What Gilchrist does not tell Raya is how the Israeli government has now allied Israel with various dictatorial countries in Latin America, providing them with arms, money, and "advisers" and even offering the guaranteed services of their lobby with the Senate and House of Representatives in Washington. He keeps to himself how the Israeli leaders stress their democratic traditions when in effect they keep supporting some of the most repressive regimes in the hemisphere with the means to remain repressive. When congressmen who returned from Latin America raised this issue in closed congressional hearings or even in the press, they were told by members of the Central Intelligence Agency that such "support from a responsible ally gave the United States leverage with those countries that it would not otherwise have." In one of his columns he almost called "Pimp and Circumstance," Gilchrist described the implications that he thought this had for the United States. This earned him the usual barrage of letters and denunciations, including one from the responsible ally's ambassador, who wrote, "When you are in the business of arms manufacture, you have the right, even the obligation, to sell to anyone who has the money to buy. That's simply free-market capitalism on an international scale." Gilchrist was tempted to reply that nations were not exactly the counterparts of department stores and that those who sold arms to known tyrants had to share at least some of the guilt when those arms were used to kill defenseless people, but he decided against it. The ambassador would probably have compared the sale of Uzis to the sale of diamonds and proceeded to shift the argument into the sphere of free trade, and Gilchrist's argument would have been lost in the give-and-take.

"But a lot of what you have written applies directly to us," says Raya.

"Maybe, but remember that when something is happening to you directly, you tend to see it in terms of everything else, and you also see everything else in terms of it. It's human nature."

"But you describe the situation perfectly."

"Well, regardless of that, I'd appreciate it if you'd print out all we've done here in a final draft, and that will finish what we came to Saranac to do. After that, we'll have some dinner, and I'll drive you to the airport, and you'll be back in Washington with your uncle in time for a snack and a cup of coffee. I'll call him and tell him when your plane is scheduled to arrive at National."

Raya has been listening carefully. When Gilchrist finishes, she says, "I've enjoyed working here, Mr. Gilchrist, and I appreciate your inviting me. I know why you did it. And I appreciate how you listened to what I told you yesterday. It embarrassed me to say what I said, but I felt I had to tell you. It's as if you are the only one who understands, really understands."

"Don't give it a second thought, Raya."

"Now," she says and then faces the computer, "I'll print out everything. Except the last sentence you told me to cancel."

As he watches her proceed with the printing, Gilchrist tells her, "You can talk to me anytime you think it would help, Raya."

She continues to work, but Gilchrist is sure she heard what he said.

10

LESS THAN TWO DAYS after his return from Saranac, Gilchrist is at his desk in his Washington apartment, proofreading the final page of his Latin American manuscript when the telephone rings.

"Hello."

"It's Tab, Gil." Tabry's tone is not what it usually is. There is a touch of apprehension in it.

"What's up, Tab?"

"I don't know how to say this."

"Just be frank."

"I think you've underestimated your charm with young women."

"Get to it, Tab."

"It's my niece, Gil. I think the girl's fallen . . ."

"Raya?"

"Yes, Raya. It's not apparent in anything she says. But I can recognize all the signs. And it's not some kind of infatuation. It seems much deeper than that. And it's all directed at you. I think I'm partly to blame for this, but it's not something that I thought would happen."

"And?"

"It's not because of the trip to Saranac. I'm not talking about that. It must have started before that. It's just that I didn't see it until she returned from Saranac. She seemed like a different person, more open one minute and then all of a sudden more depressed—and all for no reason." He pauses. "It's you, Gil, because of you. I don't know any other way to explain it."

"Just a minute, Tab. I don't know if you're right about this or not, but let me remind you that this whole arrangement was your idea. I wasn't for it from the beginning."

"I understand all that. And I'm not accusing or anything like that." There is silence for a moment before Tabry resumes. "I'm not suggesting that you initiated anything. I know you better than that. Please don't put that interpretation on it. This is not a matter of placing blame. If anyone deserves the blame, then I'm the one. I just completely overlooked the effect you have on women. It's always been one of your strong points, and it hasn't diminished over the years." Another pause. "You were the first American that Raya met. And she not only met you, but worked with you on a regular basis. The end result is that Raya thinks of you as a kind of hero. You have an international reputation. Important people call you on the telephone. She sees the company you move in. That's very heady wine for a girl from my part of the world."

"You underestimate your niece, Tab. She's not a victim of that kind of wine or anything like that. She's as intelligent as they come. I don't mean informed, well educated, and the usual. I mean intelligent. She can read between the lines." Gilchrist shifts the receiver from one ear to the other. He resists the satisfaction he feels from having learned of Raya's affection for him, more pleased than he is willing to admit, but he thinks he sees and understands what Tabry is driving at. "What do you want me to do, Tab? Let her go?"

"I don't know. I just don't want to make her a complication in your life or vice versa. I don't want to see her hurt over something that neither of us anticipated." He waits. "What do you think?"

"At this point I'm not thinking. You're doing the thinking. I'm just listening. I'll do what you want, what you think is best." Gilchrist's feeling of being pleased by what Tabry has told him suddenly turns into vexation. The fact that Raya cares for him and, from Tabry's account, seems to care more than casually touches something within him that he feels has never been touched before. But, knowing how readily the male of the species makes allowances for preferable self-deceptions, he distrusts even the pleasure that he now feels from knowing what he formerly suspected but has had confirmed by Tabry as a fact.

"If it's possible for you, Gil," Tabry says, "I'd appreciate it if you would let her down easily. You have more experience in these matters than I do. Perhaps her job with you could taper off gradually. That way she would not have an excuse to see you. I mean, she would not have occasion to see you. Socially, we don't see much of one another anyway, do we?"

"There's no such thing as letting somebody down easily, Tab. And if what she feels for me is as real as you say it is, it's not going to evaporate if we suddenly become strangers to one another. The exact opposite could happen. You're kidding yourself if you think that distance is going to solve anything." He shifts the receiver back to his left ear. "Raya is supposed to come back to work here on Monday to finish a few things. Let's follow that schedule and see how things go for a week or so. If I sense that there is no change in her, I'll think of some way to cool off the whole situation. I should be able to come up with something if I'm as qualified as you think I am." Gilchrist listens to his own voice as if it might be coming from someone else's mouth, and he wonders if Tabry is sensitive enough to detect what he detects. Is he lying to himself? And if he is, why is he?

"Gil, you can blame everything on me if you want. I know that I'm the one who put you in this fix, and I know that you didn't do anything to encourage what's happening. Before I called you, I wondered if I should just keep silent and let things go on. As a matter of fact, I haven't even asked you how you feel about her, what your feelings are . . ."

"My feelings aren't relevant, one way or the other."

"But how *do* you feel?"

"She's a first-class girl, Tab. I'm flattered that I'm on the receiving end of her feelings, but I'm a bit older . . ."

"Not that much older."

"Don't give me an opening like that, or I'm just liable to think that you're becoming a matchmaker."

"Well, I had to ask. My mistake was that I never took the possibility of her falling in love into consideration when it came to you."

"No one ever takes it into consideration. Falling in love is the universal accident."

"Well, I trust you no matter what you decide to do. I want you to know that. I also want you to know that you have my thanks in advance no matter how you decide to handle this."

"Don't thank me yet. I don't know what the outcome will be, and neither do you."

"That's true." A silence builds itself between the two before Tabry says in a completely different tone of voice, "How are things coming with your book? Raya told me a little about it."

"Slowly. Too slowly. The older I get, the slower I write. And it's always harder."

"Just like living, I suppose."

"Maybe. What about you? How's the anniversary issue of the journal coming?"

"I work on it every day. I should have it all put together by the end of the month, maybe sooner. And there are a few other things happening, and they look promising."

"But you can't talk about them yet, right?"

"Not now, but I will. And you'll be the first to hear."

"Just remember I'm a newspaperman, Tab. Don't tell me too much off the record."

"I knew you long before you were a newspaperman."

"You're too trusting."

"I'll risk it."

11

GILCHRIST KNOWS that Raya will arrive promptly at nine o'clock. One of the qualities that he recognized in her from the beginning of their work together was her scrupulous punctuality. Since returning from Saranac, Gilchrist has neither seen nor spoken with her. All that he now has in his mind's forefront is what Tabry broached to him during their phone conversation. Suddenly, even as he thinks of that or perhaps because of what it has prompted him to call to mind about Raya, he remembers, like an image imposed upon another image, the vased lilacs that she placed on his bed stand in Saranac before she left.

He sips more coffee from his third cup of the morning. He feels a certain discomfort that is equally divided between anxiety and fear—anxiety because he really wants to see Raya, wants her near so that he can taste her presence, wants his eyes to have their fill of her, wants to smell the quiet, fresh scent that is as proper to her as her smile, and fear because he hates to be at the mercy of his anxiety. For an instant he has the feeling that his very personality is abandoning him, is no longer his, no longer subject to him alone but to the personality of a girl he has known for just a few months. He asks himself again and again and again and again why he can't see her in the purely biological way he sees or has always seen other women in his life. Perhaps it is because she is not American. But no, he has known many foreign women who have never had this kind of effect on him. Perhaps it is because she is younger—but not that much younger—than he. He dismisses this as well because he has never sensed to date any evidence of age in himself or any ebb in his capacities. If anything, he knows the contrary feeling of being at the very peak of his powers. It is—it must be something else, he tells himself, something that discomforts him like an unhealing or an unhealable wound. He swigs the cooling coffee from his cup and asks himself if his discomfort is not derivative of some residual desire for Raya masquerading as concern. He knows from his own experience and observation the many guises that Pan can assume, and the avuncular or paternal impulse has always been one of the most commonplace. He wonders if it could be as simple as that. No. It couldn't be, or he would know it or should have known it by now. He reflects on how he has desired women in the past to see if a similar pattern is discernible now. Sometimes it was the simple need to possess sexually what he found attractive or desirable. The women Gilchrist chose at such times were invariably willing companions with whom he satisfied himself, and he cared little if they were satisfied or not. Then there were times when desire offered itself as an escape from loneliness or as a way of ridding himself of his residues or as a vengeance, a choice, a habit, a right, a tactic, a rejuvenation, an exercise, a tip, or an experiment. If what he feels for Raya is but a variation on the chromatic scale of his previous romances, Gilchrist is certain that he will know it in good time. The interim, he admits to himself, will be discomforting but revealing. But if he discovers something else in the process, something entirely different, what then? And what will he do in the meanwhile? Work as usual? What else? Gilchrist is ping-ponging the alternatives in his imagination when he hears Raya at the door. As soon as he sees her, his questions vanish. His anxiety and fear cancel one another, and he absorbs her presence until he knows the same satisfaction he has known just after he has written an American sentence as well as it could possibly be written, which, for Gilchrist, has always been a form of ultimate perfection.

"Good morning, Mr. Gilchrist," Raya says and smiles before proceeding directly to the computer.

"Good morning."

Gilchrist watches her inspect the papers on her desk.

"You have nothing new for me?" she asks. She is still smiling. "These are the pages I finished before we went to Saranac."

"Nothing new, I'm afraid."

"Is there something you would like to dictate?"

"Actually, nothing, Raya. I've just been proofreading what we did in the mountains. Polishing a phrase here and there." Gilchrist finishes the now cold coffee in his cup in one long swallow and stands. "Frankly, Raya,

I just don't have much here now for you to do. I should have called you before you left to come over here to save you the trip." Observing her, Gilchrist can see the echo of her original smile leave her face completely. In that instant she seems to turn into a younger girl, becoming someone who is disappointed and perplexed and incapable of understanding why and momentarily unwilling to try. Gilchrist can see from her expression that she seems to be blaming herself for this.

"Would you prefer I come back tomorrow, Mr. Gilchrist?"

"I'd like to say yes, Raya, but tomorrow looks as if it's going to be the same as today." Gilchrist raises his shoulders and drops them. He smiles slightly but not quite successfully. "It's just one of those dry periods. They come now and then to a writer. I try to write, but there's no juice."

Raya begins twisting a button on her blouse. Gilchrist braces for tears, but Raya, with a hard swallow and the slightest tightening of her jaw, comes to terms with herself, and the moment passes. "Perhaps," she begins, "there is something you're not telling me, something about my work . . ."

"No, of course not. No hidden reasons, Raya. Honestly."

"Perhaps I presumed too much by telling you what happened to me . . ."

"No, nothing like that . . ."

"I hope I didn't embarrass you by leaving the lilacs for you in your room. I realized afterward that it might have seemed too forward of me, but I wanted to show you in some way that I appreciated . . ."

"The lilacs?" Gilchrist says, frowning like a man who cannot quite remember the reference. He is *acting* totally now, and he only hopes that the act is persuasive.

"Yes, I left them in a vase in your room at the cottage. It was just my way of thanking you."

"Oh, the lilacs. *Those* lilacs. That was a nice touch, Raya. Didn't I thank you for them? I should have. It just slipped my mind, I guess." Gilchrist keeps trying to act as blasé as possible. He notices that Raya seems more and more hurt by every word he says.

"I'll just finish the filing I started before we left and leave after that, Mr. Gilchrist. I don't think it will take me very long."

Gilchrist walks into the kitchen with his empty cup and returns to find her busy with folders and papers at the filing cabinet.

"How's your uncle this morning, Raya? He and I have a meeting next week to look over the final proofs of the anniversary issue of the journal."

"My uncle is fine, Mr. Gilchrist. Thank you."

"Your uncle is a remarkable man, Raya. Ever since he was in college, he seemed to know exactly what he wanted to do or rather what he had to do, and then he went ahead and did it. I'm just the opposite. I know what I'm doing, and I know what I have been doing, and I know what I think I can keep on doing. But I don't know what I should want to do, if you understand what I mean." Gilchrist rethinks what he has just said and realizes that putting into words what was previously an amorphous series of insights into himself has suddenly exposed his real self. His words to Raya have provided a truth about himself that is truer than he realizes.

"But you are a writer . . ."

"No, I don't mean that. I'll keep writing, I suppose. It's my life, my way to earn a living. But my subject's the world. I pick and choose. I don't have what your uncle has—a mission, a specific purpose, something like that."

Raya is silent. Gilchrist feels the space between the two of them come alive with questions but no answers. He concentrates on the patterns in the carpet until the patterns, like bathroom tiles or repeated designs in wallpaper, mesmerize him to the point of dizziness. He listens as Raya shuffles the folders in her hands. It's like listening to rolling thunder from a great distance. Suddenly, the thunder stops, the way a forceful sentence comes to a complete stop at a period. Gilchrist looks up to see Raya slide the lateral file drawers shut. She leaves her hand momentarily on the handle as if to catch her balance. Again Gilchrist suspects she is fighting tears, but she simply turns her back to him and faces the file.

"Raya."

"Yes, Mr. Gilchrist," she answers, still facing away. Her voice is firmer now, but he can still feel her will in it to keep it from wavering.

"Don't be discouraged or draw the wrong conclusions because my work, or rather your work with me, has dried up. These times come and go. I know a lot of better jobs you can have in a minute. All I have to do is pick up that telephone, and you can have your choice of four or five . . ."

"But I am not permitted to work like that in America, Mr. Gilchrist."

"There are ways around that," Gilchrist shrugs and resumes. "Working with me here is really not enough for a girl with your talent. And I'm not just flattering you or complimenting myself when I say that. I know how good you are. And you must know how good you are, and, if you don't, you should. It's not that I . . ."

"You don't have to say any more, Mr. Gilchrist. I understand." She lifts her purse from the desk and walks toward him. When she stops in front of him, she keeps looking into his eyes, not so much for a hint of seeing something in them she wants to see but just to show him that she can accept what he is telling her, that she can face him, regardless.

"I don't know what conclusions you're drawing from all this, Raya. There's nothing personal in it. All I've been trying to tell you is . . ."

"You've already told me, Mr. Gilchrist," she says and looks directly into his eyes. "Everything you didn't say told me."

"What does that mean?"

"It means I understand. It means I'm going home now, Mr. Gilchrist." Still looking unflinchingly at him, she continues, "You've been very generous to me, and I want you to know how much I appreciate it. And I appreciate how you want to find another job for me, but I think I should do that for myself when the time comes."

"As you wish, Raya, but if you change your mind, just call."

"Thank you," she says and smiles a smile that ends as quickly as it began. "Thank you for everything." She turns, walks to the door, opens it, and leaves.

Gilchrist watches the closed door as if he expects it to speak to him. After several minutes he goes to his desk and drops into the swivel chair behind it. "Very noble of you, old Gilchrist," he says to the empty room. "Very damn noble. Now what?"

12

GILCHRIST IMAGINES that he is sinking. For more than two hours he has been on his back in bed, but the sleep he thirsts for does not come, and it seems as distant now as it appeared when he first came to bed. He reaches toward his bed stand and switches on his shortwave radio. The various frequencies clash and growl as he searches for a clear channel like a man trying to solve a combination lock on a safe and waiting for his fingertips to tell him that the tumblers are in the right alignment. Finally, he locates a voice. The accent is Scandinavian. Gilchrist guesses that he is listening to Danish, and he is mildly amused by how much Danish sounds like English spoken backward.

It's been a week since his meeting with Raya. He envisions Raya's face in the darkness, hears the special tone and rhythm of her way with words, sees her walk to his apartment door and open it and then close it behind her. The door keeps opening and closing and opening and closing like a scratched recording that will not proceed beyond the scratch so that it keeps repeating and repeating the same two or three notes forever until they become, like torture by water drops, a route to madness. The voice from Denmark becomes the undersong for the whole scene, and Gilchrist puts his palms to his temples as if to keep his head from bursting.

Earlier that evening he had dinner with Ruby in an attempt to re-create and recontact a life that his preoccupation with Raya had subordinated for months. As they were splitting a hefty slice of German chocolate cake for dessert, Ruby said, "You're good and smitten, Dodge. I thought I'd never live to see the day, but that day has dawned damn loud and clear."

"Don't start moralizing, Ruby. It doesn't sit well with dessert."

"I'm not moralizing, and you know it. I don't know this girl or anything about her pull on you, my buckaroo, but you're kidding yourself even further if you're telling yourself that you don't feel a thing for her."

Gilchrist lifted his coffee cup to his lips and sipped and then kept the cup at lip level as if to hide behind it.

"The trouble with you, Dodge," Ruby continued, "is plain ordinary 'male trouble.' It comes with the installment plan."

"And what's that?"

"Do you really want me to embarrass you by telling you to your face? Do you want me to spell it out for you?"

"Why not? I can spell. I can take it."

"The trouble with you is that you can't love without having. That's your problem. I don't know what's driving it. Maybe it's just a carryover from the revenge you've been taking out on the female sex because of that girl who stood you up at the altar, but you've gotten yourself in the grip of something that even a wizard like you is going to have trouble handling, let alone solving." Ruby pushed her dessert to one side and put her elbows on the table and added, "I wouldn't be telling you this if I didn't feel something for you, Dodge, even though I know you don't feel the same about me. For you, I'm just Ruby, and I'm there for the asking, and I've always been there for you. But that's another story, and I have no one to blame for that but myself. And if you want to know the God's truth, I'm jealous as hell, and I envy that girl for what you feel for her, and I only wish that you felt that way about me. And that's not an easy thing for a woman like me to admit, believe me." She paused to evaluate the weight of her words on him, but he remained impassive. "Actually, my real reason for leveling with you is that I don't think that you realize what's happening to you."

"Tell me."

"I can't tell you better than you can tell yourself. My God, haven't you learned one thing about women from all the women you've known? Or was it all just a game to you, just skin-deep? Or are you just one of those typical romantics, absolutely typical? Maybe that's all you are. Maybe it's just as simple as that."

"I'm still listening."

Ruby was becoming irked, wondering if he was really listening to her or just tolerating her until she stopped. She could not keep the chagrin out of her voice. "You just really used every woman who came along—me included, by the way—if she fit into your dreams or your schemes, but underneath it all you kept room for the special case, the special woman who'd be the answer to everything and break the pattern of your life that you couldn't break by yourself. And what happened? The special one just happened to come along. And your problem now is that you can't adjust to it, can you? You're trying like hell to pretend it's just a passing thing, but it's not working. And you still have the nerve to take me out to dinner just to distract yourself. Your real problem, Dodge, is that you can't admit to yourself that you have feelings, real feelings for this girl . . ."

"Is that everything? Have you finished your analysis?"

"Yes, that's everything. The fact of the matter is that you're no different from anybody else in the same fix. It's been going on for centuries, or haven't you noticed?" She paused and sat back, letting her hands rest on her lap. The anger faded from her face like a blush, and she let it go. She ran her thumb several times over the edge of the place mat. "Seriously, Dodge, I don't mind having dinner with you, even under these circumstances. In fact, I appreciate it because I've missed you. And I'm a little flattered that you've come back to me like this, even though it's for the wrong reason. At least, it shows me that you trust me that much. And if a night out with me will buy you a little time, I don't mind. We owe that much to one another. Besides, I've been doing a little dating lately. An Israeli. He's on temporary assignment here. He's an official. I met him at the embassy, and we've gone out a few times. He's educated, sophisticated. I've always enjoyed the embassy circuit, and he takes me to all of the social functions. It keeps me in circulation, and, if you're not in circulation in Washington, you might as well be living in Des Moines." She paused and smiled. "You're going to have to face the music sooner or later with this girl, Dodge. If you really love her and if she has the same feelings for you, then you're going to change or be changed. And that's an exclusive occupation. You're on your own with that. Outsiders like me are not welcome." She leaned across the table again. "Besides, you've had your own way for years now. Maybe you need an experience like this to help you make your life real again. I think the only thing that's bothering you now is that you, Dodge Gilchrist, the great operator and calculator, didn't pick the time and the place and the person. You're not in control this time, and that's a position you've never been in before. But it's a very democratizing experience. You're going to learn that you're just like the rest of us."

"You sound as if you're getting just the right amount of pleasure out of telling me this, Ruby."

"Pleasure? Why should I get any pleasure out of it? If I'm right, it means that I'm out of the picture. Permanently. And I'm pretty sure I'm right."

As he relives his conversation with Ruby in the restaurant, Gilchrist turns on his side in the bed. The radio voice from Denmark recedes like a mountain echo and is replaced by static. Ignoring the static, Gilchrist thinks over what Ruby told him earlier and is amazed at how precisely she has seen into the iris of his unrest. Her sensitivity surprised him, and he realizes that he had never seen that side of her, never before been confronted by—what should he call it?—her wisdom. He reaches across the bed stand and switches off the radio, but the silence of the room becomes so overpowering that he immediately switches it back on and leaves it on. "My God, Gilchrist," he says to the darkness, "it's really something when you need static for company."

Gilchrist has always taken a certain energy from self-reliance—a self-reliance that his finely toned body and his intelligence and education have together created. Whenever he needed the strength to confront and solve anything, he merely had to reach back, and the strength was there. But now there is only strangeness, as if his mind is no longer his instrument but his tormentor, as if his body's very mortality is weighing upon him rather than enlivening him, as if he has somehow become alienated from himself.

As he stares into the darkness, he sees for the first time into his dilemma. All that he has suppressed now surfaces. For so many years he had simply regarded women as a series of females; they simply were what he was not, and it was their embodiment of what he thought he needed from them when he needed it that made their lives relevant and complementary to his own. That they had families was of little interest to him. That they had problems was of less interest to him. That they had convictions and ambitions interested him least of all. It was their presence that he wanted, the scent of their welcoming bodies, the tactile knowledge of their private accesses.

Gilchrist confronts himself with these conclusions not so much as conclusions but as accusations. Convinced and, in a sense, convicted by their correctness, he realizes that he has *used* women, and he wonders if his feelings for Raya are simply an extension of his proclivity—a desire to possess what he has not yet used. He has never admitted this to himself in these terms, but now he does. If such are his feelings for Raya, then she presents herself as just another one of his consumptions, even though she is as yet a consumption-to-be. But this still does not explain the change that he feels in himself—a change that Ruby seems to have already detected despite his efforts to conceal it. He reassures himself, but only momentarily, that Ruby's reaction to his absorption with Raya could have been as undisguised a thing as jealousy. He keeps picking at these insights like a man trying to unravel tangled yarn or untie a wet knot. It leaves him more confused.

Gilchrist has never been a man who sought to dignify or legitimize his liaisons. They simply *were*, and then they were not, and that was enough. He was not like a doctor he knew from Bethesda who had a similar generic interest in women but who finally felt an obligation to marry each of his paramours so that his lovers eventually and predictably became his wives, and then they became his ex-wives as new lovers replaced them. When Gilchrist asked him why he felt he had to marry, the doctor explained that marriage had the advantage of raising sexual experience into a sexual life, that he was a man by nature "uxorious" (the doctor's word) who needed a steady and "habitual" (the doctor's word again) sexual life. Gilchrist concluded but never said to the doctor that merely legitimizing sexual experiences did not make them anything less or more than experiences. They differed from Gilchrist's naked promiscuities only in the sense that they were ultimately "dignified by legitimacy," which, to Gilchrist, created a difference in name, not nature.

No, the special regard he has for Raya seems to be removed from his usual pattern. But Gilchrist cannot give it a name. He knows enough of human nature to realize that obsession deferred or denied for the best of reasons is not necessarily obsession neutralized. On the contrary, he knows if his feelings for Raya are more than this, if there is something else that he cannot identify, then he will recognize it in time because it will be unignorable. But what then?

The ring of the telephone bursts like an explosion in the darkness. Gilchrist switches off the radio and lifts the receiver to his ear.

"Dodge?" The voice is Ruby's.

"Yes."

"Did I wake you up?"

"No, I wasn't sleeping."

"Have you been watching television?"

"No, what's up?"

"It's not good news."

"What is it? Tell me."

"It's your friend. It's Tabry."

"What happened?"

After a slight pause, Ruby says, "He's dead. The report came over just now. A house fire. They found him, but it was too late to save him."

"My God!" He waits. "Is that all?"

"The girl's alive, Gil. She apparently wasn't in the house but came back after the fire started. She tried to save him, but she couldn't. I think she was hurt doing it. The report just said she was hospitalized. That's all I know."

III

The Time of Night

13

"I TOLD YOU that we'll continue to investigate, Mr. Gilchrist."

The detective that Gilchrist is speaking to is holding a small pad on which he has already made a number of notes. He has identified himself as Martin J. Cobb, placing particular emphasis on the *J* as if there is another detective in the department with the same first and last name and with whom he does not want to be confused. Gilchrist notices that Cobb's hair is cut short enough to bristle, and he has the square-faced jaw of a fullback or a linebacker. Like most modern-day law enforcement officers, he has all the answers and the prudential manners of a man who has been briefed by lawyers about how to perform his duties, how to ask and respond to questions, how to be legally correct.

"I happen to know," Gilchrist says, "that that fire could not have been started by a man who didn't smoke."

"This individual could have been smoking, or he could have been careless in some other way. I put both possibilities in the report. We found no evidence to indicate anything else, but we'll continue to investigate." He pauses. "You say he didn't smoke, but we found a half-smoked cigar beside the sofa."

"He didn't smoke. I've known the man for years, and I can vouch for that."

"Maybe he decided to experiment." He pauses again. "As I said, we'll continue to investigate."

"When?"

"First thing tomorrow morning. I have two men on duty tonight at the site to prevent any pilfering, and at 0900 tomorrow morning I'll be back with my team, and we'll look at everything again in case we might have missed something. It's a police matter now, Mr. Gilchrist, and I promise you that we know what has to be done."

"Cigar or no cigar, don't you think it's odd that a man is not able to get out of the ground floor of a house that's on fire? The fire chief and the doctor in the emergency room told me that eyewitnesses said that his niece found him on the floor in the living room and dragged him on the porch when that cornice fell on her. Don't you think that he could have saved himself if he knew that his house was on fire? All he had to do was smell smoke and then walk out."

"He could have been asleep, or he could have been intoxicated. We have no way of knowing his true condition at the time of the fire unless we conduct tests and . . ."

"Come on, Cobb, I happen to know he never drank. Never drank or smoked. And he was the lightest sleeper I ever met. I lived in the same dormitory room with him for more than three years, for God's sake. I know what I'm talking about."

"Mr. Gilchrist, my team and I will do our job at 0900 tomorrow morning, and if we discover any evidence of foul play, you'll be the first to know. I promise you that."

"Are you going to put in your report the possibility that he could have been set up by certain people who wanted him to die 'accidentally' in the fire?"

"I don't put anything but facts in a report. I'm not in the business of making assumptions."

"Well, I am. I know that he was living under risk. He was shadowed all the time, and there were threats. I know the facts about this. It's my business."

"If we find any evidence to suggest the scenario you're sketching for me, there will be a hearing, and you can be present at the hearing if you think you can shed any further light on this incident." Cobb looks directly at Gilchrist as if to indicate that this is the end of the conversation.

"There's one more thing."

"And what's that?" Cobb asks impatiently.

"I'd like to be sure that all of Tabry's books and papers that have been taken from the house are under lock and key until I can examine them. I have a statement in writing and notarized that identifies me as the one who would be responsible for his effects if anything happened to him."

"Everything that was not burned is already in our warehouse. If you can produce the statement that you just mentioned, we will release all of Mr. Tabry's effects to you. No problem."

"I'd like to know what you have in your report about his niece, Raya Tabry."

"I can read you the chronology."

"Go ahead."

Cobb removes a trifolded sheet of paper from his inside coat pocket, opens it, and reads from it, "At 10:12 p.m. on August 14 an alarm was turned in by a neighbor of the deceased. At 10:22 firefighters arrived on the scene. At 11:05 the fire was partially contained. At 11:08 the niece of the deceased arrived on the scene and rushed into the house while the fire-fighters were still engaged in tamping down the fire. Within minutes she emerged attempting to drag the deceased through the front door. Two fire-fighters, who had discovered the body of the deceased a few minutes earlier themselves, were assisting her. Before they were able to carry the deceased clear of the structure, a cornice of the porch fell, striking the niece of the deceased on the right temple, rendering her unconscious. The firefighters arranged for the deceased and his niece to be transported by ambulance to the emergency room at Georgetown Hospital. Mr. Sharif Tabry was pronounced dead upon arrival. Cause of death was listed as asphyxiation. Miss Raya Tabry was taken immediately to the neurosurgical unit, and there . . ."

"It's definite that she wasn't in the house when the fire started?"

"Affirmative. We checked on her whereabouts that evening, and we learned that she had been working with a printer on a project of Mr. Tabry's . . ."

"It probably was the anniversary edition of his journal."

"In any case, the printer said after we tracked him down that she had left his office shortly after 9:45 p.m. and proceeded to walk home. Then he added that the project, whatever it is, is now on hold, and he asked if there was someone in authority who could tell him what should be done."

"I'll contact him. I know all about that."

"Do you want the name, address, and telephone number of the printer?"

"Yes."

14

"SINCE MISS TABRY has no next of kin, I'm going to tell you exactly what her condition is and what we can and cannot do and expect. From what you've told me, you are now the only person who has any direct connection or responsibility in this matter. My name is Dr. Voss, Mr. Gilchrist. As a matter of fact, we're neighbors. I have an apartment two floors below yours."

"I didn't know that. I don't know many of the other tenants. I'm not there most of the time."

"But I am, so I recognize your name, and, of course, I read your columns. I know your work. I respect it." Having allowed himself a personal moment, the doctor shifts back into his professional tone. "I'll be frank with you, Mr. Gilchrist. I want to be as candid as possible with you about Miss Tabry's prognosis."

Gilchrist nods, noting that the doctor—a man of perhaps fifty with a Lincolnesque slouch, thick brown hair going uniformly gray from peak to sideburns to crown, and a habit of smiling reassuringly between sentences—is of that small group of men who prefer to deal with facts rather than feelings or false hopes but who never separate facts from their human connections. As he always does when dealing with professionals of this character, Gilchrist prepares himself to hear the worst first. He is not disappointed.

"Head wounds are really beyond prognostication, Mr. Gilchrist. My own view is that this patient, by all rights, should never have been able to survive to this point, considering the nature of the trauma."

"But she did."

"Exactly. And we're dealing with the patient in just this way. We'll continue to monitor her carefully, very carefully. As you know, we've induced a deeper coma, but that was and remains essential to keep the pressure down. Any rise in blood pressure or temperature at this point could cause the brain to swell, and, as you know, that could be fatal."

"I understand that."

"Good. Now I must be frank with you. Just this morning I completed a small but important surgery that relieved pressure on Miss Tabry's brain. The drainage is continuing, and the results so far have not been discouraging. Let me put it positively. I mean that the results have been encouraging within the limits of what was attempted. That's all I can say at this point."

"And . . ."

"Everything else is the same. Her heart and other vital organs are good. But the head injury is serious. For neurosurgeons, Mr. Gilchrist, the brain is the whole ball game. For us, the entire body exists only for the support of the brain and its functions. The body ingests, rids itself of waste, inhales oxygen, reproduces itself, and so forth, but all these are at the service of consciousness. Consciousness is all. And the brain and consciousness are synonymous in medical terms. And that for us means that consciousness and life are synonymous."

"How does that apply to Raya? To Miss Tabry?"

"Well, I'll give you the worst possibility first, and that is that the patient may not survive. At the moment there seems no imminent danger of that, and that's something I could not have said as recently as last night. The second possibility is that the coma may be prolonged. Prolonged indefinitely. And that could confront us with a complete set of additional problems, not only medical problems but financial and moral problems. The third possibility is that she could emerge from the coma with certain, well, certain impediments. What these impediments might be we have no way of knowing until they reveal themselves. The fourth possibility is that she might emerge from the coma and make a complete recovery. I've seen this occasionally in my practice. Not often, but I've seen it, and I've seen patients recover completely from injuries more serious than Miss Tabry's. There must be some therapy, of course, but there could be complete recovery."

Dr. Voss waits and studies Gilchrist's face as if to be certain that his listing of the possibilities has been completely understood. Judging that it has been, Dr. Voss continues. "That's all I can tell you at this point. In cases like this it's best, best psychologically, if you can keep from thinking about the future. I know that this is really impossible, but it's better to think how far we've come since yesterday. I don't see how she survived the first night. But she did, and that creates possibilities that are hidden from us right now."

"Is there anything I can do?"

"While she's in coma?"

"Yes."

"Frankly, we don't know what reaches a patient in a coma like this. All we know is that the brain keeps working beneath the coma."

"So thought is still happening, is that what you mean?"

"We have no reason not to think so. And the best therapy, according to our research, seems to be for someone to talk and engage the patient at the level of the patient's deepest interest. One sentence might do the trick. For many of the patients here in comas we keep radios going most of the time so that there is always sound in the air. Some sound is better than no sound at all."

"If I sat beside her and talked to her, would that help?"

"It could, of course. It wouldn't hurt."

15

GILCHRIST SITS beside the bed and studies Raya's face. She is lying on her back under a single sheet. She looks like someone who is not quite asleep. Her hands are at her sides.

For more than two weeks Gilchrist has come to her hospital room every afternoon. On most afternoons he sits in silence. At other times he reads his newspaper column aloud as if expecting Raya to comment on it. At other times he simply begins a conversation and then stops when he realizes that the answer he is expecting is not going to be said.

On this particular day Gilchrist says, "I buried your uncle in the rain, Raya. A lot of his students came to the funeral and some colleagues. Afterward I had whatever was salvaged from the fire brought to my apartment. Not furniture, nothing like that. Just his papers and his books. There were back issues of the journal, books in Greek and Latin, reams of letters bound with rubber bands, some lecture notes. Almost all the papers were warped from water damage, or else they were singed and smelled of smoke, but they were still readable. Then I found a note that Tab wrote to remind himself to call the printer to proceed with the anniversary issue of the journal. I've decided I'm going to take that on myself, Raya. That will be a better memorial for Tab than anything else I can think of. But the one thing I can't get out of my mind from the funeral is how all those students just stood there in the rain when it came time to bury Tab. A few of them had umbrellas, but most of them had nothing, and it didn't matter to them. It was their last tribute to a man who must have given them a lot. It brought tears to my eyes, and that's unusual for me."

16

"HER TEMPERATURE continues to be normal."

"What about the coma, Dr. Voss?" Gilchrist asks.

"Still status quo, I'm afraid. I have nothing new to tell you about that. But all the vital signs are good, and that's encouraging."

Gilchrist almost tells Dr. Voss that he is beginning to tire of the word *encouraging*. It is part of the argot of officialdom that he, as a writer, loathes. Government officials are "concerned." Diplomats are "cautiously optimistic." Doctors are "encouraged."

"Another thing I noticed yesterday," Dr. Voss says, "is that she has some muscular response. She responds to stimuli to the hands and feet. This means there is no paralysis."

"What about the ability to take food? How long will it be before you can take her off the glucose?"

"That's not an easy matter, Mr. Gilchrist. Feeding Ms. Tabry by mouth is not possible. She's incapable of the simple act of swallowing. If we try to force something like that, we run the real risk of having her aspirate the food. That could lead to asphyxiation, and Ms. Tabry . . ."

"Excuse me, Dr. Voss, but why not call her by her name? Her name is Raya."

"I can, but I prefer not to, if you don't mind."

"Frankly, I do mind."

"Then you'll simply have to mind, Mr. Gilchrist. It's a matter of professional practice with me. I don't mean to sound clinical about Ms. Tabry, but I find that I do my work better if I think of my patients simply as patients at this stage. And at this stage it hardly matters one way or the other, does it? It certainly cannot matter to the patient."

"It matters to me."

Dr. Voss shrugs.

"Is there anything more you want me to know?" asks Gilchrist, beginning to stand.

"Actually, there is," says Dr. Voss and indicates that Gilchrist should sit a moment longer. "How the brain regenerates from an injury of this kind is never clear, Mr. Gilchrist. We know many things about the brain, but its healing and regenerative powers remain a mystery. There's no way to prognosticate because there is no sense of proportion. Sometimes it takes so little to kill a man or a woman, and at other times a massive blow might result in just a minor injury. In the same sense, the brain has that kind of vulnerability, that kind of resilience."

"We've talked about that before, Doctor."

"Yes, we have, but I'm repeating it because there's been a development with Ms. Tabry. A minor development, really. Only a hint. Just a hint. This morning I examined her as usual. And I talk to her during every examination for the same reason that I've asked you to talk to her. And at one point I asked her, as I've done many times before, to squeeze my hand if she could hear me. And just a fraction of a second after I asked her to do that, I felt her fingers flex around my hand. It was for just an instant, but it was not something I imagined. One second, and her hand was completely limp. Then there was the slightest pressure. When I asked her a second time, I felt nothing. But there was a response the first time. I'm as positive about that as I am about anything."

"That sounds like the best news we've had yet."

Dr. Voss returns to the chair behind his desk and sits down. He does not slug himself into the seat but sits with the same sense of control that characterizes everything he does. He removes a tobacco pouch and pipe from his desk drawer and proceeds to fill the pipe bowl with tobacco.

"Do you mind if I smoke?"

"Not at all," says Gilchrist. "I have a cigar once in a while myself. A pipe I've never tried. Too much trouble."

"You have to enjoy the 'trouble' to be a real pipe smoker. And I enjoy it, to tell you the truth." He strikes a match and passes the match flame over the bowl of the pipe. In a moment the fragrance of pipe tobacco fills the room. "It's none of my business, Mr. Gilchrist, but do you mind if I ask you about your friendship with Ms. Tabry's uncle? It must have been rather close for you to take the pains you're taking with his niece."

"No, Dr. Voss, I don't mind your asking."

"Had you known one another for many years?"

"We went to Georgetown together, roomed together, graduated together. But his country had been occupied, and he couldn't go back there after he earned his degree. He went on to do graduate work in England and then returned to teach Greek and Latin at Georgetown. He founded a journal there and a foundation to support it, and that became his personal resistance to the occupation."

"Was he married?"

"No. He put everything into his work, and he was the kind of man who could do that. There are men like that. He'd been trying for years to bring his brother's daughter to the United States—to bring Raya to the United States after his brother was murdered—and finally it happened . . ."

Even as he was speaking, Gilchrist relived the night when Ruby called him to tell him of Tabry's death. He remembers how he hung up the phone, stunned, and then dressed and drove to Tabry's house. A few firemen were still there, dousing the smoking ruins or rolling up the flattened hoses and loading them in spools back on the trucks. One fireman told him that Tabry and his niece had been taken to Georgetown Hospital, and Gilchrist sped there. When he finally located the policemen and doctors in the emergency room, he was told as tactfully as possible by the doctor on duty that Tabry was pronounced dead on arrival and that Raya was being treated for a head wound. One policeman interrupted to say that she had been struck by a falling cornice as she was trying to drag Tabry from the flames in the living room.

"What caused the fire?" Gilchrist asked the policeman.

"We're investigating that."

"What have you found so far?"

"We think he must have been smoking, then fallen asleep with a lighted cigar in his hand, and that set fire to the sofa in the living room. We found a cigar butt."

"What if I told you that he didn't smoke?"

"We'll include that in the report."

"That's it? Just include it in the report?"

"It will be part of the investigation."

"And the girl? What about her? Where is she?"

"It's too early to tell," said the doctor on duty. "The head wound is serious, and she's unconscious. We're treating her for a probable concussion now, but we'll be taking more X-rays and a scan."

"Who's the doctor with her now?"

"Dr. Voss. He's the head of neurosurgery here."

"Can I see him?"

"I'll ask."

"But first I'd like to see Mr. Tabry. He was my best friend . . ."

"The deceased?"

"Yes."

The doctor led Gilchrist to a curtained cubicle at one corner of the emergency room. He parted the curtains for Gilchrist and entered the cubicle with him. "We don't usually do this, but I . . . ," began the doctor.

"I know you don't. I appreciate it."

"We pronounced him at 11:43 p.m. That was almost an hour ago," said the doctor.

Gilchrist winced when he saw the sheeted form on the gurney in the middle of the cubicle. Then he walked toward it. The doctor lifted the sheet gently. Tabry's lips were slightly parted, and his eyes were not quite closed. In death he seemed to be aiming his eyes at something directly in front of him. Gilchrist walked around the gurney and studied Tabry's face from the other side. On this side, the left side, he saw a bluish mark between the end of the eyebrow and Tabry's hairline.

"What's that mark?" Gilchrist asked.

The doctor walked to Gilchrist's side of the gurney, studied the mark for a moment, and then examined it with his fingertips. "He must have fallen on something when he collapsed," said the doctor. "It's more than a bruise. Perhaps he hit his head against something."

Gilchrist stared at the doctor. He guessed that he was in his early thirties. He had a full black beard, trimmed close, and he looked at things with the eyes of a jeweler. "You think it could be more than a bruise?" Gilchrist asked.

"Yes, I would say so."

"Could he have been struck there?"

"Struck?" asked the doctor as he turned his jeweler's eyes on Gilchrist and did not blink or look away.

"Could someone have hit him there with something?"

"What are you driving at?"

"I'm asking you if that bruise on his temple could have been caused by someone who hit him there, knocked him out with some kind of weapon?"

"It's possible, yes. I mean that kind of contusion could have been caused by a blow, but my supposition is that he probably struck something when he fell."

"From the sofa to the floor is not a very long fall," Gilchrist said and waited. "Are you going to put in your report that the bruise could have been caused by a blow to the head?"

"No."

"Why not? You told me it was possible. You said so yourself."

"Because it's speculation."

"Isn't your theory about the bruise from a fall from the sofa speculation? And not a very persuasive speculation at that."

"Mr. Gilchrist, all that I'm noting in my report is that there is a contusion. I cannot surmise beyond that. Officially, that is."

"In other words, this whole business is being considered a domestic accident, something like that?"

"That's correct, Mr. Gilchrist. I would remind you that I'm a physician. I'm not a detective."

"Well, I have some theories of my own about . . ."

"That's between you and the police, Mr. Gilchrist."

17

GILCHRIST IS SITTING in the visitor's chair beside Raya's bed. He is holding her hand. He remembers Dr. Voss's telling him that there had been a definite response when Voss asked her if she could hear him. Gilchrist is waiting for something similar to happen.

He was once told that if you stand or sit close to a person who is asleep, in time the sleeper will sense your presence and awake. This will not be because of something said or done. It will just happen because the sleeper feels something or someone near. It will slowly intrude into his "space." Once when he and Tabry were roommates at Georgetown, he had entered the dorm room while Tabry was sleeping. In a spirit of experiment he tried standing as close to Tabry as possible without making a sound. In a matter of minutes Tabry was awake and talking to him.

Dr. Voss had told Gilchrist that the voice of someone near and dear to a comatose person could in some mysterious way be heard. There might not be a response, but the voice could be heard, and that would be a gain for mere consciousness, an alternative to silence.

"I did talk to the police, Raya. They listened, but I think they listened just for the record. The detective on the case is a man named Cobb, and he said that there was not a speck of evidence that the death was anything but an accident—a regrettable accident but an accident pure and simple. And the doctor at the hospital stuck to his guns that the bruise on Tab's head might or might not have been caused by a blow, and that left everything in doubt. I have my suspicions, and I think I'm right. Your uncle had some lethal enemies. They know how to act in a decisive way when they want to silence somebody, and they know how to cover their tracks. They're artists in arranging the kind of accident that killed Tab. But it was no accident. Proving that will have to wait. Right now you're all that matters to me. I really don't begin to live until I'm here with you. Time doesn't matter to me anymore. I'll stay as long as there's the last bit of hope. That's why you have to hold on. Just hold on."

18

BY THE TIME Gilchrist reaches Raya's room it is almost nine o'clock. His intention was to come much earlier, but a deadline for his column forced him to work through the afternoon and the dinner hour. Now as he sits in his usual chair and studies Raya's face, which he invariably does to see some change, some sign that wasn't there the night before or the night before that, he takes her hand in his and begins the one-sided conversation that has now become not simply a ritual but something he needs to do daily for the day to be complete and not a waste.

"I spent time with the printer, Raya. We're going ahead with the publication of the journal. I told the printer that he should print the whole edition as planned, and then we'll print an extra couple of thousand for me to plant where they will have the most influence. I'll send them all over the world to editors, prime ministers, heads of state, dissidents, whatever. I'll make sure that this is your uncle's memorial, Raya. And after I do that I'm going to devote my column to the Palestinian question on a regular basis. I see what has to be done. I went to the warehouse early this morning and looked over the books and the papers that the firefighters had pulled from the house. Almost everything was damaged by water, but I found myself reading stuff I'd never seen before, mostly from Europe, about the Middle East. It opened my eyes, really. And then I went to see the printer and read the galleys of the journal from page 1 to the end. It's a kind of testament to everything that Tab stood for."

Even as he keeps holding her hand, Gilchrist feels himself sliding slowly into sleep. It's been a long day, he tells himself, longer than he thought. He places her hand gently on the sheet, stands, and walks slowly out of the room. He is waiting at the elevator when he hears someone call his name, a nurse.

"Mr. Gilchrist?" says the nurse, walking toward him.

"Yes."

"I think you should wait here for a moment. I've placed a call to Dr. Voss."

"What happened? What's wrong?"

"I just was making my night check of Miss Tabry, and I . . ." She stops.

"And?"

"I noticed that her eyes were open. They were open, and she blinked. And then I saw she was trying to say something, but there was no voice, just her lips shaping a word. I looked very closely and leaned over in case I might hear something. Then I called Dr. Voss. He's coming directly over."

IV

The Time at Hand

19

IT IS NOW three weeks since she opened her eyes, and, however hard she tries, Raya can only remember the fire. And the images never change. She is running into the living room where the sofa and the draperies are in flames. She sees Tabry half on the floor and half on the sofa, then reaches under his armpits and tries to tug him across the floor toward the front door. All the time she is coughing because of the smoke and, between coughs, screaming, "Help! Help me, please!"

By the time she reaches the doorway, she is joined by two firefighters who push her aside, seize Tabry by the ankles and arms, and carry him across the porch to the front yard. Raya remembers feeling a hard blow to the side of her head. It comes suddenly, like a shot. And the memories stop.

From then on all she remembers is sky—a sky without a cloud through which she is floating like her own planet. She looks upward into the pale blue that has no end. She imagines that she is floating on her back in a dead sea. She cannot sink even if she tries, and she has no desire to try. It is simply enough for her to float and look upward into blue and let the sea take care of her.

Presences seem to be in motion around her. She feels them, but she does not see them. It is as if they are passing in utter silence and darkness. From somewhere in the void of pale blue she hears from time to time a voice. It is Dodge Gilchrist's voice, and he is talking to her, but she cannot understand him. She wants so much to answer him and tell him not to leave her or disappear entirely, but he continues to talk. It is as if her answering or not answering has no influence on him whatsoever.

In her memory of those moments she senses that someone else is standing beside her. She feels fingertips on her forehead and at her temples. Suddenly, it seems as if something like a nail is being driven into her skull. The pain is like a burn from a hot iron. Then the nail is withdrawn, and the pain eases for a moment but does not vanish. She feels a cool towel on her forehead, on her neck, under her breasts, across her thighs, and down her legs to the ankles. She wants more than anything to sit upright, but her body refuses. She feels imprisoned in her own skin. It is as if she is merely the occupant of her body, as if its will is no longer her will. And all the time Gilchrist is continuing to speak to her. His voice is calm, conversational. He does not seem to be aware of her predicament at all. She wants to tell him that she is listening, but her tongue does not obey her.

She lets the sea and the sky take her where they want to take her. She stops trying to speak or sit up or see or move. There are long silences during which Gilchrist is not speaking to her. When he does speak, he seems to her to be speaking through a blanket. It is his voice. Raya is sure of that. She can sense the rhythm of his words, but she does not know what the words mean. Perhaps, she thinks, he is speaking in another language.

At one point she is startled by someone who is speaking to her and calling her by name. "Miss Tabry, can you hear me?"

It is not Gilchrist's voice this time.

"Miss Tabry, it's Dr. Voss. Can you hear me? Please, squeeze my hand if you can hear me."

20

IN THE WEEKS that follow, Raya progresses through simple therapies to those that are more complex. All during this time Gilchrist is with her every day, telling her that she is coming along very well, that it will just take time until she is fully herself again, that he will be there for her. She listens to everything that he says as if each word is her link to reality itself. And Gilchrist continues to speak to her in a tone she has never heard him use before except in memories of a blue dream when he was uttering words to her that she could barely understand but which were always there for the hearing.

As the days pass, her memory slowly restores itself, and she makes fewer and fewer errors in speech. In fact, her recovery in diction and memory begins to exceed her recovery in motor movements and balance. Nonetheless, she learns to eat by herself, advancing from soft foods to regular meals. She sleeps without sedation. She is able to turn without assistance so that she can sit on the edge of the bed and dangle her feet. One morning, with the help of Gilchrist and Dr. Voss, she is able to stand.

"I feel as if I've never stood before," she says.

"It's almost like starting from scratch, Miss Tabry," says Dr. Voss, "but babies do it all the time, and they soon get the hang of it. You'll learn a lot faster than babies because your learning is really relearning."

"May I take a step now?"

"Try," says Dr. Voss.

With Gilchrist and Dr. Voss supporting her on either side, Raya lifts her right leg slightly and tries to move it forward. Again she experiences a sensation that she first recognized when she was in a coma—the sense that her body was on its own and that she had no command over it. Her leg begins to shake.

"I can't," she says. "It's as if my legs have no strength in them anymore."

"Don't be discouraged, Miss Tabry," says Dr. Voss as he helps her sit on the edge of the bed again. "You've come a long way so far. We have a lot to be grateful for, believe me."

Raya looks at Gilchrist, who is smiling at her. She turns her face away because she feels herself coming to tears. Sensing this, Dr. Voss leaves the room. For several minutes Gilchrist places his hand on her shoulder and keeps it there. Raya reaches to hold his hand. "I don't know," she says and stops. "I don't know if I can do it."

"Let's say that *we* can do it."

"You are so good to me, Dodge," she says after a moment, "but you can't take care of me forever."

"We'll see," says Gilchrist. The fact she has just called him for the first time by his first name seems almost like an act of confidence in him. He likes it.

Raya looks up at him and places his hand between her two hands and rests her cheek against their joined hands as if she is resting on the only pillow she has left. After several moments she releases his hands and grips the edge of the bed.

"I have nobody now," she says. "I have no family now. No one."

"Don't talk about that."

"But it's true." She smiles at him the wan smile of the helpless and says, "There is a saying in Arabic that I never understood until now. Women would say it if they were childless, or mothers would say it if their children had gone away to Europe or the United States. They would just wring their hands and say, 'I have no one now, no one to bury me.' I never understood what made them say that, but now I know the feeling."

"You're a long way from burying."

"But the feeling is the same."

He sits on the bed beside her and places his arm around her shoulders. She lets herself collapse lightly against him. Still in that position, she realizes that she called him by his first name. Why? Slowly, she remembers his voice in her blue dream, how it kept hoisting her out of the depths like a lifeline, how his voice drew her to him until everything associated with her previous formality with him vanished completely.

"Dodge," she whispers, "where would I be without you?"

She lets him hold her for several moments longer. The sunlight in the room brightens and then diminishes as the clouds cover or uncover the sun. Raya notices how the white walls are chalk in the direct sunlight but ivory in the indirect.

"Dodge," she says, "please give me a mirror."

"I don't have one."

"Please bring me one. There must be one in the room, in the hall, somewhere. I just want to see how I look now."

"Why? Not for me, I hope. I like you just the way you are."

"No, for me. A woman just can't go from day to day without seeing herself."

"Vanity, Raya. All is vanity."

"I don't care. I want to be vain. Please."

Gilchrist leaves the room, walks to the nursing station where he explains quickly to the nurse on duty what he wants, accepts a small hand mirror that the nurse takes from her own purse, and returns to the room. Raya is still sitting on the edge of the bed. She has the focused look of someone who is gathering the strength to face what she must face, regardless of the consequences.

"Here's the item," says Gilchrist, handing the mirror to her.

"Thank you," she says, taking it and holding it mirror side down on her leg for several minutes. Then she lifts it and slowly raises it to the level of her eyes. She shifts it even more slowly from one side of her face to the other and back again until she has seen everything she wants to see. The first thing she does is frown. Then she lifts the mirror again. She notices the scar above her hair line on her right temple. The stitch marks are still visible, and the hair in the once shaven area around the wound is little more than stubble long. Her hair looks as if a comb has not been passed through it for a month, as indeed none has. She touches the hair above the scar. She looks for a final time at the rest of her face, then hands the mirror back to Gilchrist.

"I'm not myself anymore," she says.

"Nonsense."

"I'm not how I remember me. I look so bad I can't even cry about it."

"You look terrific. Remember, I saw you from the beginning of all this. Now you can breathe and eat on your own. In no time you'll be walking. And after that the sky's the limit."

"Do you think I'll be walking soon?"

"Let's just say that you'll be on your way sooner than you think."

"I hope so. I want to start to do for myself." She pauses and looks at him. "All at once I feel so tired, Dodge." She closes her eyes and slowly reopens them. "Can you help me lie down, please?"

With one hand on her shoulders, he reaches down and lifts her legs and swings them gently on the bed as he simultaneously eases her supine. Then he adjusts the pillow for her.

"Thank you, Dodge."

"It's all part of my Make-Raya-Better Service."

She closes her eyes. Gilchrist waits by the bed to see if she will open them again. After waiting five minutes, he turns and walks on his toes to the door. He is almost there when he hears Raya call his name.

"Yes," he answers. Turning, he sees that she is still as he left her. Her eyes are closed.

"I want to say something," she says.

"Yes."

"I have never felt for anyone what I feel for you."

Her statement reduces Gilchrist to silence. It is not silence as much as it is speechlessness. He leaves the room, returns the hand mirror to the nurse from whom he borrowed it, and takes the elevator to the hospital garage. Once in his Mercedes he heads in the direction of his apartment, but just before he reaches Wisconsin Avenue, he drives straight instead of turning and parks near the entrance to the Georgetown University campus.

Having had little interest in reunions, Gilchrist has never returned to the campus since graduation, even though his apartment is less than five minutes away. He locks his car and walks back to the main entrance. He passes many to-and-fro-ing students and several bearded men who are trying their best to look like the professors they probably are. An occasional Jesuit passes as well. For Gilchrist, they all hardly exist. All that seems real to him is the campus itself and whatever it is that has drawn him back at this moment.

He imagines that he is a student again and that he and Tabry have been discussing their respective ideas about religion. Tabry has been explaining the Koranic notion of resignation. For Gilchrist, resignation and faith have always seemed surrenders to the inscrutable. For him, the only constant was self-reliance as long as that was possible. When Tabry asked him what he would do if he had to rely on something other than himself, Gilchrist had no answer. Now as he walks toward Gaston Hall, he finds himself remembering another evening. He and Tabry were walking the same path to hear a lecture by the French philosopher Étienne Gilson. Gilchrist enters the same hall he entered more than a decade ago as if he were entering a church and sits down in an aisle seat. In his memory the philosopher's speech has already begun, and he listens afresh to hear Gilson explain with continental precision how knowledge rarely leads to faith since faith is not a matter of knowledge at all but one of trust voluntarily given. Gilson is already emphasizing that faith is a gift plus a willingness to live with the trust that such faith bequeaths to the believer. For someone to believe, Gilson is saying, he must make a leap of faith, must proceed from mere knowledge to a state where knowledge is secondary, bridging the distance with belief. Gilchrist remembers Gilson's pausing at this point, removing his glasses, and adding that he certainly does not mean to deprecate knowledge because, he continues, too many believers accept too much on faith. Where it is possible to know, Gilson continues, believers should certainly strive to know because such knowledge is always (Gilchrist remembers the exact words) "a positive gain for the understanding."

That phrase has stayed with Gilchrist like a motto, and he remembers how he discussed it with Tabry after the lecture. Since he was "more or less Protestant" and Tabry a Muslim, the two shared a common impartiality regarding matters Catholic. But where Tabry believed in a personal God in a way that echoed the belief of Christians and Jews, Gilchrist believed only in the possibility of God. The idea of a personal God was foreign to him, despite his high-church upbringing, and as an undergraduate his interest in various theologies was little more than the interest of a sampler, a dilettante. Even in those student days Gilchrist placed his faith only in what he semijokingly called "Gilchrist's law." What this meant to him was that the majority of human beings were motivated by self-interest and that the only impediment to their pursuing their self-interest was the lack of the means or power to do so. In that world faith seemed irrelevant, and Gilchrist as a writer was a citizen of that world. When Gilchrist went on to international studies, it did not take him long to conclude that most if not all nations seemed to obey the same law. In such a vision of life there seemed little place for God. It was not until he heard Gilson's lecture that the true meaning and scope of faith dawned on him. Whether faith was a gift or an act was not the main point for Gilchrist. The main point was that he was confronted with the possibility of a world beyond reason but that this was completely reasonable. For Gilson, it was as reasonable for men to have a desire to believe as it was for them to have a desire to know, to possess, to eat, and to reproduce themselves. Gilchrist's reading and travel corroborated the fact that every culture on earth confirmed this need to believe in its totems, its poetry, its statues, its temples, and its tombs. Although Gilchrist never pursued this matter of faith any further at the time, he never put the question of faith entirely out of his mind. His life seemed to proceed well enough without it, except for the experience of his being jilted by Holly, which he in time attributed to fickleness or indecision or, as he once told himself, Holly's decision to pursue what she saw was in her own self-interest.

Now as he walks out of the nostalgic darkness of Gaston Hall, he feels the presence of an absence within himself. He first sensed this while he was sitting in Raya's hospital room and speaking to her night after night while she lay in a coma. Life at those moments seemed quite beyond his grasp and control, and when he reached back for the strength and forbearance and patience he needed, he found nothing there. It was no longer a matter of self-reliance and will. It came down to a sense of helplessness compounded by the fact that he discovered in himself a capacity for love and concern that he had previously looked upon as little more than a weakness.

When he returns to his Mercedes, he is sweating. He swallows hard several times, then starts the motor and resumes the short drive to his apartment. Less than a block away, he feels himself actually shuddering. He begins to wrestle with a wave of nausea.

"Come on, Gilchrist," he says aloud in the car. "Get back to basics. Breathe deeply."

He follows his own advice as he parks the car. By the time he reaches his apartment, he feels somewhat better, but there is a void within him that is swelling like a held breath, forcing everything out of his mind but an awareness of his own helplessness and weakness.

"What's happening to me?" he asks aloud, as if he has to hear the sound of his own voice to prove that he is still in control of himself. It suddenly occurs to him that he might be having some form of nervous breakdown. "God, God help me," he mutters to the darkness. He has never known this side of himself before. He has never begged God or anyone for anything. He waits. Slowly—degree by degree—he returns to his former self. He stands in place for several moments, then walks out on the balcony. The city of Washington that he acknowledges for the millionth time does not intrigue him now as it once did when he saw it as an orchard of stories waiting to be harvested. Instead it confronts him with the fact of its own indifference. Frowning, Gilchrist walks to his desk. There is a small stack of printed sheets on the desk blotter. These are part of a series he has begun on Israel and the Palestinians, concentrating particularly on the tactics of the Israeli government that influence American foreign policy in the Middle East by everything from intimidation to political contributions at the appropriate times. Gilchrist shuffles the papers, which include critiques of the oligarchy of Arafat's governing faction and of its all too obvious corruption. As he further shuffles the papers, Gilchrist is pleased with how they feel in his hands as a carpenter might be pleased by sliding his palms over the planed and sanded braces of a chair in the making. Seated now in what he considers the very cockpit of his craft, Gilchrist tries to make light of the vertigo he felt on his drive home from the campus. He tells himself that he just gave in to the fear of the moment, that he forgot himself, that the strain of the previous months had suddenly caught up with him. But this still does not explain what he has been trying for weeks to understand about himself. Why did his self-confidence all at once abandon him?

To his readership and to his fellow journalists he represented an unrepentant and unreconstructed first worlder, defining the first world, as he did repeatedly in print, as the United States plus those few countries in the world that were its dependents, allies, or imitators. In column after column he wrote that the future of the planet lay with the first world's being able to maintain its military and economic supremacy over the second (the Soviets and their satellites) and the third world (the rest of the nations of the world, exclusive, perhaps, of Japan). If trouble developed where American interests were concerned, Gilchrist was the first to advocate a "no-nonsense" confrontation, the use of "surgical strikes" if necessary, and the implementation of meticulously devised plans (originating usually in the Central Intelligence Agency) to "destabilize" governments that were unwilling to play the American game as he saw it. His Pulitzer series on the assassinations after midcentury, highlighted by the murder of John Fitzgerald Kennedy, was actually rooted in the assumption that third-world elements or factions like the Mafia employed by third-world elements were responsible for Kennedy's murder as well as others. His recommendation was that more stringent security arrangements could have averted the murder or at least created the possibility of a result that might not have been fatal. It was his insistence on security, security, security that made Gilchrist a columnist who was frequently quoted by the Pentagon and their allies in Congress.

For Gilchrist, the only gospel that made sense for American foreign policy regarding the third world was peace through strength—massive strength—and the will to use it when needed. He often quoted Winston Churchill, who was known to have said that the only thing worse than war was defeat, which meant that the only policy worth pursuing was one that would guarantee victory as the only alternative to defeat in the military sense. He backed up this view in the various talks he consented to give around the country by quoting from an obscure essay by Charles Lindbergh. In this essay Lindbergh described a time during World War II when he was flying a P-38 in the central Pacific. He was attacked by a Japanese pilot in a Zero. The Japanese pilot surprised Lindbergh by coming out of the sun behind him and closed in for the kill. Lindbergh tried various evasive maneuvers without success before he put the P-38 into a dive, knowing that the Zero would have to dive after him or lose him. At a certain point in the dive Lindbergh pulled out of it suddenly. The

Japanese pilot could not match the pullout without having his plane stall or disintegrate, and in a matter of seconds Lindbergh became the hunter and, assisted by other pilots in his formation, downed the Zero. Lindbergh concluded from this that the only thing that saved his life was the superiority of his equipment—not his skill or his luck or an error on the part of the Japanese pilot. Superiority of equipment, Gilchrist would stress in his talks, was the key to keeping peace in the world. The superiority of American armaments over Soviet armaments constituted the country's strength in the Cold War. If modern war was largely a matter of equipment versus equipment, Gilchrist emphasized, the country with the best equipment was the country that would escape the tragedy of defeat.

When Gilchrist discussed his views with Tabry, he found that Tabry would always ask the same question. If you happened to be a country that lacked superior equipment or lacked equipment of any kind, Tabry asked, how do you keep yourself from subservience or extinction if those whom you oppose have the strength in arms that you cannot possibly match? Gilchrist usually answered that such was the way of the world, that Darwinism did have a place in the struggles between nations, that there were and would continue to be wars that were simply tragic or one-sided or both, and that there were many historical examples. Then Tabry would smile and tell Gilchrist that he really had to be in his, Tabry's, position to know that the oppressed had to discover a strength that was beyond arms. At that point Gilchrist would simply shrug, and the discussion would end.

Although Gilchrist admired Tabry for his persistence and brilliance and courage, he could not help but feel that these were virtues wasted in a lost cause. The fact that Tabry's continued resistance kept the spirit of Palestine alive within Tabry himself was something that Gilchrist could not understand. After all, thought Gilchrist, Tabry was not the only displaced person in the world. What did other displaced persons do? They relocated and began new lives. Irredentism was not the answer.

It was only after Tabry's death that Gilchrist began to examine and question his philosophy. Even though he felt he could never prove that Tabry was murdered or even the victim of a carefully arranged "accident," Gilchrist did realize that Tabry's very existence as well as the influence of his activities and publications had become not simply a bother but a threat to the Israeli government. Since Tabry was not a military threat, he had to have been seen as a danger of sufficient importance in an ideological way to warrant his elimination. That made Gilchrist refocus on the political positions that Tabry had taken all his life and for which he had, as Gilchrist believed, paid the price. Tabry's stand was essentially a moral one, and it was this morality of his vision that began to eat away at Gilchrist's view of the world as an ongoing drama of self-interest and power contending with self-interest and power. If one man could by his intelligence and conviction and stamina and persistence induce a sovereign state to dispatch assassins to kill him, then the value of one man in the right cause was in some mysterious way a match for that state. Gilchrist found this formulation both intriguing and confounding. Moreover, his feelings for Raya had succeeded in making the entire matter not merely ideological and political but personal. Because of this he felt himself being drawn deeper and deeper into the vortex of Tabry's and Raya's orientation. Indeed, he felt himself actually becoming *them* in outlook and sensitivity, and this simultaneously put him in touch with certain things in his own personality that he did not know existed. He was changing, and he could sense the change even as it was happening.

His decision to underwrite the final costs of the publication of the anniversary issue of Tabry's journal was motivated primarily by his friendship for Tabry as well as his wish to make the issue Tabry's memorial, but as weeks passed and the publication schedule of the journal moved from galleys to the final proofs, Gilchrist took a deeper personal interest in the contents of the journal itself. He read and reread all the articles, not simply as a proofreader but as someone to whom the words were now more than print on a page. He did not read them as much as he drank them, ate them, let them turn into himself. He strengthened and revised sentences and passages in the essay of his that Tabry had chosen to include in the journal until it no longer had the intent of his original conception but was entirely new, almost revolutionary. He mentioned several times in his own syndicated column the upcoming appearance of the journal, and he urged his fellow journalists to consider it for review or as a future subject for their own columns.

Gilchrist was never a man to whom change came easily. On the contrary, he took a certain pride in not changing, as if persisting in his views or habits even in the face of opposition or consequence was by its nature commendable. But now he was beginning to see the irrefutable truth of Tabry's positions on the Middle East replacing his own. His columns captured this change as it evolved. His emphasis was no longer on answers but on questions. His editor warned him that he was turning into Socrates and warned him that it was always more dangerous to raise questions than to provide answers. "You're bewildering your readers, Dodge. They're no different from all other ordinary Americans in this country, and what they don't like is to be bewildered. They would feel much better if you returned to your own self and your own style, the one that they've grown used to, the one where your position is known in advance. That way you're in focus, and you stay in focus. Otherwise, you're just a blur to them. They won't give you hemlock to drink, but they'll gradually ignore you. Do you understand me, Dodge? You're a columnist, for God's sake! So just write a goddamned column the way you did before. Three hundred words twice a week. Is that asking too much? Up until now you've been able to do that without working up an intellectual sweat. Now you've got this Palestinian bug up your ass. For the past month you've been sounding like Hamlet!"

Now as he sits at his desk and shuffles his papers into order, Gilchrist feels for the first time in his life that what he wants to write from now on will be more than journalism, more even than trying to gain some perspective on the daily or weekly or monthly panorama. He realizes without evasion but with some reluctance that he has never really stood for anything that was morally crucial—not in print, not in his own life. He has argued positions of varying political and social import with more than adequate persuasiveness and skill, but they were never matters of life and death for him. Even his prized pieces on the assassinations had been primarily investigative. In that series and in various others he had followed the logic of possibilities as far as the evidence and his own ingenuity could carry him, often going beyond the factual to those unknown and unknowable areas where one man's theories and conclusions were as good as any other man's since both, being speculative, were not subject to total refutation. He had, in brief, never put his very life on the line by taking a position in which he believed without reservation. Sophistry had been his journalistic profession—highly engaging and well-written sophistry but sophistry nonetheless. One of his colleagues had once called him "Bill Buckley without a base," and, although he resented it at the time, it described him more accurately than he would have been willing to admit.

Placing the thin stack of papers to one side of his desk, Gilchrist swings around to his computer. For fifteen minutes he types without stopping: "One of the most basic of all ethical tenets is that few people commit immoral acts in full awareness of their immorality. Actually, what makes such acts committable is an illusion of self-justification, and this illusion often persists long after the act is committed as a balm against guilt. Once this mentality takes command, these same people, particularly if they happen to be government leaders, become involved in making ends justify means. They make devils of their enemies, calling them inhuman or worse, and this justifies any and all attempts to eliminate them from the face of the earth. From such seeds grow genocides, and the only restraints to such behavior are lack of total kill-power or whatever invisible deterrents the common opinions of mankind may exert. The leaders of such governments would never consider themselves murderers. But they are. In the international sense they are war criminals. But, as we learned from World War II, for political leaders to be regarded as criminals, it is essential that the murderers be caught and tried, which is to say that to be a war criminal, one must first lose the war—a conclusion that is as lamentable as it is true . . ."

This is the beginning of the first in a series of articles that Gilchrist will write about the Israelis and the Palestinians. In his third article he will imply strongly that Tabry's death was not an accident and explain why eliminating Tabry was a necessity for those who feared his attempts to form a government in exile and that Tabry had already been approached by officials in the Department of State to form such a government and was in the process of doing so at the time of his death. Gilchrist will subsequently shrug off the State Department's predictable denial of its complicity with "the late Professor Sharif Tabry" and continue with the series until his editor suggests that he become involved in another subject, that a good columnist ("And, damn it, you just happen to be a good columnist, Dodge!") cannot afford to become a Johnny One-Note, that the paper "has to respect the sensitivities of its advertisers," and that said advertisers are not without concern for the very country that Gilchrist has decided to make his target of opportunity at the moment. Gilchrist will listen and then continue with the series.

For weeks after the publication of all the articles, every newspaper in which Gilchrist's column is syndicated receives and prints letters to the editor from officials, professors, quacks, moderates, and immoderates, all of which are routinely forwarded to Gilchrist. He ignores them all on the basis of an old premise he once heard from a columnist of yesteryear who, facing similar attacks on a totally different issue, told him that in such straits you should always to be "more *for* what you are *for* rather than more *against* what you are *against*." Because his silent disdain only provokes his opponents further, he is asked on one occasion to receive a visiting delegation of two men and two women from the Israeli Embassy. He welcomes them in the customary manner, listens to them in silence, volunteers nothing, retracts nothing, and thanks them for coming. Shortly after that Gilchrist begins to receive on a regular basis the telephone calls at three or four in the morning that Tabry once told him he habitually received. Gilchrist changes his telephone number twice, but the telephone calls keep coming.

During this entire period Gilchrist visits Raya regularly. Her progress is slow, but there are no reversals. She is fully able to feed herself, to comb her hair, to see to her own hygiene, and to walk the length of the hall with support, first from orderlies, then with a cane. Each time Gilchrist sees her, he waits for her to ask him to walk with her to the solarium at the end of the hall and back until it becomes a daily ritual.

"I love to see green, Dodge. It means there is life out there."

She stands beside her bed, and she lets him take her arm. He feels for a moment as if he is escorting her to a formal dinner or a dance. They move down the hall with an almost stately slowness that makes the moment seem more precious that it would seem otherwise. She is still unable to lift her feet when she walks so that she moves ahead by sliding her slippered feet across the waxed floor in short strides.

"You'll make a great cross-country skier," says Gilchrist. He enjoys kidding with her like this because it brings a lighter dimension to their conversations. And she responds in kind. Even though her body is weak from many weeks in bed, she has survived the accident mentally without any complications.

"What is that?"

"It's skiing on level country mostly. You just stride out on your skis and cover the distance by pushing yourself with poles. It requires almost the same motions you're making now. Sliding motions."

"Will you teach me to do that when I am stronger?"

"Absolutely."

"I'll probably fall."

"Probably."

He feels the pressure of her grip on his arm. He has never had anyone depend on him for anything, and the knowledge that Raya needs him to help her walk, needs him totally and without pretense—this fills him with a sense of his own indispensability. The feeling is new to him.

"Do you like snow?" she asks.

"Sure. Why do you ask?"

"You mentioned cross-country skiing. You need snow for that."

"It would be tough without it."

"We do not have snow in my country. Sometimes in the mountains in the north there is snow, but not much. In Lebanon, there they have snow in the mountains all year."

"That's the only place where I like snow—in the mountains. Here in the city it's a problem. It turns everything into a mess."

They pause for a moment. He can see that she is tired even from the short walk from her room. She smiles at him, half in gratitude, half to show him that she is getting stronger but still has a way to go.

When they finally reach the solarium, Raya slides with him toward the bay window so that she can feel the sun on her face. Gilchrist notices that the scar beneath her hair line is completely healed, although the color of the scar is not yet the color of her skin. It is no longer red but a nameless shade between pink and purple.

"I love the sun, Dodge. It makes me feel alive."

"You can see my car from here," Gilchrist says and points.

She looks where he is pointing and lets her gaze traverse the foliage beyond the parking lot. At last she focuses on one tree, and she lets her eyes drink their fill of it.

"What kind of tree is that, Dodge?"

"Which one?"

"The one by itself over there. No, not where you're looking. The one with the dark-red leaves on the other side of the street."

"Japanese maple, I think. Yes, Japanese maple."

"It reminds me of an oriental dancer. The branches are like the arms of a dancer. So graceful. Sometimes Dr. Voss helps me walk here, and I just stand and look at that tree. It gives me—how can I say it?—it gives me courage." She pauses and smiles at him. "You may not believe this, but I always wanted to be a dancer."

"It's not too late."

Instead of answering, she looks at him directly, and her eyes fill all at once with tears.

"It's not too late, Raya," says Gilchrist. "You can be a dancer yet. Everything's still ahead of you. Everything's possible."

"But I have nobody now. There's no one left for me. After Uncle Sharif . . ."

"You have me. Don't forget that."

He feels her grip tighten slightly. Slowly, he turns with her, and they start the slow walk back from the solarium to her room. When they reach the doorway, Raya stops and looks at him until he finally returns her look.

"You don't have to answer this if you don't want to, Dodge."

"I don't mind your asking," Gilchrist responds after a long pause.

"Why are you devoting yourself to me?"

"I just want you to get better."

"Are you doing this for Uncle Sharif?"

"No."

"Is that the truth?"

"Yes. You don't have to harbor any doubts on that score. I loved Tab like a brother, but what I feel for you is separate. I'm not here to pay a debt to his memory, if that's what you mean."

They continue walking until they reach her bed. Raya seats herself on the edge of the bed, and Gilchrist sits beside her. Their eyes are at the same level, and Gilchrist looks into her eyes steadily. It is not a stare on either side. It is as if their eyes are like thoughts or bodies in contact.

"Raya," Gilchrist says finally. "For years I've been the most self-sufficient man in Washington. I have a reputation for it. Until I met you, I never really needed anybody. No, that's not the right word. I mean I never really cared for anyone, cared in a way that inconvenienced me, made inroads on my life. I never needed to care. Then you happened. I sensed a difference in myself from the beginning, but I ignored it. Then when we were in Saranac, I felt something for you that I couldn't ignore. It drove everything else out of my mind."

She looks away but only momentarily.

"When you left Saranac," he continues, "your absence was the only presence I felt. It filled the whole cottage." He looks at her directly. He takes her hands in his. As soon as he does, she looks down. He sees a single tear slide down her cheek and glance off his knuckle, then another. "Maybe I should stop talking now."

"No," she answers in a whisper. "No, please."

"What I'm trying to tell you, I suppose, is that you mean more to me than I can put into words. If that's what love is, then I really love you. You. As you are. I won't change."

After a pause Raya whispers, "Dodge, tell me what to say now."

"Say what you want. Say what you feel. Say anything, or just say nothing. It doesn't make any difference. It won't change anything in me. I'm just telling you this because there's no one else who has a right to know except you. If you don't feel the same toward me, say it straight."

She works her hands free of his and joins them on her lap. He sees that she is still coping with what he has just confessed to her. She nods her head several times, understanding, wanting to understand.

"Dodge," she says.

"Yes."

"Would you help me? I just want to lie down."

"Sure," he says as he removes the bathrobe she had draped over her shoulders and then supports her as she lies back on the bed.

When she is settled, she reaches down and draws the sheet over herself. Then she closes her eyes and remains so still that Gilchrist thinks she is asleep. He is about to turn and leave the room quietly when she opens her eyes and finds him. She says in a voice he can barely hear, "I feel the same for you, but I can't express it the way you can."

"You live it. And that's better. And harder. And truer."

"Did you feel like this when we worked together?"

"What do you think?"

"I think I'm a good worker. I do some things very well. But I'm not pretty. I'm not what you think of as pretty."

"Who said you're not pretty?"

"I say I'm not. And right now I'm worse than ever. I keep hoping that my hair will grow in so that I can brush it and brush it and brush until it does what I want it to do. I miss doing things like that. It's something that every woman likes to do for herself. I want to be prettier than I am right now, prettier than I feel."

"That's not important enough for you to worry about."

"But it is important. I'm nothing like the women you have known."

"How do you know about them?"

"Let's just say I know." She looks at him. "I have something I want to say, Dodge. I made it my business to know more about you than I really had any right to know. And the only thing that made me want to know more and more was that you were unique to me. You were—I don't know—like sunlight. You were everywhere I looked." She runs her fingers along the edge of the sheet. "And now that you've told me how you feel about me, I almost can't believe it's true. I want to believe it, but I can't. Perhaps when I'm stronger, when I'm myself again, I'll be able to accept it, but now I can't."

"I'm not going to change."

"Everybody changes, Dodge."

"I'm not everybody."

Raya closes her eyes again and joins her hands at her waist. For a while Gilchrist just studies her, wondering how she could have thought of herself as not being pretty. He follows the arch of her eyebrows, the intersecting eyelashes, the lips that are not quite touching one another. She has lost some weight because of her weeks in the hospital, but the result is that this has only sharpened her features rather than distorted them. He avoids looking at the slowly vanishing scar near her hair line and tries to see her as she was in Saranac. Except for the weight loss that has given her face a more ascetic as well as a more athletic look, she really has not changed. To Gilchrist she looks even more attractive, even though he realizes that she would be the last to admit it.

"You're very pretty, Raya. You're more than just pretty. You're beautiful."

She does not open her eyes, but the start of a smile softens her lips. "Thank you."

"You look a little like Audrey Hepburn."

"Do I know her?"

"An actress."

"And I look like her?"

"You're both beautiful in the same way." He waits to let the compliment sink in. "Dr. Voss thinks you'll need only two or three weeks more of therapy before you'll be able to maneuver by yourself."

"Does that mean I have to leave here?" she asks, opening her eyes.

"Well, he didn't exactly say that. He just said . . ."

"But that's what it means, doesn't it?"

"Well, yes, that's probably what it means . . ."

"But where can I go?"

Gilchrist sits on the edge of the bed. "Even after you leave here, you'll still need therapy now and then. Someone will have to come where you are and show . . ."

"But I have nowhere to go."

"You have my apartment, Raya. I didn't want to bring this up now, but now's as good a time as any. I can hire a nurse to be with you during the day. It's a good place to live, not far from stores and . . ."

"Do you mean you're giving me your apartment?"

"Well," Gilchrist says and smiles, "not completely. I'm afraid I come with it in a way. I was planning to sleep on the daybed in the study and leave the bedroom to you. That way I can work without bothering you, and you can have the run of the place when I'm not there." He stops and waits for her response. There is no expression on her face, and she has closed her eyes again. Forgetting what he has just said to her, he finds himself wondering for a moment why it is that only the most attractive women tend to think of themselves as unattractive. Even at her present stage of recovery, Raya impresses him as having a face that might be profiled on a coin. He notices, as he noticed from the start, that her nose is perfectly classical in the Greek and Roman sense. There is no bridge, and the line from forehead to the tip of her nose is straight.

"I don't know what to say, Dodge."

"When you have nothing to say, say nothing. That's an old Irish proverb."

When Raya remains silent, Gilchrist realizes that in some unspoken way she has accepted the offer of his apartment. He had prepared a complete brief of arguments to persuade her if she balked. He is relieved that he never had to use any of them.

"I have to be leaving now, Raya," Gilchrist says and stands. "You did fine on your feet today. Tomorrow you'll do even better." He leans toward her and kisses her on the forehead and then kisses her again where the hair has almost completely covered the scar. "That should make it heal completely. A nurse told me that once."

"Was she pretty, this nurse?" Raya asks, her eyes still closed.

"Not bad." Gilchrist walks to the door but keeps his eyes on her to see if she will open hers and look at him, but she does not.

Raya keeps her eyes closed long after Gilchrist is gone. She would like nothing more than to sleep and wake up in the middle of the month to come. The prospect of the daily therapies that await her seems more like a sentence than a benefit, and she feels her muscles tighten when she thinks of it. It does no good to tell herself that she should be glad to be alive, that her recovery has been, in Dr. Voss's own words, nothing short of miraculous, that her prognosis is excellent. All that she is sure of is that what happened did not have to happen. But it did.

Reaching across her body with her right hand, she seizes the sheet and snaps it like a cape clear of her body. Then she raises herself on her elbow and wills her legs over the side of the bed. She comes to a sitting position and remains that way momentarily, gripping the side of the bed to keep herself from going farther forward, backward, or sideways. Still gripping the bed, she gauges the length of the room and estimates that it will require five full strides for her to reach the door. Since she knows she cannot stride, she multiplies by two. She will slide each foot across the floor in ten separate movements as she did when Gilchrist held her by the arm on their way to the solarium. She feels she must prove to herself that she can do it alone.

Slowly, she slides her legs off the bed until her feet touch the floor and ease themselves into her slippers. She feels like a girl lowering herself into a dark pool and waiting for her feet to touch bottom. Then she stands, still touching the bed with her fingertips for balance. After a second or two she lets her hand fall to her side. She realizes that it is the first time she has been able to stand by herself. After inhaling deeply, she takes the first stride by skating her slippered right foot across the floor for a half yard or so. Now it is the left foot's turn to slide ahead. When she tries to bring her right foot alongside her left, she imagines that the floor is beginning to slant sharply to the left. Then the doorway lists to the right. The floor suddenly becomes a sea. When Raya raises her hands to steady herself, she realizes that she is on the floor. She actually did not feel herself fall. She lets her cheek touch the cold tile and waits for the room to steady itself. She looks around the room from floor level. A pair of trousered legs approaches her.

"Miss Tabry, what are you doing? What happened?" It is Dr. Voss's voice. "Here, let me help you. Are you hurt?"

She lets herself be lifted upright and half-carried back to her bed.

"I was trying to walk by myself," she says.

"You shouldn't try that alone. Not yet," says Dr. Voss, leaving her supine. "Did you hurt yourself?"

"No. I really didn't know I was falling."

"Move your arms for me, please. Good, good. Now your legs."

"I have to learn to do things by myself, Dr. Voss. I can't stay like this."

"There's plenty of time to be independent. You have to trust my judgment on that. This is something that can't be rushed."

"But I can't expect Dodge to take care of me like a baby."

"He understands the situation completely. And he wants to help. No one is forcing him to do a thing. For all those weeks you were in a coma that man was here with you every night. He is here now because he wants to be and to do what he is doing." He waits. "It's obvious that he cares for you."

"But you don't understand . . ."

"Even a doctor can understand that."

Raya relaxes. Dr. Voss still stands beside her. He is studying her even as she speaks to make sure she has not injured herself.

After several moments pass, Raya says, "I know why he is doing these things for me. I really do know. But you don't understand what it means to be loved when you aren't able to do anything except appreciate what someone you love is doing for you. When you are always receiving . . ." Raya pauses and looks to Dr. Voss for assurance. "I thought that he was doing these things in memory of my uncle. They were friends for years, you know. But I was wrong. He's doing what he's doing just for me. He finally had to tell me that because I almost forced him to say it. Now that I know how he feels, I'm like a person in a trap because I feel the same way. I want to reach out to him, to get well, to walk, to be complete as soon as I can. I want to be—it's not the right word—equal. I want to be able to do things for him, and I can't. And knowing that I can't is too much for me."

Dr. Voss watches her pleading eyes for a moment before he looks down and concentrates on his own folded hands.

"You have to understand how I feel, Dr. Voss. I have no friends here in America," she says and pauses. "I have no one else to talk to about this."

Dr. Voss nods. Looking at the determination in her eyes, he finds that he cannot return her stare. That stare remains with him after he leaves her room, remains with him for weeks thereafter as the therapy continues. Slowly, she masters, sometimes painfully, always tirelessly, each exercise he devises for her until she is able to walk the full length of the hall by herself, descend and ascend flights of stairs, and speak entire paragraphs without garbling a word.

V

Time in the Balance

21

THE LETTER in Gilchrist's hand seems like something alive as he turns it slowly to the light. The handwriting on the white pages blurs until he brings the pages to eye level and rereads what he has already read twice. Having memorized the salutation ("My dearest Dodge . . .") and the first sentence ("I cannot help but write this letter, but I want you to know that it is because I love you more than I can say in these words . . ."), he proceeds to read what he is still trying to understand but cannot accept. The letter continues: "I consider myself so lucky, Dodge, because of what you told me. For months I've been trying to understand why you are so sure you love me, but I can't. I really can't. I seem so ordinary to myself, but you are so out of the ordinary. I am someone from a country the whole world is trying to forget, and you are from the greatest country in the world. And you are known throughout the world. You were Uncle Sharif's best friend. You're even making sure that his work does not die, and I know the risks you are creating for yourself by doing this. And you stayed close to me after the accident. Dr. Voss told me that you stayed and talked to me every night while I was in a coma. You talked me back to life. You helped me to walk and speak again. You were never impatient with me. Every time I wanted to give up and just let life or death do what it wanted with me, you wouldn't let me. I could not have come back without you. And now you've given me a home in your home, and you make sure that someone is always with me when you are away. And I could do nothing for you in return. Once I told you that I wasn't able to show you how grateful I am, and you just looked away and said I didn't have to do anything. You made me feel as if I just had to breathe and stay alive, and that was thanks enough. And that is why I am writing to you now. I am a coward, Dodge. I don't have the courage to talk to you face-to-face and tell you what is in my heart, what I feel for you. But I cannot just be one who receives anymore, my dearest. You can't understand what it means to a woman to know that there is nothing she can do for someone she loves—nothing. She feels herself shrinking. She begins to feel unnecessary, and no woman wants to feel unnecessary. I know you love me, Dodge, in your own way, but I must find a way to give back in my own way. Because I'm just beginning to feel well, I have asked Dr. Voss if he will help me go away for a time so I can heal by myself. And then I can return to you with something within me that is mine and mine alone to give you. Dr. Voss has found a place where I can go. He even made it possible for me to do a little work there. He thinks that typing will help my coordination. I know that you'll be able to find me if you try, Dodge, but please don't try. Please don't. Give me the time I need. Please do this for me. You are in my thoughts and in my heart forever. I love you, and I pray every day that God will keep and bless you. Please understand, Dodge. Yours, Raya."

Gilchrist stares at Raya's name at the bottom of the page, and it is as if he is staring at her face. Then he looks at the entire letter again. The handwriting is firmer at the beginning than at the end, as if her will were stronger at the beginning and then grew gradually weaker as she went on.

The weeks preceding this moment gave him no hint that she was going to do what she did. He remembers the day he brought Raya from the hospital to his apartment. He relives the way he pushed the wheelchair through the apartment doorway, and Raya is asking him why she can't just walk in.

"I'm strong enough to walk now, Dodge. Let me walk by myself."

"Let's play it safe the first time."

"But it's only a few steps."

"No deal. Permission denied."

Once inside the apartment, Raya surveys the room and says, "Everything looks just the same. But your desk looks terrible."

"Work. Work does that. And you have to remember that I have the best sense of disorganization and chaos in Washington."

"Your desk will be my first project."

"All those papers have been like that for weeks now. They can stay that way a little longer."

"But it will give me something to do. I have to do something besides those exercises. They're so boring."

"Exercise is enough for now. Dr. Gilchrist insists on that."

She smiles at him and then, putting her hands on the arms of the wheelchair and giving him a playful smirk, forces herself out of the chair like a swimmer emerging from a pool and then walks with only the slightest unsteadiness to his desk before turning and facing him again.

"Ten whole steps, Dr. Gilchrist. All by myself. Aren't you proud of me?"

"Wrong adjective."

"Why? Can't I use *proud* that way in English?"

"*Grateful*'s the word, Raya."

The playfulness leaves her expression. She smiles a serious smile. Then she returns slowly but with new assurance back to the wheelchair. After putting one hand on the arm of the wheelchair, she smiles again at him and says, "Dodge, you always manage to say something that touches something in me that makes it so hard for me to answer you."

"Precisely what I intended. I prefer my women silent."

He gives her his arm, and they walk together to the balcony and look out at the city.

"Washington still looks like Washington," says Raya.

"Well, it hasn't been that long since you saw it from here."

"That was another life ago."

"Right now is the beginning of a new life."

The new life becomes routinized within a week. Gilchrist works during the day while the nurse stays with Raya. At dinner the nurse leaves, and Gilchrist and Raya eat together and share their separate days until they become the same day for both of them. On those few evenings when Gilchrist must be away to honor a speaking engagement or write his column from another city or take care of final details regarding Tabry's anniversary issue of the journal, he has the nurse remain with Raya.

One evening while he and Raya are having coffee after dinner, Gilchrist notices that she seems apprehensive.

"How were the exercises today?"

"Good. Dull but good," Raya answers. She takes a sip of coffee from the cup and waits for the rest to cool.

"Do you want to elaborate on that a bit?"

"No," she answers and adds, "I took a telephone call for you today."

"And?"

"It was meant for you." She pushes her cup to one side of the table. "It was a threatening call."

"How threatening?"

"Threatening. It was a threat to your life."

"Don't you believe in crank calls?"

"I don't understand that word."

"A crank call is a call made by someone who wants to get a cheap thrill."

"It wasn't that kind of a call. You know what I mean. The nurse told me she took a call like that last week, but I didn't tell you about it."

"You should have."

"Is it because of the work you are doing on the journal? Is it because of what you are writing in your columns?"

"That's part of it. It goes with my job, I suppose," says Gilchrist. He sips his coffee and then saucers the cup.

"Uncle Sharif used to receive calls like that. I was there when two of them came."

"I know. He told me about it. He wanted to keep you clear of that stuff, and now you're right back in it again, thanks to me."

"Do you think Uncle Sharif would want you to risk your peace of mind or even your life for him? Do you think he'd want that for you?"

"How can you ask me that, Raya? You know what your uncle stood for. His work meant a lot to a lot of people. It meant a lot to Palestine. I'm just trying to keep the fire from going out, that's all. It's damn little, really."

"But you have your own work."

"Well, maybe this is my work now. Maybe I've been doing the wrong kind of work all these years and not admitting it to myself."

"No, you shouldn't say that. You should . . ."

"Please, Raya, let's not go on with this. It's much too personal a matter with each of us, and it bothers me when I have to argue with you. Life's too short to waste it on disagreements. I'm sorry you got the telephone call. I'll contact the telephone people tomorrow and have the number changed again. That should help."

"Does that mean we'll be living in fear every day, living at the mercy of the telephone or whatever . . . ?"

"I don't know. I hope not. There's no way to know."

Raya stands and takes her cup and saucer to the sink. She lets water run into the cup from the faucet. Then, after setting the cup on the sink rack to drain, she remains standing, and the water from the faucet continues to run. Gilchrist, hearing the water, looks at her but says nothing. Quietly he rises from the table, stands beside her, and twists the faucet that shuts off the water.

"I don't know if I can stand it, Dodge," Raya says. "Even now I keep thinking about the fire. I thought I would be able to get over it, but I'm not getting over it. I'm not as strong as my uncle was or as you are. If anything were to happen to you now after what has already happened, I don't know what . . ."

"Nothing can happen to a newspaperman, Raya. It's against the First Amendment."

"Don't make light of it, Dodge. I know what the risks are."

"Try not to think about it."

Raya shakes her head in a slow and decisive no. When Gilchrist attempts to put his arm around her, he feels her shrink away from him. She reminds him of someone who has just warded off a blow and is preparing to ward off another, and another, and another.

22

ON THE FOLLOWING DAY Gilchrist has his telephone number changed. For a week or more after that there are no additional threatening calls. Gradually, the matter of the telephone calls becomes a secondary issue for Gilchrist. What comes to replace it is the result of a meeting with Ruby.

While driving back from Dulles Airport where he has gone to interview the president of Finland, Gilchrist decides to stop for coffee and a snack in a mall near Vienna. It is not until he is seated and surveying the room that he sees Ruby sitting at an adjoining table. She keeps looking at him as if her stare will magnetically make him lift or turn his head and recognize her. Within a few seconds the tactic works. He returns her smile. Ruby then grinds the cigarette she has been smoking into a tight butt in an empty dessert dish while Gilchrist leaves his table and joins her at hers.

"I thought only women like me visit malls like this at three in the afternoon," she says as he sits across from her. "How can the world spare you, Dodge?"

"Why don't you ask me how I am?"

"I know how you are. I have eyes, and my eyes tell me that you look terrific, as usual. But what brings you to the bourgeois world halfway between lunch and dinner?"

"I had to interview a Finn at Dulles. This was a good place to stop on the way back, and I was hungry."

"Well, there's nothing mysterious about that, is there?"

"Not that I can see."

"What are you interviewing a Finn for? Judging from what I've been reading in your columns lately, that's a little north of your current range of interests."

"How many times can a newspaperman interview the president of Finland out of Helsinki?"

"Don't they use Andrews for that kind of visit?"

"This was different. He was here for private reasons. I got a tip, so I came."

Ruby shakes another cigarette from a pack in her left hand and waits for him to put a match to it for her. He does, and their eyes meet through the sudden surge of smoke that settles between them.

"It's a little painful for me to see you, Dodge. It's good, but it's a little painful."

"Do you want me to leave?"

"That won't help."

"Let's find another subject to talk about than Gilchrist."

"Like what? I don't know a damn thing about Finland," she retorts and mashes her cigarette into the same dessert dish.

"Do you always take one puff from a cigarette and then do that?"

"I shouldn't smoke anyway. I just do it to keep myself occupied." She pushes the dessert dish away. "Your articles lately have just one subject, Dodge. You've got Israel into your craw big time. It's as if you have nothing else to write about."

"There are a lot of other things to write about, but I'm just not interested in writing about anything else at the moment. This is the one subject that's been distorted and distorted in the media for decades, and I think it's eating away at our foreign policy so that it's no longer ours. I feel a responsibility to rectify the situation."

"All by yourself?"

"You know what they say, Ruby—'One man plus the truth equals a majority.'"

"How do you know you have the truth, the whole truth, and nothing but the truth?"

"Not all of it, but I'm learning."

"Are you doing all this for the sake of your friend, that professor from Georgetown who died in the fire?"

"Yes and no."

"You don't have to be evasive with me, Dodge. There's nothing wrong with that, you know."

"Nothing wrong with what?"

"Making somebody else's cause your own. In some quarters it's even regarded as noble."

Ruby starts to shake another cigarette from the pack, decides against it, and lets it slide back into position among the tight white cluster of cigarettes still left.

"How about you?" Gilchrist asks. "How have you been?"

Ruby shrugs as if the question is irrelevant. "I heard that the man's niece is recovering now."

"She's with me."

"So I've heard."

"Where did you hear it?"

"Around. There are people who know you who also know me. They weren't telling me a state secret."

"It's no secret. I would have told you in the course of events."

"You don't owe me an explanation."

"I know I don't. But I would have told you."

"Thanks, Dodge. It's nice of you to say that. It feels good not to be completely ditched."

"That can never happen, Ruby. We have too much on one another."

"Dodge," she says emphatically and looks at him, "quite apart from us, I have to tell you that you're playing hardball with this Palestine-Israel issue that you're devoting all this space to in your columns. I suppose you know that."

"The answer is affirmative."

"Do you believe in what you're saying that much? I mean, do you believe in it enough to put your reputation at risk like this? Some people tell me that you might even be putting your life at risk."

"The answer is affirmative as well."

"I've been with some Israelis lately, people from the embassy. They're not amused. It's a matter of life and death to them."

"I'm not amused by them either, so we're even."

"My friend at the embassy . . . ," she begins.

"Is this the same one you told me about, the one you met at the embassy? The one who impressed you?"

"You remembered that?" she says and smiles.

"Maybe I know him. What's his name?"

"His name is Gelb, Seth Gelb. He's here on temporary assignment."

Gilchrist remembers the talk he had with Raya in Saranac. Wasn't Gelb the name of her interrogator? He frowns, remembering.

Without letting her eyes fall from him, Ruby says, "I know how much this girl means to you, Dodge. I'm woman enough to detect that. But I think I know you well enough to say that Dodge Didier Gilchrist is too much a pragmatist to get involved with a losing cause. And if this issue is anything at all, it's sure as hell a loser."

"Come to the point, Ruby. You're saying one thing, but you mean something else."

"The point is that I hope you see that love is one thing, while having the courage to take on a lost cause is something else. You can't risk your reputation and your well-being because what you feel for that girl is somehow entwined with the cause that her uncle lived for . . ."

"And died for."

"Regardless," says Ruby, annoyed by the interjection, "what I'm driving at is that you can't mix ideals that way. I've tried it myself in my life, and the results are disastrous. You have to believe in what you're doing for its own sake, Dodge."

"And?"

"Everybody but everybody in Washington thinks that you've changed your stripes because you're playing Lochinvar to that girl you're nursing back to life in your apartment. And there are a lot of people who think you'd change completely if that girl were suddenly out of the picture. That's why you're not being taken as seriously as you would like in some quarters. People are just waiting for you to revert to the former Dodge Gilchrist, and they think that in time you will."

"They can think whatever they want."

"But only you really know if what they think is true, Dodge." She waits, then adds, "You can tell me, for God's sake. Is it true or not? You're not the first Casanova who thought that some vestal virgin would turn his life around and make him *good* again all at once." She waits again. "You don't have to answer me, but you have to give yourself an answer. Maybe you've already done it. But I think too much of you to keep my mouth shut about this. Personally, I admire what you're doing, what you're writing, what you're saying, and I don't give a damn if it's part chivalry or part anything else. As a matter of fact, I think that what you're doing should have been done a long time ago by a lot more people. But it's risky, and for your own peace of soul, you ought to think long and hard about what I'm trying in my own blunt-and-Ruby-way to tell you."

"I'll think about it, Ruby. In fact, I've thought about it a lot already." Gilchrist cannot bring himself to tell her that he has not come up with any answers.

"One thing about a losing cause, Dodge, is that you lose. And you sure as hell have backed a genuine loser."

"What if I happen to believe that the only causes worth backing are losing causes?"

"Well, if that's what you really believe, then you have to live with it. And I don't know if you're the kind of man who can live with that. And if you find out that you can't, you're just liable to take it out on that young woman, and that will ruin both your lives."

Gilchrist looks at Ruby as if he is seeing her for the first time. "Ruby," he says, "you have your own way of amazing me, do you know that? You have more than six million reasons not to say what you're saying, but you say it anyway. Why?"

"I have to leave now, Dodge. I have an appointment in Arlington." She stands and gives Gilchrist a half smile. "You can chalk up what I said to old time's sake. I'm not the most diplomatic woman on earth. I just say it straight out." She pushes her chair flush against the table. "Good luck with all this, Dodge. Take care of yourself."

Watching her leave, Gilchrist realizes how much he will always admire the enigma that is Ruby . . .

Gilchrist's conversation with Ruby occurs exactly one week before his "marriage." Or was it simply a solution? The letter from the authorities at the Immigration Office simply stated that the temporary visa for Raya Mirene Tabry was scheduled to expire in less than a month and that, at the end of that period, the aforementioned Miss Tabry would be required to leave the country.

"Where can I go, Dodge? I can't go back," Raya said after reading the letter.

"Let me look into it."

Gilchrist quickly learns that the various rules and quotas vis-à-vis immigration are as rigid as canon law. Raya's only options are to leave the country and request reentry or to be adopted by or married to an American citizen. Gilchrist is told by immigration officials that the laws have little flexibility for someone in Raya's position. It is then that he seriously begins to think of marriage as a possible solution.

"There is no reason that it has to be anything but a paper marriage, Raya," Gilchrist explains to her.

"But isn't it possible that I could leave the country and then apply to come back? I could go to Canada. I think I'm strong enough to do that."

"Negative. Dr. Voss told me that you need another three months of therapy at the minimum. And besides, where could you go in Canada or anywhere else? Who would be there to look after you? I'm no Florence Nightingale, Raya, but I'm not bad, and when it comes to you . . ."

"Oh, please, Dodge, it's not that. It's not about you at all. You must know that. It's just that I can't see myself going through the acts of becoming a citizen and a wife as if I were buying a newspaper or a dress. Marriage is something special for me, but getting married just to get around a law makes me feel—it's hard to say—cheap and dishonest."

"It's not dishonest, Raya. It's done all the time. And the hard fact is that you don't have many options."

"But it's still dishonest. And it's with the wrong motive."

"All right," says Gilchrist, seeing that his pragmatism is going nowhere against her sincerity. "It's dishonest. But blame the motive on me. We can do what I'm suggesting for all my dishonest reasons, or we can go and make our case just as we are—on the merits—and see what happens, and one thing that might very well happen is that you will be asked to leave the country anyway."

"You sound so sure about that."

"Fairly sure. I also think that this whole business might have been brought to the attention of the Immigration Office by one of Tab's—one of your uncle's—standing enemies just to make life a little more interesting for us. Sometimes all it takes to wake up the right government agency is one telephone call. Somebody just might have made that kind of telephone call about you."

"But why?"

"Anything to create a problem, Raya. Even if we somehow beat this rap, there will be others down the line to put down. We're up against some people who specialize in making life as difficult for us as they can, sometimes inside the system and sometimes outside the system. For the moment I think they're working inside the system . . ."

Several days pass before Raya tells Gilchrist that he can proceed as he suggested, that she will do whatever he wants, that she still thinks it's dishonest, but . . .

All the procedures after that become purely clinical. Gilchrist collects the necessary papers, completes them as required, presents himself with Raya at a clinic for the required blood tests, and then drives with her at a fixed time on a fixed day to a local magistrate who performs the ceremony in less than six minutes. Afterward, he drives southward along the Potomac to a small seafood restaurant below Mount Vernon. It is the first time that he and Raya have been out of his apartment together for dinner since the day he brought her from the hospital.

After ordering dinner for the two of them, Gilchrist looks at Raya and smiles hesitantly. They are sitting opposite each other at a circular place-matted table, and they sit for a long time without speaking—he, because he can think of nothing reassuring to say other than what he has already said, and she, because the flurry of the events of the day and of the days preceding has left her benumbed by regulations and procedures that have touched the marrow of her life in ways she is reluctant to think about.

"Dodge," she says so quietly that he barely hears her.

"Yes."

"Why are you doing this for me? Why have you been doing all these things for me?"

"One question at a time."

"Tell me, Dodge. I know you have tried to tell me, but I have to hear it again, especially now."

"Raya," he answers but does not look at her, "I don't know if I can explain why."

"Dodge, you're a writer. You have all the words to say whatever you want to say. Be honest with me, please."

"Well . . . ," he begins, then loses his focus and, despite trying not to, regains it. "Well, I'm doing it because I don't want you kicked out of the country on a technicality, especially now."

"You're not answering me." She sits back in her chair and waits.

Gilchrist straightens a wrinkle in his place mat by ironing it steadily with the base of his right hand. He keeps up the ironing motion long after the wrinkle has disappeared until Raya places her hand on top of his to still it.

"What I feel," says Gilchrist, "is not easy to put into words." He sandwiches her hand between both of his and looks into her eyes like a man testifying under oath. "Listen to me. I'm a journalist. I've seen hundreds and hundreds of people as a journalist, and I've known hundreds of other people socially as well, here and all over the world. Many of them were women. I've studied them. I've talked to them. I got to know many of them, some as friends, some as more than friends, some as enemies." He irons another imaginary wrinkle from the place mat with his elbow. "I've closed the book on all that. That Gilchrist is over now. Gilchrist the celebrity is over now. I look back on those years, and I'm almost ashamed of them." He pauses. "You're unlike anyone I've ever known. It's not even original to say that, but I'm saying it anyway. When you were lying there in a coma, I let my heart do all the talking. I said everything to you that could be said about how I felt. And then you awoke. Even now when I look at you, I can't believe that you came through all that. I think I have to be imagining you. Does that make sense? You don't do it by doing anything at all. Who you are does it."

23

STILL CARRYING her letter and reading it again and again as he walks, he enters the bedroom to find the closet empty of her few dresses, skirts, and blouses, the drawers of the bureau similarly empty, her toiletries in the bathroom gone. He sits down on the edge of the bed and finishes reading her letter for the fourth time. Although he now knows her letter almost by heart from salutation to conclusion, he concentrates on every word as if it were a poem whose inner meaning would reveal itself only if it were given his quintessential attention. Then he folds it and reinserts it in its envelope.

The telephone rings like a message from another world. Gilchrist strides back to his desk and picks up the receiver at the end of the fifth ring.

"Raya," he says, half expecting to hear her answer.

"Mr. Gilchrist." It is a man's voice.

"Yes. Who is this?"

"This is Dodson at the print shop."

"Yes, Mr. Dodson. How are you?"

"Well enough, I suppose."

"Good. What can I do for you?"

"Well, Mr. Gilchrist, I don't know exactly how to begin to tell you this. But let me say at the start that this story has a bad ending."

"Go ahead. Tell me."

"You remember that the anniversary issue of the journal was at the binder's last week."

"Yes."

"It was returned to us for shipping yesterday, and we were all set to box the journals and send them out first thing tomorrow morning. In fact, I checked the entire order myself about two hours ago before I locked up."

"Well, what's the problem, Mr. Dodson?"

"The problem is that I had to come back to the shop for a package I left here—a birthday present for my grandson—and I saw that someone had broken in. Nothing's missing. I gave the place a good search before I called you. Nothing was touched except the anniversary issues of the journal. Whoever broke in spilled oil paint over the entire shipment. Ruined the whole run, every single copy, not one worth a damn." He pauses. "The police are on their way. But as far as I can tell, the ones who broke in were here for just one purpose. Nothing but the journal was touched."

Gilchrist sags into the chair beside his desk. "You say the entire run is lost?"

"I checked every stack myself. There's this black paint over everything. It's a damn mess." Dodson pauses, and Gilchrist can hear him talking to someone. "Excuse me, Mr. Gilchrist. The police just came. Just hold on for a minute." Dodson resumes talking to the police. "Sorry, Mr. Gilchrist. I had to explain a few things to Inspector Cobb here." Gilchrist remembers the name. From where? He associates the name with the fire at Tabry's house, the emergency room at Georgetown Hospital, the inquiry. "I want you to know that I'm really sorry about this. I know what the anniversary issue meant to Mr. Tabry and what it means to you. We took every precaution, believe me. It looks as if there was someone who was just waiting to ruin everything at the last minute, the whole job."

"Thanks, Mr. Dodson."

"I'm really sorry, Mr. Gilchrist. It's as much a loss for me as it is for you."

"I'll let you know in a few days if there is anything we can do . . ."

"It's really too bad. These people knew just what they were doing, Mr. Gilchrist. They were out to destroy the run, and they did."

VI

The Time Preceding

24

NOT THAT IT had been much different from what he expected. He had read enough about Israel to know what its internal and foreign policies were. But knowing in theory, as he knew from his experience as a reporter, was never the same as knowing in fact, and now, at the conclusion of his two-week stint in Israel, he knows much more in fact.

Sitting in the airport lounge and looking out at the very hills that Tabry had told him so much about over the years, he feels himself party to an old dispute. He recalls Tabry's visceral resentment of the government's indifference to the displaced Palestinians, its arrogance when it was reminded of its exclusionist policies, its barely hidden scorn for the "occupied."

The days of the previous weeks relive themselves for Gilchrist as he waits in the lounge for his return flight from Tel Aviv to New York, but first he remembers how he stood in his editor's office one day after he opened Raya's letter in his apartment and decided he had no choice but to respect her plea that he not try to find her.

"Why in the hell do you want to go?" asked the editor. "You haven't exactly put yourself in their good graces. I doubt if they'll even admit you. And if they do admit you, I doubt if you'll have freedom of movement in the country to find anything worth writing about."

"I want to take a crack at it. I'm an American, after all. They might make life a bit difficult for me there, but I doubt if they'll deny me entry. That would make them look bad."

"Have it your way."

"Have passport. Will travel."

"Need visa. Don't forget that part of the slogan."

Two afternoons later Gilchrist was amazed that it took less than twenty-four hours for him to receive his visa.

"Enjoy your trip to Israel, Mr. Gilchrist," said the embassy official as he stamped his documents. "Perhaps this visit will help you clarify your view of us."

During his flight from New York to Tel Aviv, Gilchrist tried to sleep, but he thought only of Raya. His memories of her were so raw and painful that he periodically stood and walked up and down the commodious aisles of the jet and tried to distract himself by looking at the faces of the passengers.

Seated now in the airport lounge and surveying the very runway he had landed on two weeks earlier, Gilchrist knows that he is being watched. His "watchers" have made no secret of their assignment. They are the same men who tracked him during his entire stay—except for one night. He realizes now that it was that one night that made the whole trip worthwhile. But that night had not happened until he had been in the country for eight days.

During those eight days he was escorted to farms, offices of politicians, newspaper editors, and those he came later to identify as "government-approved" authors. From the politicians he learned little. True, there was an opposition party, but its views vis-à-vis the Palestinians were not radically different from those of the majority party.

"We must ensure the survival of the Jewish people as a majority here," a former prime minister told him.

"But the demographics don't favor you."

"Then we will have to find a solution that guarantees our majority status."

"Is it a matter of majority or exclusivity?"

"We cannot permit our culture to be diluted, Mr. Gilchrist."

"Your culture or your power?"

"I see no point in continuing this conversation."

The newspaper editors whom Gilchrist saw spoke openly of dissent in the country, but it was dissent at the fringes of power.

"Do you think it possible for there to be a 'Tom Paine' in the journalism profession here?" he asked one editor.

"We have them now. Avineri and others. But they are marginal. They run the risk of being accused of disloyalty to the people, their own people. No journalist here could survive long with that kind of reputation."

"What if his case were not against the people but against the government?"

"The response would be the same. For many here, the government and the people are one entity."

"I see," said Gilchrist. The answer sounded like an excerpt from one of Johnson's speeches during the Vietnam War.

The authors with whom Gilchrist had government-arranged appointments were barely known outside of Israel. One had written an epic about the early pioneering days when the first immigrants created and named their own city. Another was more or less the official speechwriter for political figures of prominence. "It so happens," he said, "that the views of these men and my own views are one and the same." A third had just received a medal for fostering solidarity between the political and literary "communities" in the country. Gilchrist had long since tired of the word *community* in the political argot of the United States. It often was one of Safire's creations that covered everything from gangs to racial and ethnic blocs, all of which were, to Gilchrist, a step in the wrong political direction. Finally, when Gilchrist asked about two of Israel's most distinguished writers, he was told that they were on sabbatical in Europe.

"Are these government-sponsored sabbaticals?" he asked.

"No government funds were involved. These writers went as private citizens."

"That sounds more like a vacation than a sabbatical," Gilchrist interjected and paused. "Are their families still here? Perhaps I could interview the wives."

"Their families are with them. One of these individuals is in Tuscany. And the other, who knows."

"Will Elon be coming back? Will either one be coming back?"

"Possibly."

"When?"

"That is entirely up to them."

"Are they in fact coming back ever?"

"That is entirely up to them."

On his fifth day in the country Gilchrist requested a meeting with the minister of internal security. He was told the minister's name. He kept telling himself that he had some special reason to remember the name—Gelb. He was told that the minister would meet him in Jerusalem at his hotel.

As soon as he saw Gelb's blond hair and brown mustache, Gilchrist recalled what Raya told him in Saranac. For a few moments Gilchrist was tempted to confront Gelb with what he knew of him and name names and exact circumstances, but he thought better of it and confined himself to the political questions he came to ask. But as Gelb was about to leave after more than a half hour of answering Gilchrist's questions, Gelb said, "It seems that you have become friendly with one of our former detainees who is now in the United States. A certain Miss Tabry."

Gilchrist nodded. He realized at once that the time for formalities was over. The conversation would proceed without pretense or diplomacy on either side. Gilchrist sensed that Gelb was prepared for this, since it was he who had brought up the subject. Instinctively, Gilchrist distanced himself spiritually from his role as a visiting journalist, bracing himself for whatever was in the offing. He also studied Gelb with even closer scrutiny, noting that the almost equine and somewhat lean shape of Gelb's face, which the brown mustache, drooping at either end, made even leaner, was belied by the man's body. It was the body of a heavier man, but the weight was concentrated in the chest and shoulders so that it appeared that the face and body were at odds.

"An intelligent young woman, Miss Tabry," Gelb was saying. "Her father and her uncle were long-standing enemies of ours." He paused. "We detained her briefly just as a precaution."

"A precaution against what?"

"Against whatever."

"Do your laws permit that?"

"Of course. Of course, we go on the principle that the government cannot wait to imprison someone until he . . ."

"Or she."

"Until he or she actually commits a crime. Thus, we act before he or she actually commits the crime. That way the crime is never committed."

Gilchrist smiled at Gelb until his smile seemed to mystify him.

"Does that remark amuse you, Mr. Gilchrist?"

"It intrigues me, frankly. If jailing someone based only on suspicion is made legal, it would seem that everyone on earth is jailable, since no one knows for sure when anyone might commit a crime."

"When you have lived with terror as long as we have, you would not find such procedures amazing, believe me."

"Don't you see any terror in the fact that you can arrest or harass someone just because you think he or she *might* commit a crime?"

"We prefer to call it prudence. A government's first responsibility is to ensure its own security and protect its people."

"How many people have you arrested like this? I read a report from Amnesty International as well as the International Red Cross that you have more than ten thousand political prisoners here."

"A biased report, obviously," Gelb said and hoisted his belt, which had begun to slip down so that his pants were sagging. "There are people in this world who are our permanent enemies, Mr. Gilchrist. Even in those two august organizations that you just mentioned, there apparently are such people."

"That has echoes of Zabotinski."

"You have read Zabotinski?"

"I've read *The Iron Wall*, if that's what you mean. His thesis was that you create a state and surround it with an iron wall until your enemies are defeated and then negotiate with the remainder—the surplus population."

"That's not quite the same as the preventive detention we practice here."

"But it's a result of the same mentality, isn't it? Someday you might enclose the entire country within a wall in the hope that you could live in total security."

"Some here have already suggested that, but I would call that an unnecessary expense at the moment."

"But it could happen someday if you keep the same mind-set," said Gilchrist and paused. He was becoming more and more convinced that he was dealing with a dogmatist. He had actually expected more Machiavellian responses from Gelb. Instead he was getting reaffirmations of already established policies or evasions. As a journalist drawn to "hard news," he was bored. And he could feel himself becoming angrier by the minute.

"Do you mind if we visit one of your prisons?" Gilchrist asked.

"If I let you visit the prisons, how would I know that you would not be as negative as Amnesty International or the International Red Cross?"

"You wouldn't know."

"Then why should I take you?"

"Because you know I'm a good newspaperman, and I would let the facts speak for themselves."

Gilchrist saw that he had Gelb checkmated. For a moment Gelb ignored the corner in which he had painted himself and waited for Gilchrist to introduce a new subject.

"If the facts about the prisoners contradict what Amnesty and the Red Cross wrote, I'll let the truth be known in my report," said Gilchrist.

"You are not exactly a friend of my government, Mr. Gilchrist. Why should I expect you to be our defender in your columns?"

"I'm not sympathetic with the policies of your government vis-à-vis the Palestinians, that's true. But I have given my reasons publicly." He paused. "I don't play fast and loose with the truth. If I see that the prison reports were wrong, I'll give my reasons in print. You know I'll do that. My reputation bears that out."

"Very well, then," said Gelb. "I have appointments this afternoon, but I'll pass by your hotel with my driver tomorrow at 9:00 a.m. and take you myself to the nearest facility. You will find it fairly typical, I believe."

"Fair enough. I'll be ready."

As he remembers that meeting with Gelb, Gilchrist smiles and walks to the window of the airport lounge that permits him a complete view of the city and the hills around it. It recalls the view he had of similar hills on the outskirts of Jerusalem. The new apartment buildings in the surrounding settlements seemed to enclose the city like a palisade. It makes Gilchrist think of an article he wrote several years earlier about the palisade mentality in foreign affairs. He wrote then that such a mentality was a return to the atavism of the Maginot line, a reliance on the illusion that safety could be guaranteed if you shielded your population behind barriers, whether the barrier was a fortress of missiles or, as was true in Berlin, behind an actual wall. The fortresslike ring of apartment buildings, all uniformly grayish and identical in their precast specifications, seemed to

Gilchrist to be an obvious indictment of the mentality that conceived it and of the government and even of the people to whom such a mentality was a comfort. As he watches, he feels that the buildings seem to have a smothering effect on the city they enclose. And this helps him understand why so many Israeli intellectuals and writers had decided to immigrate or to oppose the successive governments that had perpetuated this policy. Gilchrist himself could no more imagine himself living in such an environment than he could imagine himself living in a locked room. As a writer, he would feel strangled.

He remembers that he felt the same sense of strangulation when he accompanied Gelb to the prison on the morning after their initial meeting. During the drive to the prison, Gelb explained that he would permit Gilchrist to see how the prisoners were housed and treated but that he would not permit interviews.

"Why?" asked Gilchrist. He was determined to question every dictum that Gelb advanced.

"To a prisoner, Mr. Gilchrist, an interview is like a microphone to the world. He knows that he will be heard, so he talks and talks and talks. If he says things that are, shall we say, inaccurate, then it places me in the position of clarifying an inaccuracy. I don't have time for such clarifications, Mr. Gilchrist."

"So I'm going to have to rely only on what you tell me, is that the case?"

"That and whatever you'll be able to see with your very eyes."

What Gilchrist saw was ward after ward of neatly made cots with a prisoner at attention beside each cot. It was like a military inspection. As Gilchrist walked by the prisoners, he noticed that each was looking directly ahead, as if any deviation might be regarded as a crime or infraction and be punishable as such. Afterward, he was escorted to a dining hall, which was scrubbed and in almost immaculate order. Finally, Gelb took him to the compound itself where the prisoners, when they were not on work details, were permitted to exercise and, for an hour each day, smoke if they wished.

"Where do you get the cigarettes for them?"

"You provide them. The cigarettes are American."

Finally, Gelb and Gilchrist visited the infirmary. Gilchrist met the doctor and nurses on duty, then surveyed the ward where only a single prisoner, covered to the waist with a sheet, lay faceup in bed. As Gilchrist passed the bed, the patient followed him with his eyes. Gilchrist smiled at the man, but the smile was not returned.

"What's wrong with him?" Gilchrist asked Gelb.

"Overexposure to the sun. He was on a detail outside the compound, and he worked without a hat. He should be able to be released tomorrow."

After returning to his hotel after the tour of the prison, Gilchrist began to wonder if he had let himself become propagandized by his own antipathy to Gelb and his associates. His conscience as a journalist began to trouble him. He had just seen the "facts," and these "facts" did not conform to what he had expected to see. Could Amnesty International and the International Red Cross have exaggerated their findings? Then he remembered Raya's account in Saranac about her interrogation by Gelb. This had certainly not been imagined. Gilchrist concluded that Gelb might have called the prison the night before and had it carefully prepared for his visit. That could easily explain the spit-and-polish appearance at the facility. But, even so, wouldn't the prisoners have tried to tell him something with their eyes at least? He had looked hard into the eyes of many of them and had come away with nothing, not the slightest suspicion, not a skeptically lifted eyebrow. But, Gilchrist theorized, what if the prisoners had been told that he was an official or an ally of the government? Then they would have had every reason not to convey anything at all.

"You see," Gelb had said on their drive back to Jerusalem, "we are not as barbaric as you were led to believe, Mr. Gilchrist. In fact, our standards are higher by far than those of any others in the Middle East. I'm sure you're familiar with prison conditions in Syria, Egypt, Iraq, and Turkey. They are barbaric. We have nothing in common with them."

"Are all the prisons like this one?"

"This is typical, I would say. I thought I made that clear before we came."

By the time they reached the hotel, Gelb had completed his description of the Israeli government's reliance on computers and such to store information about all those within the country and abroad who were regarded as "enemies of the state."

"Our system is as sophisticated as any other in the world, and that includes your Federal Bureau of Investigation. In fact, the FBI has borrowed many of our techniques."

Gilchrist nodded. He was letting it go in one ear and out the other.

"By the way, Mr. Gilchrist," said Gelb as he escorted Gilchrist to the door of his hotel, "my guest told me this morning that she knows you. She had no idea that you were here. She said you were good friends in the United States."

Gilchrist stopped and faced Gelb. "What's her name?"

"Levenson. Ruby Levenson. She told me that you knew we were friends. She'd mentioned it to you in Washington."

"She did mention it. I'm surprised she's here."

"I insisted. She needed to revisit Israel." He paused. "I'm sorry you won't have a chance to see one another while you're here. We're leaving this evening to attend a conference over the weekend in Geneva. But she did ask me to give you her best regards."

For the balance of the afternoon Gilchrist remained in the hotel, working on his reports, verifying facts by telephone, and thinking of Ruby. Why had she come with Gelb? How could she have known he was in Israel, since only he and his editor knew about the trip? Why did she ask Gelb to remember her to him? To leave him perplexed? Did she hope that he would take the initiative and call her? Even as he put this question to himself, Gilchrist was tempted to call her and then decided against it. But why did she want him to know that she was in the country? Each time he reached this point in his thinking, he came up with no answers.

When he went to supper, his two watchmen were in the lobby as usual. They followed him into the dining room and seated themselves three tables away, all the time pretending that they did not know that Gilchrist knew who they were but knowing that he knew that they knew that he knew that they knew. If their presence was not the annoyance it was, Gilchrist would have found it comical.

Glancing off and on at his watchmen, Gilchrist tried to distract himself by thinking of Raya and found it easier than he realized. He smiled.

He enjoyed thinking of her. For days he had forced himself not to think of her, had concentrated exclusively on his work, had more or less Novocained his memory. Now her sudden presence in his mind removed the annoyance he felt toward his watchmen and put Ruby Levenson out of his mind entirely.

"Are you Mr. Gilchrist?"

Gilchrist looked up to see the headwaiter at his side. "Yes, I'm Gilchrist."

"You're wanted on the telephone, sir."

"Where's the phone?"

"Follow me, please."

Gilchrist did. After the headwaiter handed him the phone, Gilchrist held it for a moment and looked back to see if the watchmen had followed him. They were still at their table, scrutinizing him over their menus.

"This is Mr. Gilchrist," he said, turning his back to the dining room and cocked the receiver to his ear with his right shoulder.

"Gil?"

Gilchrist knew exactly who it was but was not anxious to admit it. "Who is this?" Gilchrist asked, feigning it.

"This is Ruby. How are you?"

"Fine. Surprised, but fine."

"Did you get my message?"

"Yes," he said. "Yes, Gelb told me, but I thought you'd be on your way to Geneva by now."

"I decided to stay. At least for one more day. I'll catch a flight tomorrow."

"And your host? Is that the right word for him?"

"He left more than an hour ago. I'll meet him at the Beau Rivage tomorrow night."

"Well, he's not one I would have picked for you, Ruby."

"How long are you staying in the country, Gil?"

"Just a few more days. Then back to Washington."

"Is it possible that we could see one another before you go?"

"There are two undercover men watching every move I make, Ruby. They're a grown-up version of the Katzenjammer kids, and they're trying their best to be professionals. It's not quite working, but they're working hard at it, and they have the noses of bloodhounds. I don't think it would be wise if they followed me to a meeting with you while your 'host' and probably their boss happens to be out of the country, do you?"

"I should have guessed that. They shadow a lot of Americans here. Especially people like you." Ruby paused, and Gilchrist could almost hear her thinking as he waited. "Do you want to see me, Gil?"

"Yes," said Gilchrist, and then he immediately wondered why he had said it.

"Then I'll let you worry about decoying your shadows. I'll have dinner waiting for you."

"Tonight? I was just sitting down here to have dinner."

"It has to be tonight. I'm leaving for Geneva tomorrow, remember?"

"Yes, I remember."

"Tell any taxi driver to bring you to the Gelb villa. They all know where it is."

"What if I can't shake them?"

"Then we'll have to settle for this phone call, I suppose. Good-bye, Gil."

Gilchrist placed the receiver on its cradle. He waited by the phone for several minutes. A Gilchrist he thought he had buried began his quiet resurrection—Gilchrist the planner, Gilchrist the angler, Gilchrist the happener.

Instead of returning to his table, Gilchrist strode directly to the table where the Katzenjammers were sitting. They were still studying their menus.

"Gentlemen," said Gilchrist, "it seems that I have some work that must be done right now. I'm going to pass up dinner and go up to my room and do what I have to do. Enjoy your dinner, and I'll see you both in the morning."

Both men looked up at Gilchrist with an almost planned look of incomprehension. Gilchrist left the dining room. By the time he reached the lobby, he saw that the Katzenjammers were behind him. He waited by the elevator and saw them take their usual positions, one in a chair beside the main and only entrance to the hotel, and the other to the left of the elevators.

Once in his room, Gilchrist telephoned room service and ordered coffee and a sandwich. Then he waited . . .

A half hour later when the bellman came with his sandwich and coffee, Gilchrist knew that the only way he could leave the hotel without being detected was to leave by a door other than the main one. And he also knew that he had to return the same way. His knowledge of hotels told him that the service entrance was the best option as well as the least conspicuous.

"Tell me," he asked the bellman, "how long are you on duty?"

"Until tomorrow morning, sir."

"Listen," said Gilchrist and gestured for the bellman to be seated. "I need your help in a matter."

"Yes, sir, if I can . . ."

"I have an important appointment tonight, and I need to get to it and back to the hotel as, let's say, as quietly as possible. I'm not going into detail, but I must go and return without being observed. It's not criminal or underhanded or anything like that. It's purely personal. So I need your help to do this. I'm willing to pay you well for your trouble."

"The money will not be necessary, Mr. Gilchrist. I'm aware of the fact that there are two security men in the lobby."

Gilchrist looked at the bellman with surprise. "What do you mean?" he asked.

"You are known to us, Mr. Gilchrist."

"Are you with the police?"

"No. I mean you are known to us. Palestinians. My people. We know how you have defended our cause in your writings. I am a Palestinian from a village near Bethlehem. It will be an honor for me to help you."

"My God! I can't believe this."

"Do you want to leave now?"

"As a matter of fact, yes."

"Can you follow me, please?"

Together they left the room and proceeded to the service elevator, which the bellman summoned by inserting a small key into a mechanism in the wall.

"So you need a way to get to your appointment?" asked the bellman.

"Yes, I do."

"My brother Nadeem is a taxi driver. I will have him take you."

"What's your name?" Gilchrist asked.

"Samir," answered the bellman as they entered the elevator and descended in silence to the subbasement. The doors opened, and Gilchrist followed Samir through a white-washed hall toward a gray door. Once through the door they were standing on an inclined ramp.

"Follow me, please, Mr. Gilchrist," Samir said and led him through an alley to the main concourse in front of the hotel where a row of six taxis was waiting, front bumper to back bumper for half a block. Samir proceeded directly to one of the taxis, leaned in through a window on the passenger side, and conferred for a minute with the driver. Then he opened the rear door of the taxi for Gilchrist and said, "This is my brother Nadeem. He will take you wherever you wish to go, and he will wait for you and bring you back to the hotel. The door in the subbasement will be left open for you. I'll make sure of that myself. Here is the key to the service elevator. You will need it to return to your room without going through the lobby. You may return it to me tomorrow."

Gilchrist entered the taxi. He had expected his departure to be much more complicated and hazardous than it turned out to be, and he felt the welcome but still uneasy satisfaction of someone who has been inundated with too much good luck.

"Thank you, Samir," he said to the bellman, who was still standing like a soldier on post beside the taxi. Gilchrist offered him a tip in dollars.

Refusing the tip simply by withdrawing his hand and placing it over his heart in the Arabic manner, Samir said, "It is an honor to help you, Mr. Gilchrist."

The driver started the taxi and steered quickly out of the concourse to the main road. Gilchrist noticed that the driver resembled his brother—slight but muscular, spade faced with black and curly hair. He saw that the driver had a mustache, while Samir was clean shaven. Other than that difference they could have been twins.

"Did Samir tell you where . . . ," Gilchrist began.

"Are you the Gilchrist? The one who writes?"

"Yes." He paused. "Do you know the Gelb villa? I have to go there."

"Yes, yes, I know, but why are you here?"

"To write."

"Are you going to write about this Gelb?"

"Among others, yes."

"Why do you go to his house? He is the son of a dog. He is not worth your ink."

For the rest of the drive there was no further comment from Nadeem. When they reached Gelb's villa, Nadeem coasted the taxi to a halt and turned off the headlights. He pointed to the villa to assure Gilchrist that he had brought him to the right place. "I will be here when you come back, Mr. Gilchrist. If they make me move, the police, wait for me here. I will come back."

Gilchrist nodded and stepped out of the taxi. He walked slowly up a lane lined with ferns to the villa—a blue stucco modernistic bungalow with a porch floor of hexagonal purple tiles—and knocked on the door.

From the moment that Ruby opened the door, Gilchrist knew, really knew, that he should not have come, that he was not the same Gilchrist, and she was not the same Ruby.

"Gil," said Ruby, smiling. "You did it. I knew you would." She moved closer to him and, without kissing him, touched her cheek to his. "Come in, come in."

He told himself that he should turn and leave, make some excuse, do something, but he was trapped by his own momentum from having come in the first place. Something about her manner was too light, too dismissive of the frankness that usually existed between them. He studied her as she led him by the hand into the dining room. She seemed to him to be slightly heavier, and her hair was cut short and colored darker than he had ever seen it. And her voice was throatier, her manner more practiced, less spontaneous.

"I hope you like roast beef and tossed salad. Basic American fare. I put the meal together myself. The servants are gone, except for Eli."

"Eli?"

"The man you saw when you came up the lane."

"I didn't see a soul."

"Well, he probably didn't reveal himself. Eli's our private guard. Protection seems to be necessary these days, according to Seth. He has a dangerous position in the government, you know, and we have to take certain precautions. I told Eli that you were coming. You might not have seen him, but I'm sure he saw you."

"Didn't you qualify it by saying that I was *probably* coming?"

"I didn't think that was necessary. I knew you'd come," she said and smiled, adding, "And I was right, wasn't I?"

The dining room table was shaped like an oval. There were two place settings, one opposite the other. Four candles were burning in a candelabra in the center of the table.

"It looks nice, but it's not very practical. I'm going to move my place to the side of the table so I can be closer to you and actually see you. Otherwise, I wouldn't be able to see you through the candelabra." She moved her place setting from the head of the table to the side, smiled Gilchrist into his chair, and then excused herself so that she could bring their meals in from the kitchen.

After she had brought in both meals, she placed her hand on Gilchrist's forearm and said softly, "It's so good to see you, Gil. I really wasn't as sure as I just sounded when I said I knew you would come, but I'm glad you came. I appreciate it."

"I suppose I could ask why, but that might poison the atmosphere."

Smiling quickly, she withdrew her hand and said, "Still as direct as always, aren't you, Gil."

"I've always found it saves a lot of breath and spares us a lot of hypocrisy."

Ruby sliced a small triangle of roast beef from the flat rare piece on her plate and forked it neatly into her mouth. Gilchrist did the same, and for several moments the two of them ate together quietly.

"Why are you so thick with this guy?" he asked.

"I'm not exactly sure. He has a certain style. He's decisive. I like that."

"He's not for you, Ruby. I wouldn't trust that guy any farther than I could throw him."

"He's talking marriage."

Gilchrist looks at her and smirks.

"I was looking for some encouragement from you, Gil."

Gilchrist pushed his dish to one side and said, "Ruby, I think I'd better leave. I was crazy to come here in the first place. Neither of us is going to feel very good about this an hour from now. Neither of us needs this."

"I do."

"Why?"

"I don't know. I just do. Does everything have to have a reason?"

Gilchrist stood and walked out of the dining room to the front door. By the time he reached the door, Ruby was beside him.

"Gil," she said, "don't leave, please."

"What's the point? You're going to ask me my opinion about this joker, and I'll tell you. You'll hate yourself for asking my opinion, and I think I won't like myself any better for giving it, and that means we'll both end up with ill feelings. At least we can spare one another that."

She turned away from him. When she faced him again, she was holding back tears, but Gilchrist could not tell if they were real tears or not. "You don't have to be sorry for anything, Gil. I probably deserved everything you said, maybe more."

"Good night, Ruby. I'm sorry I spoiled your last night here, sorry it turned out like this."

"Are you, really?"

"Good night, Ruby." Gilchrist put his hand on the doorknob and turned it so that the door opened a jot.

"I only stayed here tonight because of you, Gil," Ruby said.

"If that's the truth, you weren't thinking straight for either one of us."

"It's the truth."

"What was supposed to happen?"

"Nothing," Ruby answered and paused. "Something." Another pause, but shorter. "Anything." She stepped next to him, putting her hand on his shoulder and letting her body touch his. She took his hand in her free hand, brought it to her lips and kissed it, then held it to her cheek, then against her breasts.

"It's too late for this, Ruby."

"Is it? Really?" She positioned herself in front of him, locked her hands behind his neck, and rested her head against his chest.

Gilchrist could feel something fluttering in her left breast, like a little muscle gone wild. Then it stopped. For a minute he was back in his Washington apartment with her when they first met. He knew then that he could do whatever he wanted to do with her, as he had done previously on other occasions, and she wouldn't stop him. Whether it was a residue of his old affection for her or his dislike of Gelb he had no way of knowing, but he felt the old urge of yielding to the invitation of her body when he put his hands on her shoulders and backed her away from him.

"Ruby," he said, "this is crazy. You know it, and I know it."

"I only know that I'm not lonely when I'm with you."

"You're thinking with your glands, Ruby." He took a step back. "Have a good trip to Geneva. It's a good Calvinist town, and you'll forget all about this. Let's leave it at that. No winner. No loser."

He opened the door and exited quickly, shutting the door firmly behind him. He thought he saw a man in the darkness, but he did not stop to make sure. The taxi was still waiting at the end of the fern-bordered lane. Nadeem started the motor and made a U-turn back to the city.

"Shall I take back to the hotel?"

"Yes, might as well."

"You know this Gelb is the worst of all of them, don't you?"

"Worst of all of whom?"

"The worst in the whole government. They are all criminals, but he is the one who keeps his foot on our necks." Nadeem stopped at an intersection and spat out the window. "I think it was Gelb who killed Sharif's brother. And Sharif also."

"Sharif?" asked Gilchrist.

"Sharif Tabry. And his brother, the poet. They were both from our village."

"Are you from Sharif's village?"

"Yes."

"Sharif was my best friend. Did Samir tell you that?"

"This was already known to us, Mr. Gilchrist. We know about you and Sharif, and we know what you are doing for us when you write. If you were not known to us, would I be talking the way I am talking now to you?"

Gilchrist watched Nadeem accelerate quickly out of the intersection. They drove for a short time in silence.

"How far is Sharif's village from here?"

"Five kilometers."

"Can we go there?"

"Now?"

"Yes, now."

"Of course, we can go there." Nadeem stopped and turned halfway around in the driver's seat. "Why do you want to go to Tabry?"

"To Tabry?"

"My village. It has the name of the family. The government people want to give it another name in Hebrew, but we reject."

"I want to see it. I haven't seen it. They'll never take me there officially. I want to talk to the people there." He waited. "Will you take me there?"

"As you wish."

Nadeem made an abrupt right turn and within minutes was heading due west. He drove with the sure speed of a man who knew the road from memory.

Gilchrist looked out of the taxi's rear window and caught a glimpse of Jerusalem below the vivid stars . . .

The mayor of Tabry was a thick-shouldered man of fifty or so with a grizzled triangular mustache, the peak of the triangle touching the base of his nose and flaring downward to the corners of his lips in isosceles slants. Nadeem had told Gilchrist en route that the mayor had lost his right leg a year before when he went to start his booby-trapped Land Rover. There were several other mayors of towns on the West Bank who had been severely injured in similar attacks.

"Tabry welcomes you. The village of Sharif Tabry welcomes you, Mr. Gilchrist," the mayor said after Nadeem introduced him to Gilchrist. Later, in the living room of the mayor's stone-block house, Gilchrist met several men and women as well as three students, a boy and two girls.

"These pastries come from Nablus, Mr. Gilchrist," said the mayor after they were all seated in his living room. "They have no rival. They are stuffed with cheese and pistachio nuts. We call them *knafy*. I missed them when I was studying years ago at the University of Texas. I'm a civil engineer by profession. I taught at our university before it was closed because of the Intifada. So I returned here to my village and became, as your hosts say in their newspapers, 'political.' There are many men like me—doctors who gave up their practices, lawyers who did the same—all of them professional people without a profession except to become 'political.' Why?

Because freedom comes first. You can't practice your profession unless you are free. Please, try the *knafy*."

Gilchrist lifted one of the cakes, which looked like a turnover, and bit into it as the mayor continued.

"Actually, our problem here is both a political one and a psychological one. It's political at heart, but it has overtones that any psychologist would understand. The fact is that we are occupied by people who think we are a hindrance. But we are permanent. That makes us a permanent enemy to them. They've become paranoid about it. And they have the power to live out their paranoia, so they make it hard for us because we are within their control. We are in the belly of the lion, so to speak. They make us wait for work permits. They arrest us whenever they choose because we are who we are. They close down our universities, which means that they want to keep our children illiterate. They do not want us to excel, and they are frustrated because, no matter what they do, we do not succumb."

"You resemble the Irish that way, Mr. Mayor," said Gilchrist, swallowing the last bite of *knafy*.

"The Irish?"

"For centuries they lived under the British heel. They were regarded just the way the Israelis regard the Palestinians. The Irish answer was to become more Irish, and eventually they prevailed."

"We will prevail as well. They tell the world that we receive better wages, better medical treatment, better everything under the occupation. But we are not free. To be free, you must control your own destiny. A man can have everything—money, clothes, food—but unless he has political freedom, he is still a slave. And to many Israelis we are meant to be their slaves. They say it openly. They think we are animals. That is why we oppose them with something that is stronger than their power. Let me give you an example. Last week one of their soldiers was on guard duty just a few kilometers from where we are now. A child, a little boy of seven, came and stood this far from him." The mayor then indicated a distance from where he was sitting to the wall opposite. "This little boy of seven knew that this soldier was our enemy. He carried a handful of little stones, and he began to throw them, one by one, at the soldier. Little stones, you understand, the size of pistachio nuts. They could not hurt anyone. When the boy ran out of stones, he went and collected more and kept on throwing them at the soldier. Naturally, the soldier became annoyed and tried to scare the boy away. But the boy kept coming back. No matter what the soldier did, the boy kept coming back with his little stones. After a while the soldier moved to a different position, but the boy kept throwing stones at the spot where the soldier had been standing. The soldier had nothing to fear from a child of seven, but in a way the child had defeated him."

Nadeem, the taxi driver, waited until the mayor was finished and then said, "Sometimes I have to drive people to the border. I mean, I used to drive them. Now I tell people that my cab is not good enough to travel the distance, and they get someone else. But I know how they search us at every checkpoint. They never search their own people. Sometimes they take us into a booth and make us take off our clothes. That is part of their war against us."

"What's the point?"

"To shame you. Do you know how it feels to stand naked in front of someone? They make you stand that way in front of them until you think you have no dignity. They search your clothes. Then they search you. They look in your mouth. They have no shame. They search you in the back where your dirt comes out. They have men and women in the same booth. They examine a man's wife in front of him. If the man makes a move to stop him, they say he is 'obstructing.' But imagine having to look at a guard who is putting his finger into your wife. Or your daughter. But they do it, and there is no one to stop them. They say it's part of their security. I spit on their security."

"We have many stories, Mr. Gilchrist," said the mayor. "It is inhuman to live under occupation." He turned to one of the students, a boy in his late teens. "Tell Mr. Gilchrist what happened at the university last Thursday."

"After they closed the university," the boy said in slightly accented English, "a group of us tried to get into the library. When we reached the campus, we saw four soldiers in a lorry at the entrance. They got out of the lorry when they saw us. We turned and ran. They didn't chase us. Instead they laughed at us. We could hear them laughing when we reached the top of the hill. Then Efrem and Wadie picked up some stones and started to throw stones down on them. They stopped laughing. They started up the hill after us. One of the soldiers stopped and pointed his rifle at us. We all dropped down on the ground. There was one shot, then another. Finally, I couldn't stay on the ground any longer, and I stood up and ran. Two of the soldiers chased me and caught me. They threw me on the ground and kicked me. One hit me on my head with his rifle. Afterward they dragged me to the lorry and drove me to the interrogation center. At the center they called me a trespasser and said that my father and my mother were going to pay a fine for what was done. I said we were very poor. They told me that we would be made to pay in other ways. They said they were going to make an example out of me. I said that all we had was our house. They kept me at the center all day. At night they sent me home. That was three weeks ago. Since then the soldiers have come two or three times to look at the house. We don't know if they will use bulldozers on the house the next time they come. They've done that with other houses in the village. They come and tell the family that they have ten minutes to collect what they have and leave. Then the bulldozer crushes the house, or they use dynamite. The family is left with nothing but what they can carry. So far we are lucky. My side still hurts where they kicked me. For one week after they kicked me, I passed blood in my water. There is still blood now, but not as much."

The girl beside the boy waited to see if he was going to continue. When he nodded to her that he was finished, she said, "The first time the university was closed, I was part of a manifestation. Some of our American teachers were not going to be permitted to teach because the government said they were not impartial . . ."

"They accused them of being sympathetic to our situation here," interjected the mayor.

"A group of us gathered in front of the dean's office," the girl resumed, "and started to chant that we wanted our teachers back. There were soldiers all around the building. We stood about twenty meters from them and said the names of each of the teachers that had been dismissed, one by one. Suddenly, one of the soldiers fired his rifle over our heads, and we turned and ran. There were other shots. I saw two of my friends fall beside me. They were both shot in the legs. That was the government's policy at the time—to shoot protesters in the legs. Here." She pointed to the calf of her right leg. "Here, you can still see where I was shot." The girl had fierce tears in her eyes as she pointed to a scar left by the wound, a pink zigzag below the knee. "But what happened in my uncle's village was worse."

The mayor lifted his hand to intervene, as if the girl had already said enough, but the girl ignored him.

"The soldiers came to my uncle's village just after midnight. They gathered all the men over eighteen in the square, including my uncle. They accused them of plotting against the settlers. Then they marched them into the olive orchard. There were more than twenty. My uncle told me afterward that they made them all lie facedown on the ground. They tied their hands behind their backs, and they tied their legs together at the ankles. Then they stuffed rags in their mouths so that no one could hear their screams. Then the lieutenant ordered the soldiers to use clubs or the butts of their rifles and break the arms and legs of all the men on the ground. Some of the soldiers refused, but the rest of them obeyed. There were many of them who broke their clubs doing what they were ordered to do. They did this to everyone but my uncle because they wanted him to go back to the village and tell everyone what had been done and to take it as a warning." She paused. "To this day that is still spoken of as the 'Night of the Clubs.'"

Gilchrist made notes as she spoke, and he continued to write as every other person in the group related some incident of abuse. There was some overlap in the stories so that he often heard different versions of the same thing, except for one instance. One of the students explained that he had been arrested during one demonstration and that the soldiers began to break the arms and legs of the demonstrators. Gilchrist had heard this described as a "moderate form of punishment" by Jeane Kirkpatrick, the country's spokesman at the UN, when he inquired into the matter before he left Washington. The student, his arm still in a cast, held it up as evidence after he gave his testimony.

Even as he made notes, Gilchrist could not help but think of how similar abuses and punishments had been visited on the colonists by the British prior to 1776. He had even pointed out the parallels in several of his columns. The eventual reaction of the colonists provided the very language that Jefferson immortalized in the Declaration of Independence, and Gilchrist had quoted it verbatim in the same column: *"All experience hath shewn, that mankind are more disposed to suffer, while evils are sufferable, than to right themselves by abolishing the forms to which they are accustomed. But when a long train of abuses and usurpation, pursuing invariably the same Object evinces a design to reduce them under absolute despotism, it is their right, it is their duty, to throw off such a Government, and to provide new Guards for their further security."* The only difference, as Gilchrist saw it, was that the people he was now listening to had no means to overthrow their oppressors, at least no means to overthrow them by force of arms, as had the colonists. In the words of the mayor, the Palestinians were indeed in the lion's belly.

Gilchrist remembered how in subsequent columns he had described how other downtrodden peoples had managed to resist oppression until a victory of sorts was theirs: the Irish, the Indians under Mahatma Gandhi, the emancipated slaves in the United States fulfilling the exhortations of various leaders from Frederick Douglass to Martin Luther King. But he also noted the history of the American Indian tribes and other aborigines around the world who had survived only marginally and without a full political dimension. And then, of course, there were the Armenians and Assyrians before them who had almost been erased from the face of the earth because of genocidal policies. The Nazi-murdered Jews of Europe were an even more recent example. So, he concluded, it was possible for an oppressed people to be expunged entirely or to be held down and abused long enough for their spirit and identity to be permanently bent.

Scanning the faces of the villagers before him, Gilchrist could see a curious combination of an attitude of undefeat with an acceptance of temporary defeat. And there was a sense of tiredness as well, the kind of tiredness he had seen in the faces of soldiers who knew that battles other than the one they had just survived were waiting and would inevitably follow, and that others would follow—battles without end. It was not lack of courage that he saw in their faces. It was more a look of forbearance. Perhaps, Gilchrist thought, this was the ultimate courage, the courage not to give up regardless, courage in the face of hopelessness. Their expressions said that there would be no defeat as long as something within them kept saying, quietly but persistently, no.

After the villagers left the mayor's house, the mayor and Gilchrist were alone.

"That was the true face of Palestine, Mr. Gilchrist."

Gilchrist nodded, folded his notebook, and slipped it into his pocket.

"As long as Israel has the support of the United States for its policies here and the means to implement these polices, there will be resistance. Israeli law is applied in unequal ways, beginning with those Palestinians who are still in Israel proper. The Nationality Act of 1952 makes Israeli citizenship possible for non-Jews only after the fulfillment of a number of 'unspecified conditions.' And then there is the Land Acquisition Law of 1953, which authorizes the government to expropriate without the consent of the owners any land belonging to the Arab owners living in Israel. And yet the Palestinians still in Israel pay the same taxes as the Israelis pay, but they remain the poorest in the country, with inadequate textbooks in their schools and with a shortage of teachers. And their political representation is such that they can vote only for those nominated for them within the framework of established national parties. That's the pattern for the future in the country itself, and for those of us under occupation, restrictions are even worse. You've probably already been told about them by Nadeem."

After they left the mayor's house, Nadeem drove to a small cemetery where he said that Sharif Tabry's brother was buried. Gilchrist inspected the mound that was marked by a flat, unmarked stone with the name—TABRY—nicked across it in English as well as Arabic.

"They shot him after they deported him to Lebanon," said Nadeem. "And they made sure that they shot him around his mouth because he had the mouth of a poet. That dog Gelb was the one who ordered it."

"How do you know?"

"I know."

As they drove back to the hotel, Nadeem stopped the taxi at the top of a small hill and said, "Sometimes I stop here in the morning and wait for the sun. I lean against that tree over there and smoke a cigarette, and then I feel the sun coming up behind me like wings. And the wings reach around me and stretch out over the whole country and make it shine like gold. It's the first sun of the day. It's not bright enough to hurt your eyes, so I can watch it." He paused and asked, "Do you want a cigarette? They might be too strong for Americans. Turkish."

"Why not?" Gilchrist answered, accepting the cigarette and letting Nadeem light it for him. Nadeem then lit a cigarette for himself, and both men smoked in silence.

Nadeem stepped out of the taxi and opened the door for Gilchrist. Together they walked toward the tree that Nadeem had mentioned. Nadeem took a final draw on the cigarette he had been smoking and flicked it away.

"Once I was arrested with my older brother Braheem," Nadeem said. "It was two years ago. There had been some problems, and the military police were arresting everybody. You know how they react when they are having trouble with us. They arrest everybody. And then they interrogate." Nadeem leaned against the tree and looked out at Jerusalem. "They tied our hands behind our backs with that plastic tape they use now and made us sit in the sun while they called each of us in for questioning. And they had us blindfolded also. They do that so that you feel more alone. There was no other reason to blindfold us. What could we be looking for? But with your eyes covered, you feel all by yourself, and that is why they do it. You don't know what's coming or who's coming. It's like you are in a prison cell. Only *you* are the cell. They took their time questioning us. In the first day they interrogated only six men. All day, only six men. And the rest of us sat blindfolded in the sun with our hands tied behind our backs. If you called one of the guards and said you had to go to the toilet, he told you to go where you were sitting. So you had to ask the man beside you to zip down your pants in front so you could do what you had to do. The guards didn't object to that. They wanted everything to be difficult for us. And after you relieved yourself, you had to sit down beside what you did. And if you had to do the other thing, then the man next to you had to help you get your pants down, and you just squatted where you were and did what you had to do. There was no way to wipe yourself. For two days we sat in our own filth. It was supposed to be a lesson to us. Then on the third day they released all of us, except for my brother Braheem. They had nothing to charge us with. We knew it, and they knew it. But they take full advantage of opportunities like that to torment us, to attack our dignity, to give us a bad morale."

"What did they do to your brother?"

"They kept him because he was the oldest. They wanted to make, how do you say, an example. They kept him for two more weeks in prison. Then they took him to the border with Lebanon and told him to start to walk. He had nothing but the clothes he was wearing. They deported him. He can never come back. So he was in Beirut for one year and made enough money to go to the United States. And that's where he still is. In Washington. He works there with people who make furniture. He has skills with wood. He tells us that he is all right, but we want to have him back with us."

"How do they treat the ones they keep in prison?"

"Like dogs. Worse than dogs."

"I visited one yesterday. It looked better than many others I've seen in my life."

"They knew that you were coming. Who took you there?"

"Gelb."

Nadeem gave a staccato laugh. "He is the supervisor of all the prisons. He showed you only what he wanted you to see. They had Sharif's niece there before Sharif arranged for her to go to the United States."

"I know that."

"How do you know?"

"She works with me in Washington. Sharif asked me to find work for her, and I did." He paused. "Did they abuse her when she was in prison?"

"I don't think so. They knew that she was not political. I think they just wanted to frighten her. With my sister it was different."

"Was she arrested?"

"Twice for protesting. She was very political. The second time they sentenced her to be in prison for two years. She would not see us when we came to visit her. She never wrote to us. But we learned later from someone who was there with her that they did bad things to her. That was probably why she would not see us. And she never wrote."

"Even now?"

"There is no now."

"What do you mean?"

"Dead," said Nadeem. "They found my sister in her cell. She made a rope from her dress. They found her hanging. It was an accident, they told us." He coughed out his staccato laugh again and walked with Gilchrist back to the taxi. After they were seated, they remained silent.

"Are you all right?" Gilchrist asked.

"Yes," answered Nadeem. "It is difficult when I talk about these things."

"Do you think I'll have trouble getting back into the hotel?"

"No."

"Are you sure?"

"My brother is there. There will be no problem."

25

GILCHRIST WAS ALMOST finished shaving his right cheek when Ruby telephoned him. She told him she was in the hotel restaurant on her way to the airport and had to see him. He informed her that he was under constant surveillance and then asked her again if she thought it was a good idea for her to be seen with him since it was certain that this would be reported to Gelb. Her answer was that she had told the two Katzenjammers that she had left a piece of luggage back at the villa and wanted them to retrieve it for her. She figured that it would take them about one hour round-trip.

"Okay," said Gilchrist. "Just let me get the soap off my face."

Ruby was seated at a table set for two in a corner of the dining room. As a matter of habit, Gilchrist looked briefly for the Katzenjammers. The only other people were a group of American tourists. Their Philadelphia accents were unmistakable to Gilchrist as he passed their table.

"Well," said Gilchrist, seating himself across from Ruby. She was smoking the inevitable cigarette and wearing sunglasses with purple frames inset with punctuating rhinestones in the lenses themselves. "This is a surprise. I didn't expect to see you."

"I gave myself an extra couple of hours to get to the airport. I just wanted to talk to you."

"Anything wrong?"

"I didn't like the way our evening ended. It's been bothering me ever since." She gestured with the half-smoked cigarette in her hand, took a final puff, and then ground it in the seashell ashtray in front of her. She kept grinding it as she continued. "I didn't want things to take the turn they took, but how I am before I see you and how I feel after I see you are always two different things. I can't quite reform myself."

"You make too much of that."

"Well, I had to say it to you, face-to-face."

"When's your flight?"

"I have time." She crossed her arms over her breasts and sat back in the chair. A waiter came to their table, smiled, and eased a menu in front of each of them. Then he filled their glasses with water and left.

"Well," said Ruby. "How has it been for you here?"

"You mean the geography?"

"Everything."

"Enlightening. Let's leave it at that."

"Are you getting the story you came to get?"

"In pieces. I'll have to pull it all together when I get back to Washington. But right now I'm too close to it. And I still want to see people who are not *official*, if you know what I mean. That poses some problems. I just can't believe that this insurrection on the West Bank and in Gaza and the way it's being crushed hasn't provoked some dissent. Where are the dissenters?"

"There are some."

"Well, this revolt isn't going to evaporate. It's just the overflow of all the underlying tensions, and there's a whole philosophy of political resistance behind it. The Israeli government is treating it like a local brawl that will blow over if they can just find some way to contain it, round up the organizers, and have the patience to wait it out. Meanwhile, the daily death count goes up and up."

"I've had my own disagreements with Seth about that."

"About what?"

"About Gaza and the West Bank. And I'm not the only one who has disagreements, believe me. A lot of my friends in Washington are tied in knots about this, and that goes for a lot of Israelis, too. People like Chomsky, Avineri, Shahak, Elon, and Rinehart write about this all the time. Not everybody's happy watching Israeli soldiers shoot these rioters or beat them with clubs and all the rest of it. So don't think you're the only one who has moral scruples, Mr. Dodge D. Gilchrist."

"Is that what Gelb calls them—rioters?"

"What he calls them is beside the point."

"I hope you know the kind of a guy you're involved with, Ruby."

"Let me worry about that, Gil. But getting back to what we were say-ing—the fact is that Jews aren't supposed to treat other people like this. I tell Seth that, and he tells me that American Jews don't understand what Israelis are facing. He tells me that I don't realize what a fight for survival means. He doesn't want young Israeli soldiers doing what they have to do, but there's no choice. That's his position, and that's the government's position."

"Is it yours?"

"Hell no. I tell him that nobody ever won everything in the long run by keeping people down, keeping them under the gun."

"What does he say to that?"

"He just tells me I'm naive. It's getting to be a real sore point between us." She paused, and for a moment Gilchrist had the impression that she wanted to change the subject completely. "It's not something that goes away, Gil. Every day there's some new event on television or in the papers or just by word of mouth. There's no letup. It makes me sick. I'm not saying that I'm the greatest Jew on earth, but I am Jewish, and I'm not ashamed to say it. I'm proud of it. I think Jews have made one hell of a contribution to the human race on a lot of fronts. And that's why this Palestinian business makes me sick. Why in the hell can't they have a state, for God's sake? Let them have it. It's better than killing them day after day in public view, isn't it?" Her emotions were getting the better of her, and she tensed for a moment to keep them from overwhelming her. "Besides, look at what this is doing to us. We're always on the defensive. And we keep giving the same old answers, and they don't convince anybody. Nobody believes us any-more when we say that the real terrorists are hiding behind civilians and the rest of it. That's why a lot of people like me think that what we're doing to Palestinians right now is un-Jewish. We don't say it out loud because . . . Well, we just don't. We don't go public. But that doesn't mean we don't have our own opinions, our own reservations. And that's one reason I don't think it's fair of you to lump everybody who supports Israel into one big ball and say we're all for breaking arms and legs of every kid who throws a stone at some teenage soldier who's stuck with keeping some kind of order in the streets. There are people I could name for you who don't agree with that policy at all."

"It would help if they were more vocal about it. It doesn't do any good to disagree and then keep your disagreement private, does it? If they were just a bit outspoken, I'd be the first to give them all the ink they needed in my columns."

"It's not that easy, damn it." She realized that she was speaking too loudly when she saw the Philadelphia tourists turn their heads in her direction. Speaking with the same intensity but in a lower voice, she continued, "Do you think it's easy for any Jew to say in front of the whole world that he thinks Israeli policy is dead wrong as far as the Palestinians are concerned? Gil, you have no idea of the pressures that can be mounted against you if you say something like that. I've had people I know and respect tell me off when I speak about what's wrong over here. I've lost two friends because of it. A lot of them tell me I have a short memory, that you can't deal with people who are determined to wipe you off the map, who can kill children as readily as they can kill soldiers, who do whatever the PLO tells them to do, who warn that you're lost if you so much as give up an inch. And they keep it up until you feel like a traitor or else just too stupid for your own good."

"Does that kind of stuff intimidate you, Ruby?"

"You're damn right it intimidates me. I'm no patsy. You know me well enough to know that. I have as much moxie as you or anybody else, but I'm not good at playing me-against-the-world."

"Forget the world. What's shameful or wrong about saying just what you see?"

Ruby studied him with a look of exasperation combined with disbelief. She waited to see if his expression would change, but it remained exactly the same. For a moment she thought of picking up her purse and leaving without saying another word. She went so far as lifting her purse before she suddenly put it down so forcefully that the contents fell on the floor. Gilchrist reached down and retrieved a small package of Kleenex, a lipstick cartridge, a change purse bulging with coins, a Tampax still in its sleeve, and a pair of keys on a ring. He placed them on the table beside the empty purse. Ignoring the retrieved items and the purse itself, Ruby stared across the table at Gilchrist as if they were both engaged at a climactic moment in a game of chess.

"Gil," she began, "I know you're a smart man, and you have a lot more experience in public life than I have, but I want you to hear me out. There's a big gap in your understanding of this whole situation, and I'll try to fill it in if you let Ruby Levenson give you a different kind of history lesson." She toyed briefly with the lipstick cartridge. Then she seemed to be embarrassed as she surveyed the rest of her personal paraphernalia on the table and hurriedly stuffed it back into her purse. "Did I ever tell you that my people came to the States from Russia?" She waited. "Well, they did. My grandfather came to America from Russia. He was a tailor, and he made his living as a yard-goods cutter on Seventh Avenue in Manhattan. But every night he came home and told his son—my father—what it was like in the 'old country' before he left. And over the years my father told me. I heard so much about the Cossacks that I thought I would go nuts. Cossacks here. Cossacks there. Cossacks all over the damn place. I heard stories of Cossacks swooping down on Jewish villages and putting everybody to the sword and burning everything to the ground. In the beginning I just listened and didn't believe it. And then came Auschwitz. And after that I believed everything. Russian stories. German stories. Everything. I just couldn't see how people could do that to people. Well, you and I know that they sure as hell did. And they did it to millions. Why? Because they were Jews. That's all."

"Ruby, you're preaching to the choir on that subject. I'm not one of those who say that Auschwitz never happened. I've been there. I've seen the evidence. I've met some of the survivors."

"My father took me there when I was a freshman in college. And if you're a Jew, your education begins right there. You learn that a lot of grandfathers and grandmothers and fathers and mothers and sons and daughters were reduced to soot and smoke over there. And you don't forget that, believe me." She paused and looked directly at Gilchrist to see if her words were having any effect on him. Satisfied that they were, she resumed, "That's the gap in your understanding, Gil. You're not a Jew, so you can't be expected to have it. But if you're a Jew, you look at things differently once you understand what happened to a good many people of your kind just a generation ago. That leaves a mark on you for life. I became so ultra-Jewish after that that I even came to Israel before I graduated from college and lived in a kibbutz for more than ten months. I saw how the Palestinians were treated when I was a kibbutznik here, but I really didn't pay much attention to it. I figured, well, they lost the war, so what the hell. There were winners, and there were losers, and they just happened to be the losers. I didn't even want to understand their side of the story. And once when two or three Palestinians made an attack on our kibbutz and killed three people before the soldiers shot them dead, I wanted to understand them even less."

"What made you change your mind about that?"

"Israelis made me change my mind. My own people. They talked about Palestinians as if they were animals. And you know what you can do to people once you convince yourself that they're less than human." She waited, rethinking the consequences of what she had just said. Then she shook her head in a fast negative as if the conclusion was too disagreeable to consider. "It's the courage of these young Palestinians that gets to you, Gil. They take on army units from one of the best-trained and best-equipped armies in the world, and all they have in their hands are stones. And every day some of them die for it. It's really gotten to me. At first I just talked about it. As usual, some of my friends told me that I was just foolish. They reminded me that stones were lethal weapons, after all. For a while I believed that. I convinced myself that our reaction was just a matter of self-defense. Then I asked myself if I could come out into the street with a stone or two in my hand and face a trained soldier with an Uzi in his. I even asked Seth that, and he shrugged it off. But I couldn't get it out of my mind. There was a kind of lopsided courage in these confrontations. I knew that an Uzi has a lot more lethal power than all the stones in Israel. And I knew that the Palestinians knew that too. They knew it before they came out into the streets to challenge us. It meant that they were somehow braver. When I thought that way, all of my arguments about self-defense just melted away. And once those arguments were gone, I didn't have anything else to put in their place." She looked down at the table, shaken by her own admission. Then she continued in a tone of voice that sounded more like a plea than a contention, "What are we going to do, just go on killing these people indefinitely? These are people under occupation. We have them surrounded. We can go into their houses or deport them or interrogate them or kill them anytime we want. But does being able to do all of that give us the right to do that? And when we do, what does that say about us? What kind of people are we turning into anyway?"

"Ruby, you're coming to the point that's been where I've been for months now. All I do is write about what you just said now. That's really all I do. But because I'm public about it, all hell breaks loose. Letters to the editor, telephone calls, the whole nine yards. The other day I quoted one of the top generals in the Israel Defense Forces. He was talking about the Palestinians in Gaza and on the West Bank. He said—and I'm quoting directly now—that he would trap them like bugs in a bottle. He actually said that, mind you. All I did was quote what he told me. But the fact that I put it in print made me the one who was criticized, not the general. I was told that I was taking his comments out of context and all the rest of it . . ."

"Well, if it means anything to you, Gil, I'm not a devotee of the general's vocabulary either. All of the hard-liners here make me sick—Begin, Shamir, Sharon, all of them. They'll never change. Their backgrounds won't let them change. Begin and Shamir lost family to the Nazis, and they keep projecting those memories into the situation here. They're traumatized men, all of them. And so was dear old Golda. And somewhere along the line they bought into the idea that every Jew had to be Samson, the fighting Jew. Now we're stuck with the consequences. You see it from the outside, but I see it from the inside. And it's not easy to live with. It's not easy to be my kind of Jew these days. Of course, it's not easy to be a Jew anytime. But it's even harder now. These are tough times for Jewish people."

"I can understand that, but I don't see how that can be changed if Jewish people like you both here and in the United States don't start asserting themselves, do you?"

"What the hell good would it do? There are a lot of people who feel just the way I feel, but they're not the ones who run AIPAC and all the other hardball organizations. They call us liberals. And they call liberals fools. Not openly, but that's what they really think of us." She paused and frowned. "This whole business is just terrible. It's unrelenting. It's gotten to me . . ."

"It's more than terrible, Ruby. It's tragic. And it's tragic in the real classical sense because it's tragic for both sides. Everyone is going to lose, and wisdom will come too late if things go on like this. There are no visionaries on either side, no statesmen. The Israelis aren't able to expunge the Palestinians, and the Palestinians aren't able to expunge the Israelis. That's a perfect formula for mutual tragedy—deaths on both sides, losses on both sides, suffering on both sides, mourning on both sides . . ."

26

HAVING LEARNED to evade the Katzenjammers with the aid of Samir and his brother, Gilchrist was determined to meet other Israelis whom he would never have a chance to meet as long as his schedule was controlled by Gelb and his staff. He had compiled a list of names—a former general, a lawyer with the Peace Now movement, a scientist, and a poet, all of whom had taken public stances against the rejectionist positions of the party in power. With the help of Samir and Nadeem, he learned of their whereabouts and made clandestine appointments to meet with them.

General Misrahi was one of the heroes of the 1967 war. For many years his name was paired with that of Moshe Dayan in the esteem of most Israelis. Following the invasion of Lebanon, Misrahi vigorously opposed what he called the "blind adventurism" of the government and resigned from the army. Because they could not impugn his patriotism, the appropriate government officials and spokesmen habitually alluded to the views of General Misrahi as "ill-advised and capable of being used against Israel by its enemies."

"I'm regarded as an aging annoyance," General Misrahi told Gilchrist as they finished lunch on the general's patio. "I embarrass my friends in the current government, and I intend to go on embarrassing them because I think they are transforming us into the Mongols of the Middle East."

"What would you have them do differently?" Gilchrist asked.

"I would have them stop treating effects and get down to the causes, get down to the sources of the problem. We can't go on killing children like this. I say this to them openly, and they accuse me of undermining the government. And yet what am I doing? I'm just asking the right questions, the truly Jewish questions. Somebody has to ask them."

"Do you think your war record gives you some credibility with Israelis as a whole?"

"With some of them, certainly. They know in their hearts that we cannot go on like this. And everyone who thinks, *really* thinks, about the situation will come and must come to the same conclusion in time. As for the rest, well, we can't be led by the blind, can we? We're not dealing with mere civil disobedience when we talk about the problem of the Palestinians. This is a full-blown political resistance. And it's getting stronger and more deep-seated every day, and it will continue to get stronger. I draw a parallel between us and South Africa. When I say this in public, I'm accused of making an 'odious comparison.' That's the phrase they use. But regardless, the situations are not dissimilar. In South Africa the result was a redefinition of the entire country—its laws, its customs, everything. If it reverted, we would have had apartheid indefinitely, which would have meant civil war, massacres, or worse. Where could the Boers go? There had to be an accommodation. And the same is true for us. The ideal solution is at hand, as it has been for years now, but we're too blind to accept it. For a long time the Palestinians were talking about a single secular state where Jews and Palestinians could live together. That carried with it the end of Israel and Zionism, of course. But we haven't heard that song for years now. What we do hear and what we will continue to hear is a call for separate states. Adjacent, but separate. And I for one think that the Palestinians should have their state as soon as possible. This will leave our ethnic and political identity intact. And it will give the Palestinians an area where they can live out theirs."

"But how do you handle the predominant view here and in the United States that a Palestinian state will become a threat to Israel eventually?"

"How will it be a threat? First, it will need years of subventions to survive economically. Second, it has no conceivable way of being a military threat. The learned Mr. Podhoretz in your country doesn't agree with that, but Mr. Podhoretz is not a military man. I've spent my whole life in the military, Mr. Gilchrist. I know the capabilities of the Israeli armed forces on the ground and in the air. Let me remind you that we have the third-largest air force in the world. We have a highly trained standing army and an instant reserve. If we can handle all the Arab armies combined, are you trying to tell me that we will be threatened by a Palestinian state that needs every penny it receives just to survive?"

"I'm not telling you, General. I'm just posing arguments that I've heard, and I was naturally curious to hear your answers to them."

"I understand that, I understand that. I'm just being rhetorical. Please don't take it personally."

The general offered a plate of apples and grapes to Gilchrist. Gilchrist chose a sprig of blue grapes, while the general picked a plump green apple for himself. Using a table knife, he started to peel the apple, stem end first, until all the apple skin was pared away in a single ribbonlike swirl. Then he sliced the apple in equal quadrants, cored out the seeds and proceeded to eat the apple, quadrant by quadrant. Gilchrist studied him as he ate. He had a head like Michelangelo's Moses, broad at the cheekbones and almost squared from there down. His white hair was adequate, though not abundant, and it was obvious that he combed it with his fingers, if indeed he combed it at all. He had aviator's eyes so that at all times he resembled a man trained to evaluate horizons. He had distinctive crow's-feet that tightened when he smiled. He also had the permanent tan of someone accustomed to spending much of his time outdoors, and his white shirt and tan slacks gave him the appearance of a statesman or a once prominent movie star in semiretirement.

"This is a unique opportunity for us, Mr. Gilchrist," mused the general, toothpicking bits of apple from his teeth. "It's a unique historic opportunity. Let me give you a parallel. Imagine someone who is unexpectedly visited by luck or love. He wakes up and looks at the dice and sees that he has won. But he has to react. He has to deserve those quick dice. He has to fight to keep the gift of that happiness. Why? Because by the next cast of the dice, his happiness may have already passed him by. We Israelis are in exactly that position this minute."

"Then why don't more people share your view?"

"Who knows? Fear, stupidity, habit. Who knows? It's not being willing to see the obvious. But then, as one of Lebanon's great poets has written, 'the obvious is that which is never seen until someone expresses it simply.' But every time I say that the solution is at hand, I'm called an anti-Semitic Semite. Imagine that. And do you know who the first one was who said that about me? An evangelist. A Christian Zionist."

"Did you answer him?"

"Why bother? These people have paralyzed reason itself. They are living on only for the Apocalypse. They think of history as their little fairy tale. They see only what they believe. It's rubbish. Rubbish." The general shakes his head in exasperation. Then he smiles, slaps Gilchrist on the shoulder, and sits back in his chair. "I've read your columns, many of them. You have, if you don't mind my saying so, the zeal of a convert. I don't find fault with that as such, mind you, but you make the same mistake that Karl Marx made."

"Well, I've been paired with a lot of different people, but this is the first time for Gilchrist and Marx."

"The same mistake," continued the general, ignoring whatever humor Gilchrist thought he was injecting into his answer. "Marx assumed that the prevailing thoughts in a society were the thoughts of the ruling class. And you do the same."

"For what it's worth, I think that Marx was right about that."

"He was right only to the extent that he took no cognizance of counterthoughts, which can be just as powerful even though they may not be the thoughts that prevail at the moment. That's where I take issue with *you*. You aim all your criticism at the policies and personalities of the current government, and you don't give the policies of the dissenters enough attention. If you did, you might be surprised at the result."

"I prefer to deal with *real politique*, General. It's not the dissenters but the official policies and personalities of the current government that are changing history here."

"For the time being, yes. But these things can change. Let me give you an example in your own country. I visited San Francisco and was told that there was a large, politically active segment of the population composed of homosexuals. Now just suppose that a homosexual were to be elected as the mayor of San Francisco. In other words, the chief administrator of the ruling class would be a homosexual. Would this mean that the prevailing thoughts of the whole society would reflect that? I doubt it." The general finished chewing the last apple quadrant and smiled. "Enough of my theorizing, Mr. Gilchrist. I suppose you know that you are regarded by many here and in America as a complete, bona fide anti-Semite because you write what you write . . ."

"General, you should know that I'm as much an anti-Semite as you are, if that's what's lurking behind your statement."

"Nothing's lurking. Speaking personally, I know you're no anti-Semite. I've met the real ones, so I know what I'm talking about. I just want you to be aware of the fact that you could improve your stock among Jews if you were more accessible to some 'minority' views and less preoccupied with your opposition to the official ones, that's all."

"I'll take it under advisement."

"You should." The general stood and began pacing from one side of the patio to the other. He kept his head down. Gilchrist recognized the stance. Many times when he was composing a column that suddenly turned ornery, he would pace the length of his apartment in exactly the same way.

"The painful truth is that we lost our soul in Lebanon," said the general, still pacing. "It was a totally superfluous war, and we should never have gotten ourselves into it. We were led by fools who knew nothing about Lebanese politics and Lebanese history. All we succeeded in doing was losing hundreds of our own soldiers and killing thousands of people and making tens of thousands homeless. This means that we now have thousands of new enemies in Lebanon, especially in the South, that we don't need." He stopped and faced Gilchrist. "But the real tragedy of the war in Lebanon is that it compromised us as Jews. Historically speaking, the Jew is not a predator. He is at his best when he is defending what he believes is vital to his belief and his survival. In every war before the war in Lebanon, we fought with that kind of motivation, and we were unstoppable. Then, as if our experience in Lebanon were not enough of a setback for us, we faced this Intifada with no understanding of its causes and no interest in making an effort to understand. We thought if we were tough enough, it would die down. We told the Palestinians that they had better accept their political and economic servitude or we would blow up their houses, deport them, imprison them without trial, harass them, or give them four different ways to die or suffer—shoot them, crush them, bury them alive, or break their arms and legs. Imagine that as an excuse for a foreign policy. And we're still doing that, and the Intifada is stronger now that when it began. And in the meanwhile, look at what it has done to us. Our soldiers are confused and demoralized. Israelis are leaving Israel to live in Europe or America. Our country has lost its stature in the eyes of the world. And we are creating more and more enemies every day. Imprisoning these young Palestinians only confirms them in their hatred for us, and as prisoners they learn to rely on one another in ways that carry over when they are released. And most of them will have learned Hebrew in prison. Do you know what happened in Algeria when the French used techniques and methods like these? Make the comparison. How many lives did the Algerians lose? It was in the millions. The millions. But now we see that those deaths defeated France. Defeated France!"

"You don't sound optimistic."

"Not with this government. But let me be clear, Mr. Gilchrist. I'm a devoted Zionist. I still think you are wrong to imply that the policies of the present government and historical Zionism are interchangeable. I fought the enemies of Israel on the battlefield in three wars, and I would do it again tomorrow. I want Israel to be here forever, to be 'among the nations.' But I want Israel to survive as Israel. This occupation is going to ruin us. Ongoing suppression always undoes the suppressor. We're like people who are trying to hold wood underwater. When we are forced to let go—and we will be forced to do just that—the wood will come to the surface and even above the surface. I want to see us disengaged from that sort of thing. We have other and better things to do as a nation."

He paused, then continued as if he left his thought unfinished. "Some of my fellow generals would like nothing better than to attack Palestinians on the West Bank and Gaza indefinitely. Attack and pause. Attack and pause. Why? Is that a policy? And lately I've heard some other fools who want to build a wall from one end of Israel to the other as a way to keep attackers out, as if attackers invariably come on foot. Rubbish again. Don't they realize that walls have two sides? They wall out, but they also wall in. Forts are for walling out. Ghettos are for walling in. We'll have both for the price of one. Is that the way we want to live, the way we want to be perceived? We have other and better things to do as a nation."

27

"IT'S GOOD to be known by one name. Everybody knows me as Rachel. The Palestinians know me as Rachel. To the Israelis I'm Rachel. And, of course, to my mother I'm Rachel." She laughed and indicated to Gilchrist that he should seat himself beside a three-legged table where two cups of coffee were positioned opposite one another, the coffee steam rising from their brims.

"People talk about you the way they talk about the ACLU back in the States," Gilchrist said, seating himself.

"I accept the comparison," answered Rachel, laughing again. "Please, have some coffee. Nothing is worse than cold coffee."

While sipping his coffee, Gilchrist compared his impression of the woman he expected to see with the woman who was now sitting less than three feet from him. He had imagined a tall woman with an imperious manner. Instead, Rachel turned out to be a woman who was not quite five feet tall with her wiry gray hair in a chignon and all the imperiousness of a born altruist. Gilchrist knew from his own research that beneath these prosaic externals and mannerisms was the tenacity of a superb defense attorney.

"I understand that you spend 90 percent of your time defending Palestinians in the Israeli courts."

"Ninety-five percent," Rachel said with a smile. "Both courts. Military and civilian."

"Do you mind if I ask why?"

"Because I believe in Judaism. And because I believe in the law."

"A good many of your colleagues think you have other reasons, a hidden agenda."

"A good many of my colleagues are entitled to their opinion. Speaking for myself and myself alone, I can say I have one conscience to live with. That's my hidden agenda."

"Do you think you have to prove your Judaism by providing counsel in the defense of Palestinians?"

"Mr. Gilchrist, that's really a redundant question. You know as well as I that one of the strongest traditions in Judaism is our belief in justice. Sometimes we carry it too far, but it is as deep as our belief in monotheism. Usually, I regret to say, we understand it to mean only a concern for justice for Jews. But I am the daughter of a judge. One thing I learned from my father was that justice has no bloodlines. According to him, if you believe in justice, you have to go wherever it leads. And for me at this time in this country, it has led me to the Palestinians."

"Are you compensated for your services?"

"Occasionally. Sometimes I'm paid with currency. But I'm also occasionally paid with food. Last week it was with chickens."

"Does the currency come from the PLO?"

"I don't ask."

"Do you face intimidation or danger because of the work you are doing?"

"If I were a man, I think I would face a great deal of intimidation. And perhaps even some danger. But, being a woman, I don't encounter much. What little I have to deal with comes from other women, rarely from men." She sipped from her cup and indicated with a nod that Gilchrist should do the same, which he did. "I'd like to change the pattern of this interview for a moment, Mr. Gilchrist. You've been asking me all the questions. I want to reciprocate, not with questions but with a few observations. I've read many of your columns. In theory I agree with most of them. Not all, but most. And it might relieve you to know that I don't share the conventional antipathy that you have earned here among the faithful."

"Coming from you, that's gratifying."

"I'm not saying it to ameliorate you. It's simply a matter of fact, and, as a lawyer, I begin with facts. But one thing you may not be aware of is that there are some genuine anti-Semites in the United States and elsewhere who can very easily adopt your views for their own purposes. In fact, they've already done so. It may not be your intention to see this happen, and you may even condemn it and be appalled by it when it does happen, but it can happen. And the consequence is that many Jews will blame you for it."

"Will you be one of them?"

"Perhaps I will. I haven't made up my mind," she answered and smiled as much for herself as for him. "One thing I know is that you're playing with fire by taking the positions you take, and I say this as someone who shares many of your positions. But you do not share the same view of the consequences, and that's where we differ."

"Are you telling me that I'm responsible for consequences I never intended?"

"Exactly. But having gone as far as you've now gone, you no longer have a choice. And you don't impress me as the kind of man who will back off or crumble under pressure. But you have one blind spot. You have a tendency to romanticize the Palestinians. I know them well, and there are many who are as brave and focused as you are. But there are others who are not. And there are some who are simply criminals. I could tell you in detail some of the things they inflicted on the Shiites in the South of Lebanon, and they are not pretty. They include everything from petty theft to extortion. And under the main tent of the PLO there are some rather unsavory types, I can assure you. The prominent ones in the so-called leadership do their best to disassociate themselves from the less noble, let's put it that way, but the less noble are still there. And their ways of punishing traitors and collaborators are no less merciful than those of the Mafia or the old IRA. How many have been punished in the past ten months? More than two hundred, three-fourths of them killed outright. No trial, no plea bargaining, nothing."

"I'm aware of that. But they claim that these collaborators are really traitors of the worst kind. They put the whole cause in jeopardy."

"I can understand that. But it's still vendetta justice, isn't it? You might make that the subject of one of your columns, Mr. Gilchrist. You might find it quite revealing, if you did. And you will find out how they will come to regard you when you say something critical or damning about them." Rachel laughed again and drained the coffee from her cup in one sip.

28

"THEY CALL ME CRAZY. But then they call everybody crazy who doesn't agree with them. They've been calling Chomsky crazy for years, but still he goes on being Chomsky, and he has a tremendous following."

"I know your work and your reputation, Dr. Sharak, and I don't equate being brilliant and brave with being crazy, I assure you."

"Well, I appreciate your saying that. At least I know now that what I will tell you will be taken seriously."

"Quite seriously. You have my word."

"What is it you want me to be serious about?"

"The whole situation here. The prospects."

"The situation is desperate. And the prospects are bleak. Do you want me to be more serious than that?"

"That's serious enough. But could you be more specific?"

Dr. Sharak joined his hands behind his neck, leaned back in his swivel chair, and contemplated the ceiling. Behind him were shelves of books with scientific titles. To the left of the bookcase was a framed citation that Gilchrist recognized as the Nobel Prize awarded to Sharak years earlier for his work on the desalinization of water. It was partially hidden by a stack of scholarly journals tipped askew and ready to fall to the floor if they were so much as touched. Gilchrist noted finally that Sharak's desk was in chaos—papers and journals every which way and a tabloid in Hebrew on which two different pairs of reading glasses rested.

When Sharak tipped level in his swivel chair, he kept his hands joined behind his neck and looked forward and then past Gilchrist as if he were still forming a thought that kept him focusing on anything else but it. Gilchrist concentrated on Sharak's reddish forehead topped with uncombed tufts of red hair going gray. The left side of Sharak's face was a mass of scar tissue from having been burned and badly reconstructed, and his left eye

looked almost loose in its socket. A portion of his upper lip was missing so
that a single front tooth was constantly visible.

"I'm a scientist, Mr. Gilchrist, and scientists by nature and training
live in a tangible world, a world of measurables, of facts. The facts for
me are that I come from a strain of European Jewry to whom Judaism
was a responsibility as well as a faith. We fostered the whole tradition of
nonacademic scholarship. Some of the most important commentaries on
the Talmud, for example, were written by tailors and even plumbers from
among my people. We did not leave our beliefs to the rabbinate alone. We
lived our beliefs. And what we believed is what I still believe—that Jews
are destined to be a light among the Gentiles. That is my background.
And the result is that my entire allegiance is to Jewish humanism in the
classical sense, to the mission of Jews in this world, to Jews as the yeast in
humanity itself. Even though Hitler took my entire family, even though I
have only half a face from what was done to me at Treblinka, I still believe
in that. If I did not believe in that, I would have no Jewish identity at all."
He paused, released his hands from behind his neck, and let them fall on
his lap. "But those Jews who have directed the course of Israel for the past
decades have really been Jews by blood, that's all. They are simply secular
Jews. They became Jews by birth, and that was that. Today theirs is the
religion of the human will backed up by some of the best and most lethal
technology on earth, courtesy of the United States. It's a messianism of
force. The faith of these people is in airpower, soldiery, missiles. It's as
simple and fundamental as that. But peace is not created by force. It must
be nurtured. There must be trust. And peacemakers must be clear about
the risks. I don't minimize that. But life itself, as you know, is a risk no
matter how much military power you have on your side." He crossed his
arms across his chest and shrugged. "I am not an example of the Jew as
warrior. I do not believe that the mission of Jews in this world is to domi-
nate—not just Palestinians but anybody."

"I suppose you know that you're regarded as a hero by the Palestinians."

"So be it. I've spoken to many Palestinian groups in the United States
and Europe, that's true. But I have been quite direct with them. I tell them
that I totally support their goals as far as human rights are concerned. But I
don't condone attacks on the innocent here or anywhere in the world. If it

is wrong for Israelis to do this when they bomb refugee camps or bulldoze homes, it is also wrong for Palestinians to do this by infiltrating and killing people on our side of the border. I tell them they have a right to a state here. But I add in the same breath that I have as much right to be here as they do. If they should try to evict me someday in the future, I would fight them to the death. I tell them that face-to-face."

"What do they say to that?"

"What they say is not important to me. It's what I say to and for myself that is important. My problem now is that so much blood has been shed during this Intifada that I doubt if peace or even an armistice is possible anymore. But if there is any hope, it is for a two-state solution. We cannot go on living like this. We cannot let this kind of bloodletting become a habit. It makes more and more people prisoners of blind fear and blind hatred. I mean people on both sides. And what this translates into in the day-to-day world now or later is not a matter of Israel *and* Palestine but Israel *or* Palestine. That is what we are seeing in microcosm at this very minute. Every death on either side is just the first chapter in this pointless march to mutual destruction. It's very discouraging."

"Do you think a change in government would help?"

"Of course, it would help if it were a change in the right direction. But there is no leader in any of the parties who has the vision and courage to create a solution. We need a man of imagination, of stature, of vision. Like De Gaulle. We need a statesman. Instead we have leaders traumatized by their past. They are the creations of their private history, no more. It has left them frozen and paranoid. They see neo-Nazis everywhere. And if they don't see them, they create them. They think all Gentiles except these Christian fundamentalist fools are their natural enemies. They cannot tolerate dissent, particularly if the aim of the dissenters is to make them reexamine their own assumptions." He tapped his forehead with the forefinger of his right hand. "I am a dissenter. They tolerate me as a kind of fool. They laugh at me and trivialize me. They have the same attitude toward me that your government had toward Dr. Spock during your Vietnam tragedy. They said he was competent in his own professional field but totally out of his depth in war and politics. Spock said the Vietnam War was wrong. And he was in my opinion right. Give me one persuasive reason fifty-eight thousand Americans had to die in Vietnam. Just one." He waited and again leaned back in his swivel chair. "I am the Israeli Dr. Spock."

29

GILCHRIST HAD MADE IT a point to read as much Israeli poetry as he could find in translation before he came to Israel. After he came face-to-face with one of the country's leading poets, he was glad he had.

"One of my college professors told me years ago, Mr. Nagid, that the best way to understand a culture or a people is to read the work of the best poets. He added, by the way, that the least-reliable way was to rely on politicians. Not just politicians but officials of any kind, since they are maintainers of the status quo. But the poets were inclined to see beneath appearances in the present and as a result could suggest rather accurately where the present was heading."

"Have you talked to many poets here, Mr. Gilchrist?"

"None, except you. It's not exactly easy for me to make arrangements to see them."

"Well, you'll find that I'm fairly typical. None of us is in the class of my Andalusian namesake, but we try our best in our circumstances. We're not cheerleaders for the hard-liners here. This is why you should meet Pagis and Kovner and Amichai while you are here. They are among our best, and, in all candor, I include myself in that number. The problem is that most of us are compelled to be lamenters. You know Jewish history, I'm sure. There's always been a broad tradition of lamentation in our history. That's because life is always disappointing us. We've been disappointed from the time of David and Jeremiah to the present moment. Our lamentations go back that far. Sometimes there's a little self-pity in it. Not always but occasionally. But beneath and beyond that our best poetry sounds like prayer. You hear it in the Old Testament. You hear it in the great Hebrew poets of Spain. You hear it in Bialik. I call it the twisted cry of the human spirit in conflict with absurdity, which is the law of this world. It's a cry of torment, really. We excel at that."

Nagid's face reminded Gilchrist of the paintings of El Greco where all the men's faces seemed elongated, almost equine. Nagid's face made him look sorrowful by nature even when he was trying to be lighthearted. But he talked primarily with his eyes, which always seemed totally alive, as if they never rested, even during sleep.

"Are these tormented cries ever heard?" Gilchrist asked. "Are people listening to what you write, if I can put it that way?"

"When were such cries heard? We're like the prophets. We say what we see, and for that we are often excoriated or ignored. Saying what you see is a dangerous profession, Mr. Gilchrist. You're a controversial journalist. You must have some knowledge of that."

"But your books sell quite well here. I've checked on that. So you know you're being read."

"Yes, you are correct. My books do have a good circulation here, but I don't know how carefully they are being read. My book about the war in Egypt went into six printings. I don't know how many readers of that book saw it as a book against war as such. There was such euphoria in Israel after the war that our sense of the tragic completely evaporated. It was the worst thing that could have happened to us. It paralyzed our psyche." He paused. "I was a soldier in that war, and a war like that doesn't fade. The heat. The desert. And the scope. Did you know that more tanks were used in the Sinai on both sides than had ever been used in a single battle in the history of modern war?"

"No, I can't say I knew that."

"It's an impressive statistic when you compare it to the great tank battles in Europe and Russia and North Africa in World War II. But what remains with you as a permanent nightmare is not a statistic as abstract as that but what the heat in the desert did to the dead. I saw that with my own eyes. The bodies would turn into balloons, swelling and swelling until they burst through their uniforms. The bodies would keep swelling, then tear apart and explode. You can imagine." He paused, remembering. "When I returned from the war, I asked myself if the Israel I believed in was turning into another Sparta. And I regret to say that history has confirmed my fear. That's really what we're becoming—what we've already become—a modern Sparta. The first Sparta won every war it fought, but it lost every peace. It created generations of warriors who simply did not know how to live in peace and learn that the arts and skills of peace were harder to practice than all the so-called arts of war put together. That is what haunts me today. I ask myself if the business of my country is now nothing nobler than to create funerals on our side and theirs. Every day that's what we're doing, and we justify it in the name of law and order, of defense, of survival. If someone in this country or in Europe or in the United States comes up with a peace formula, what do we do? We reject it. We can't break the habit of war. Our psyche is still paralyzed. We think we can give everything a military solution, even in the territories that we've occupied now for more than twenty years."

"Are you referring to the Intifada?"

"Precisely. Our government tells the world that ours is a 'benign occupation.' And then it says that the Palestinians have rejected every peace offering made to them. But what have we offered? We say they can live in areas we specify and define. We say that we will control exit and entry. We say that we will control the water. We say we that we control the sky. What kind of an offer for peace is that? The Palestinians want sovereignty! Sovereignty! We tell them that they should behave themselves in a prison of our making, keep it clean, and not make trouble. And they resist us. Why should we be surprised? They mirror perfectly what we did against the British forty years ago. We won. And in time who is to say that they are not going to win?"

"Are you saying that victory for them is inevitable?"

"Victory or death. In the meanwhile, they will already have defeated us ideologically."

"Ideologically?"

"Yes, by letting us become oppressors in the eyes of the world and, what is worse, in our own eyes as well. That is why I said the options for them at present are either victory or death. What other alternatives have we given them?"

"But isn't that a perfect formula for tragedy?"

"Tragedy in the classical sense, Mr. Gilchrist. You're absolutely correct. We're setting the stage for that. If we continue on this course, we'll perpetuate this tragic embrace. And in time we could end up dying together, with each side believing to the end that it's right. It will be a victory of the grave."

30

BECAUSE GELB AND RUBY were out of the country, Gilchrist found himself being driven to the Ben Gurion Airport by Gelb's adjutant, a young colonel named Assaf Avrom. With his ink-black hair and swarthy complexion, the colonel could easily have passed for an Arab, according to Gilchrist's initial impression of him. In his olive uniform unbuttoned at the collar, his brightly buffed officer's boots, and his leisurely worn beret, he impressed Gilchrist as the perfect model for the military part he was playing among the subalterns on Gelb's staff. He was clean shaven and erect as a drum major and had a way of smiling that transformed his features from stern to pleasant in an instant.

"We have a good many hours before your flight, Mr. Gilchrist," said Avrom. "I thought you might enjoy a drive around Jerusalem before we go to the airport. Perhaps your schedule hasn't given you any time for sightseeing." He smiled, and his smile immediately disarmed Gilchrist of any of his reservations. He had wanted some time to himself to make last-minute notes at the airport, but he decided he could do that on the plane.

"Don't we have to allow extra time for security?"

"Not in your case," said Avrom. "I've taken care of that."

"Well, then, no problem. It will be a good and relaxed way to end my tour here."

All during the drive, Gilchrist and Avrom said little. When they passed acres of high-rise apartments that seemed to contradict the Middle Eastern nature of the environment, Avrom frowned and shook his head. Driving on, Avrom from time to time indicated a landmark or building of more than casual importance—an old Jewish cemetery, the residence of the Roman Catholic Apostolic Delegate, the gate through which Moshe Dayan entered the Old City in 1967.

"Have you and the defense minister been together for a long time?" Gilchrist asked.

"I was reassigned," said Avrom. "I've been on this assignment for eleven months only."

"Are you satisfied with your job?"

"Shall I be frank with you?"

"As you wish. It will be off the record."

"Eleven months ago I was a military administrator on the West Bank. I know Arabic well. In fact, it's my first language. My people came to Israel from Iraq. In my area on the West Bank I had no serious problems because the Palestinians trusted me, and I understood their situation. At least they trusted me until the Intifada. After that, as you know, things changed."

"Were you involved in putting the uprising down?"

"Fortunately not. I can't say this publicly, of course. But as a soldier I would have had a difficult time carrying out some of the minister's orders, particularly the one about breaking the arms of the demonstrators."

"Are you Sephardic?"

"What makes you ask?"

"Your looks mostly."

"I am. It's a very complicated history of a trek long ago from Spain to Iraq, but I'll spare you that. But I don't trace my discomfort to a difference in mentality between the Sephardic and the Ashkenazi, if that's what you're asking me. I simply think that there are better ways of dealing with the situation than the one in use now."

"Such as?"

"Such as working with and not against the infrastructure. Such as cutting back on these encroaching settlements. Such as trying to get away from seeing the Palestinians in Gaza and on the West Bank as so much cheap labor or what some call 'surplus population.'"

"You apparently don't think that any of those ideas has a chance to prevail in light of what's being done now."

"No," said Avrom as he steered around a sharp turn in the road. "No, I don't."

The bullet struck the driver's side of the windshield. The windshield did not crack, but there was a nick where the bullet hit. Avrom braked immediately.

"Out!" shouted Avrom. "Out, Mr. Gilchrist, and stay down!"

Gilchrist opened the passenger door and almost slid down to the road surface as Avrom ran from his side of the car and crouched beside him. A moment later Gilchrist saw three Israeli soldiers approaching the car, shouting in Hebrew. As soon as they saw Avrom, they stopped shouting and ran toward him. Even before they reached him, they began explaining something and pointing in the direction of a house on the opposite side of the road.

Gilchrist remained where he had slid, listening. At last Avrom walked the soldiers several yards away, and then he returned to the car.

"We have a small incident here, Mr. Gilchrist, but I think I can handle it. Please, you can stand up now." He gestured in the direction of the soldiers. "These soldiers are very young, and they fired a few rounds that weren't really necessary. Fortunately, no one's been injured, and the only damage so far is that nick in the windshield. It's a ricochet from one of the rounds they fired."

Gilchrist stood and dusted off the seat of his trousers.

"This will take me about ten minutes," Avrom continued. "We still have plenty of time to get to the airport. Would you mind waiting for me here?"

"What's the problem?"

"Well," said Avrom, waving the soldiers even farther off, "these three soldiers were on patrol, and someone began to throw stones at them. They are under orders to respond decisively, you understand, so they ran where they thought the stones were coming from and caught a glimpse of a boy disappearing in that house over there. When they went to the house and ordered the boy to come out, the boy's family rushed out of the house and surrounded them, and there was a lot of shouting. One of the soldiers was confronted by the boy's brother. Somehow he had become separated from the other two soldiers, and he lost his discipline and began firing bullets into the air. It seems then that the older brother lunged at the soldier, who thought he was in danger and fired but fortunately missed. My guess is that it was that bullet that hit our car after it glanced off something else. By then, the boy's family, including the older brother, thought that the soldiers were going to shoot them all, so they went back into the house, all of them, and closed the shutters. That's when the soldiers saw us, and here we are."

"What are you going to do?"

"I'm going to have to go to the family and ask to see the boy. I might also have to deal with the older brother before this is all over. He did exactly what an older brother should have done. He came to the defense of his brother. My soldiers don't understand that. Anyway, I think the whole situation can be handled by a firm scolding. I don't think that the family wants trouble. This has never been a trouble spot for us." He reached into the car and removed a holstered pistol on a belt and girded himself with it. "The symbol of authority," he said, smiling. "Here a man is always taken more seriously when he's armed. Please, excuse me, Mr. Gilchrist. I won't be long."

Gilchrist watched Avrom walk over to the soldiers, talk briefly with them, and then march up toward the house. The soldiers separated so that there were several yards between them and, with their Uzis aimed at the sky, waited and watched Avrom reach the front door of the house. He stood there for a moment as if expecting someone to emerge and meet with him. Then he said something in Arabic. Several minutes passed. The front door was opened, and an older man in a *khafiya* stepped out and closed the door behind him. Apparently the head of the house, the man pointed to the soldiers and started to explain to Avrom in Arabic what Gilchrist assumed was his version of what had happened. Avrom, standing akimbo, listened and kept nodding in the affirmative as if to convey to the man that he understood. The conversation continued for five more minutes. Then the man reentered the house and reappeared with the boy of no more than twelve or thirteen. The boy was followed by his mother, who was weeping and who began beseeching Avrom on the boy's behalf.

Avrom ignored the mother and spoke in Arabic directly to the boy, who looked back at him with both fear and defiance. Playing the disciplinarian, Avrom put his hand on the boy's shoulder and continued to hector him sternly but not angrily. Occasionally, he would pause, and the boy would nod a reluctant yes. Then Avrom would turn away and resume his conversation with the father.

Watching from the road, Gilchrist could sense that the situation was easing. He heard Avrom say, "Yalla, yalla!" to the boy and his mother, and they obediently reentered the house. Then he moved his gaze to the soldiers, who had slung their Uzis, barrel down, over their shoulders as if they anticipated no further need for them. The third soldier started to do the same and then, for some reason, decided against it.

When Gilchrist looked at the house again, he saw that Avrom and the boy's father were concluding whatever it was they had agreed to do. The father kept nodding to Avrom's final words in Arabic.

At that moment a man whom Gilchrist instinctively identified as the boy's older brother opened the door of the house and stepped out. He had a black mustache. He said several words to his father in Arabic, and the father walked toward him, gesturing. Ignoring his father, the brother took a step toward Avrom and said in English, "You! You leave alone my brother! You leave alone my family! You leave alone my people!"

Avrom stood his ground. Then he and the brother exchanged words in Arabic. Suddenly, the man charged Avrom. Gilchrist glimpsed the flash of a blade in the man's hand, and he saw Avrom dodge quickly to his right and reach for his pistol. By then there was contact, and the two men fell to the ground and began wrestling while the father stood to one side, screaming in Arabic and waving his arms helplessly. The three soldiers started to run toward the house, their Uzis at the ready.

Gilchrist was frozen where he stood, watching. At one point Avrom seemed to have the upper hand, but in a second the positions were reversed. Suddenly, he saw that Avrom had managed to remove his pistol from its holster just as the other man was able to disengage the hand in which he was gripping the knife. Again Gilchrist saw the flash of the blade. He followed the flash as the man drove the blade into Avrom's chest. At the same instant Gilchrist heard two pistol shots. Then there was complete silence.

The father was wailing and waving his arms. The three soldiers stopped as if they had just been given an order to do so. Gilchrist found himself walking and then running to the spot where Avrom and the older brother were sprawled.

From a distance of twenty yards the bodies of the two men looked less like bodies and more like abandoned blankets or laundry bunched shapelessly on the ground. Avrom was on his back, the knife driven into his chest up to the handle. The older brother was partly on top of him like a wrestler primed for a pin, and the blood from Avrom's wound and from the two bullet wounds from the brother were already mingling in a widening blot beneath Avrom's left arm.

One of the soldiers charged the father and pushed him down, while the other two hurried to see if there was anything they could do for Avrom. They pulled the body of the brother away. One of them knelt beside Avrom, while the other trained his Uzi on the house.

Gilchrist reached the spot a second or two later. Both of the bodies were on their backs now, and he could see that the brother had been shot twice in the face. The entire left cheek was nothing but a smear of blood and shredded flesh. The eyes were still open, and the mouth was agape.

It suddenly struck Gilchrist that he had never seen men killed right before his eyes. Five minutes earlier he had seen Avrom and the Palestinian as two living men on the earth, and now they were two corpses at his feet. The finality of the moment paralyzed him. Looking from one to the other, he could not help but notice how much they resembled each other. Avrom with his dark complexion and black hair could easily have passed for the other man's uncle or cousin. The only apparent difference was that the brother had a mustache.

The third soldier joined his companions, and the three of them looked at Gilchrist as if expecting him to tell them what to do. The father of the family was still sitting where he had been pushed. He seemed dazed. Gilchrist could hear screams and commotion in the house, and a moment later the mother and several children rushed out. The soldiers were already dragging Avrom's body toward his car. The mother of the brother who had been shot dropped to her knees beside him and began to keen and pull her hair.

Gilchrist stood there like a witness. The entire scene kept replaying itself in his mind, each time with greater vividness. He found himself remembering General Misrahi's comment about Israelis and Palestinians locked in a tragic embrace as well as Nagid's vision of the future as "a victory of the grave." He started toward the road and stopped. He took one long last look at the house, the father and mother and the children and then the dusty ground where the blood of the two dead men was already blending into a single stain.

VII

Time and the City

31

GILCHRIST REMEMBERS that Tabry once told him that Washington was a battleground. For years Gilchrist had just considered the capital as something like a field of play, a place where power was concentrated and where power made certain things happen, a chessboard with chessboard margins or rules. The chess players were transient, but the game was permanent.

Now, back for three weeks from his trip to Israel and the West Bank, he seems to feel that he is alienated from his Washington environment, that the city now has a certain falsity about it, an impermanence that is totally removed from what he has just experienced in a country whose image in the United States does not in most ways correspond with how it revealed itself to him when and while he was there.

Assured by Dr. Voss that Raya was progressing well, Gilchrist concentrated on writing a series of columns about his trip, and column after column bespoke a discrepancy between Israel as most Americans had become inured to perceiving it and the country that emerged from Gilchrist's prose—one where class distinctions often followed bloodlines, where political rights in the full sense were reserved for citizens who were Jewish, where arrests were arbitrary and where habeas corpus and trial by jury were not guaranteed for the indigenous population, where prisoners were absolutely at the mercy of their captors, where government was the very instrument that encouraged and often fomented divisiveness in the population, where private property could be confiscated or appropriated by the government for military use or development by settlers, where border settlements could be expanded across borders as "part of the natural evolution of thickening the country's security belt." On this pretext Gilchrist wrote in one of his columns that the "United States could create a belt of settlements on Canadian or Mexican soil on the pretext that such settlements were essential to the defense of Texas, Washington, Montana, North Dakota, Minnesota, Wisconsin, Michigan, Ohio, Pennsylvania, New York, Vermont, New Hampshire, Maine, and California."

As Gilchrist knew they would, his columns provoked a deluge of mail, e-mail, and recorded messages, some supportive but the majority virulently opposed. After reading one overflow of letters and e-mails, Gilchrist could not help but notice how almost all of those that were written in opposition contained many of the same phrases, as if a model letter had been used by the respondents so that their letters varied only incidentally but were otherwise clones of the original.

"Look, Dodge," said his editor after the second week of columns had ended and after he had surveyed the increasing poundage of opposition mail, some of which had originated from the offices of senators and other congressmen. "You know what I think of freedom of expression and all that goes with it. I admire your guts for what you are doing, and I'll stand behind you all the way . . ."

"I'm getting ready for the next word, which I suspect will be *but.*"

"Let me go back to what I told you before. You've become Johnny One-Note. You've got to diversify, pick other issues. William Safire does. Raspberry and Carl Rowan do. Even Von Hoffman does. Why can't you?"

"Because this one sticks like a tennis ball in my throat. I can't swallow it, and I can't cough it up. All I can do is write about it. Besides, it's the one issue that intrudes on the whole concept of citizenship for me. And for you too. For everybody. Can't you see that? I can criticize the president. I can criticize France, which is our oldest historical ally. I can criticize Jesus Christ, and no one accuses me of being a bigot. But as soon as I criticize Israeli policies, all at once the US Post Office and the Internet have more mail and e-mail than they know what to do with."

"Well," said the editor, "I frankly don't like it. I can't do anything about it, and I wouldn't do anything that smacks of censorship even if I could. You know my record when it comes to that. Besides, you're like a senior professor around here. You have tenure. You're untouchable. But I don't like the atmosphere it creates. It's a hassle that I don't need. I just think that other rights can be championed besides those of a lot of Arabs in that godforsaken part of the world. You've made their cause your own, for God's sake."

"Which means?"

"It means what it means. But that doesn't mean you can't write about rights being denied to some other people closer to home."

"Maybe I will. But what the hell does distance have to do with it? Distance couldn't matter less when it comes to human rights. I always thought, and I still think, that you are really defending your own rights when you defend someone else's. As a matter of fact, I think that's a quote from you."

The editor spun in his chair, stood, and paced the room several times. Then he faced Gilchrist and said, "Okay, okay, I'll back off. I don't like to hear my own logic used against me." He returned to his chair. "Let's talk for a minute about yesterday's column. Yesterday you brought up that business about Sharif Tabry, his death in the house fire, and the rest of the story. You didn't make any accusations, but the innuendo was as thick as piecrust. And then you slugged in that image of the phoenix rising from the ashes of the fire. What does that make you? The phoenix?"

"Maybe. But I'm just someone who's carrying on. The real phoenix is the position that Tabry devoted his whole life to. You can't burn that to ashes. In Tabry's village he's more alive today than when he was actually alive here in DC. I was there. I saw it. I felt it. That says something, doesn't it?"

"That's standard stuff for a man like that. Martyrs and movie stars don't stay buried, but you can't make too much of that. And pretty soon you'll be comparing Tabry to Prometheus—'the great forethinker who brought the fire of truth to man.'"

"What if I decided to do that?"

"It would be a bit on the melodramatic side, don't you think?"

"I always thought that the old myths are still alive and kicking if you can just find the connection."

The editor leaned forward and put his elbows on his desk. "Okay, Dodge, I quit. I'm just being a Dutch uncle because I happen to believe that that's my job. You and I go back a long way. If you want to rake up a song out of ashes, be my guest, but I still think you're narrowing yourself. And all that crap about mythology is going to go over the heads of your readership. Take it from an old sportswriter."

The effect of Gilchrist's columns on his colleagues created a variety of responses, all of which Gilchrist had heard before. One reporter, a man whom Gilchrist had known for more than twelve years and who busied himself by writing a folksy, noncontroversial column on "authentic Washington characters," told him one day, "Gil, I wouldn't touch that subject on a dare. I like my sleep. I also like to know that my car won't explode when I turn on the ignition in the morning."

"Thanks, Gus," said Gilchrist. "I knew I could count on you."

"I know how your enemies work, Gil. They come on strong and try to blow you out of the water. If you survive the first barrage, they either start whining or else get nasty. By then they know that they can't blow you away. And they're too mad to be satisfied with whining. That leaves one alternative."

Gilchrist smiled but said nothing more. Later, one editorial writer from Baltimore told him, "Gil, I agree with everything you say, but why do you have to be so public about it?"

"Well, if you agree with me, how can you not go public about it? It's a public issue. It's really at the heart of what it means to be an American citizen for me."

"I agree."

"Well, why not say so?"

"The view around here is that it would be counterproductive."

"Well, the view I have tells me that you keep quiet just to save your ass. Or should I say that you've sold your ass? Think of that each time you see the flag hoisted up over this building."

But there were other reactions to his column that were more punitive. He found that he was being asked less and less to appear on television news programs with other journalists, that an increasing number of newspapers throughout the country were "regrettably" no longer able to carry his column, that a university in eastern Pennsylvania that was planning to offer him an honorary degree had to withdraw the offer because of alumni opposition. Gilchrist was tempted to make an issue of the rescinding of the offer but decided in favor of writing a mellifluent letter to the president of the university in which he reserved his choicest prose to tell him with some candor where he could insert his degree.

Now he parks his Mercedes in its slot outside his apartment. He experiences again that sense of being in two hemispheres at once, as if some part of his identity is still across the ocean in Tabry's village. A scrim seems to fall between him and the ambience in Washington. He is waiting for these realities to disentangle themselves in his mind when he sees Dr. Voss in the apartment lobby. Gilchrist steps out of his car and waits for the doctor to pass him.

"Mr. Gilchrist, how are you? Have you adjusted to the time change yet?"

"Adjustment completed," he answers. "How's Raya?"

Realizing immediately that Gilchrist is not interested in amenities, the doctor adapts himself to Gilchrist's mood and says, "Good. Quite good. There were a few setbacks in the beginning, but now I have reason to believe that the worst is definitely far behind us. Actually, these were no physical setbacks, just setbacks in confidence."

"Where is she? Still a secret?"

"I can't break my word to her about that, Mr. Gilchrist. You know that."

"How long can this last? It's been almost five weeks."

"It lasts until Miss Tabry tells me I can tell you."

"Are you in touch with her?"

"Daily. I see her every week at least once, but I'm in touch with her by phone every evening. She's in good hands. You needn't concern yourself about that."

"Is there anything I should do? Anything that would do any good? You probably know that she is—on paper, at least—my wife. She just might . . ."

"I know about that. And I assure you that I know how hard this must be for you. But I think it's best at the moment to leave things just as they are. She hasn't had any lapses for more than three weeks now. But I want to be absolutely sure that there won't be any recurrences."

"What kind of recurrences?"

"Twice she slipped when she tried to go up and down stairs too rapidly. It was all due to impatience. It happens in cases like this. Patients try to do more than they should be doing and then get frustrated because they can't do what they want to do. Three weeks ago, for example, she was typing. I thought it would be wise for her to use some of her former skills, and I gave her a few letters to type. Suddenly, for no reason she could explain, she forgot how to type. Her fingers were lost on the keys. It lasted only for an hour or so. Then her ability came back to her. It was just a memory lapse, that's all. That has not repeated itself, so I'm encouraged."

"Do you expect that to repeat itself?"

"Frankly, no. Her recovery has been nothing short of miraculous. I'm trying to go by the book with her, Mr. Gilchrist. And I'm trying to do my best as far as you're concerned. It's just that . . ."

"As far as I'm concerned?"

"Yes."

"Can you explain that to me a bit more?"

"Well, I've come to realize that Miss Tabry is an unusual young woman. She has great courage. And she has unbounded love for you, no doubt about that. And she is intelligent. Intelligent in the human ways, the human graces. She thinks with her feelings. And that's rare, Mr. Gilchrist. What she wants more than anything else in this world is to be a total person, not just for her own sake but for yours. She wants to do for you what she knows you have done for her. It's nothing like repaying a debt or anything like that. She wants to be more than someone who receives. Those are her words, not mine. And I think she has an excellent chance to do that. And, believe me, when I tell you that she wants to do this out of love, not obligation. In fact, I think it's her right to do that, and I'm doing everything I can to see that she can do what she wants as soon as possible. I know what it means to her."

"How does she look? She was concerned about that."

"Well, I don't know how she looked before the accident, but I think she looks fine. The forehead wound is completely under her hair line now. As a matter of fact, I think she looks wonderful. Beautiful, if I may say so. It's only that I want to be sure for her sake that she does not resume what she would regard as a full life and then find that it's beyond her. That would have a terrible effect. It would undo everything we've achieved so far."

"In other words, there's nothing to do now but wait."

"I'm afraid so, Mr. Gilchrist. It might not be very long now. She'll know when she is ready before either of us knows, I'm sure. And when she does, I promise you that you'll know."

"Is it too much to ask you to tell me where she is?"

After a pause the doctor says, "I'll be seeing Miss Tabry next Monday. Let me ask her if I can tell you that."

"Fair enough."

"Thank you, Mr. Gilchrist. Thank you for understanding."

Gilchrist watches the doctor walk away, and for a moment next Monday seems like a day in the next century.

32

ON THE FOLLOWING Monday morning, Gilchrist is waiting in his Mercedes in front of his apartment. When he finally sees Dr. Voss drive out of the underground garage of the apartment in a white Chrysler two-door, he follows him through the crowded Georgetown streets, down Pennsylvania Avenue, then through several shunts to Rhode Island Avenue, and finally to the highway leading to Baltimore and Annapolis. When Dr. Voss reaches the Annapolis turnoff, he veers to the right. Gilchrist follows him at a discreet distance while always keeping the Chrysler in view. Within an hour Dr. Voss drives to the northern outskirts of Annapolis and stops at a redbrick two-story house that borders the Severn. Gilchrist watches him enter the house without knocking and close the door behind him.

Gilchrist parks his Mercedes a half-block from the house, then gets out and walks on the opposite sidewalk toward the house. The uneven brick sidewalks seem familiar to his feet. The fronts of the colonial houses (he can glimpse their modernized interiors as he passes) look as neat and welcoming as they seemed when he was last there. And they seem, like the restored houses in Georgetown, made to the measure of a man. Even though he is more than a block from the river, he can smell the freshness of the air off the water as it passes inland. When he turns, he sees Dr. Voss reenter his Chrysler, pull out, and head north for the road that will take him back to Washington.

Gilchrist notices that there are two women standing outside the door of the house that Dr. Voss entered. Raya is one of them. After the two have seen the Chrysler pull away, they speak for several minutes. Then the older woman smiles and steps back into the house, leaving Raya on the porch. Gilchrist edges behind a tree to avoid being seen. When he looks out again, he sees Raya walking southward to the center of Annapolis. Staying on the opposite side of the street, Gilchrist follows her. He notices that she does not seem to be walking with a particular destination in mind. Occasionally, she stops as if remembering something she forgot, then proceeds. At one point she picks a single leaf from an overhanging branch of a wisteria and smells it. Then, twirling the leaf by the stem as she goes, she resumes her walk.

She crosses the downtown area and heads for the docks where the dinghies, skiffs, fishing boats, and motor launches are tethered like so many waiting and tamed domestic pets. At the end of the dock she sits on a black capstan and looks down the river toward the sea. Gilchrist maneuvers quietly to a jetty behind her and studies her in profile. He sees that her hair has completely grown in, that her complexion is what it was when he first met her, that her expression, though tinged with a hint of sadness, is calm. For several minutes he is simply taken by how sadly beautiful she looks against the background of the boats and the river—the unself-conscious beauty of someone who does not know she is being observed and is consequently utterly natural, utterly herself. Gilchrist starts to take a few steps toward her. Unaware of him or of anyone or anything around her, she is looking only at the water and letting it mesmerize her.

Gilchrist stops. He wants to call to her but cannot. Breaking her mood seems to him like breaking the promise he made to himself after he read her letter as well as the later promise he made to Dr. Voss. Doing a sharp about-face, he hurries back through the crowded downtown streets and passes a placard in front of the Annapolis Colonial Inn. It stops him in his tracks. He looks twice to be certain that what he sees is not an illusion. Featured in the center of the placard is a full-face photograph of Holly. Under the photograph is an announcement that she will be speaking at the hotel after a luncheon that very day. The subject will be the last novel of the late Julian Mattimore.

33

GILCHRIST ENTERS THE INN and stands outside the door leading to the dining room. He can hear a woman who is just concluding her introduction.

"And now," says the woman, "it is a pleasure for me to welcome back to Annapolis one of our most cosmopolitan Annapolitans, Holly Mattimore."

There is a sustained wave of applause.

"Thank you for those wonderful welcoming words," says Holly. "I am truly happy to be back home before returning to Ireland so I can say a few words about one of Ireland's greatest writers, my late husband, Julian Mattimore. In each of his twelve novels we are given a different picture of different Irish people in their different lives, but collectively they are as complete a portrait of Ireland as the one we find in Joyce or the plays of O'Casey. And I had the unique privilege of being the wife of the man who made that portrait . . ."

It has the sound of a set speech as Gilchrist listens on. But it sounds even more like someone trading on someone else's talent and reputation. The deference in Holly's voice tells Gilchrist all he wants to know, and he is absolutely unable to explain why he had not suspected it from the beginning and why he had never even thought of it as a possibility in the years since. Holly is now the stereotypical memoirist on tour. When he learned of Mattimore's death two years before and then read newspaper articles afterward, he noticed that there were often semisarcastic references to "the Widow Mattimore" and how she was intent on keeping her late husband's legacy alive. It was also noted that she received fat fees for appearances. He steps slightly away from the wall and glances at Holly as she continues her opening remarks. She looks slightly heavier in the cheeks but otherwise the same. What surprises Gilchrist is that the sight of her has no effect on him whatsoever. He regards her as he might regard any woman speaking at any midday women's luncheon anywhere in America. He has heard the wives of a few recently deceased politicians speak in circumstances like this one—women whose only apparent role is to be a semi–public relations voice for their husbands.

Gilchrist feels he had heard enough. He leaves the inn, wondering what Holly's original attraction was for him and why he has wasted so many years of recrimination against other women because of that.

34

DURING HIS DRIVE BACK to Washington and to the appointment he
has finally agreed to keep at the Israeli Embassy, Gilchrist thinks of nothing but Raya. The surprise of seeing and hearing Holly and realizing
mile by mile what a fool he has been for almost an entire wasted decade
because of her—or rather his unwillingness to see her originally for the
doyenne that she was determined to become—make his thoughts of Raya
even more compelling. Having seen Raya in Annapolis for the first time
in weeks has shown him how much he has missed her, how much her
very presence meant to him at one time, and how much her absence
has deprived him of part of himself—the part of himself that she created
within him when he was actually with her. When she left his apartment
more than a month earlier, he told himself that returning to his former
self-sufficiency would be difficult but certainly possible. After all, he had
the habits of many years to fall back on. He thought that it would just be
a matter of reverting to who he used to be. But his work from then on,
including his trip to the Middle East, only made him realize how lonely
he was. With Raya he had frequently shared his thoughts even as he was
thinking them, and his knowing that she was listening, though often she
did not comment at all, somehow completed the thought for him so that
she became in a sense part of it, part of his mind, part of his life. Without
her he thought and reasoned no differently, but the dimension of sharing
or cocreating what was on his mind was missing, and the asceticism of
singular thought made him feel lonelier than he had ever felt. But in some
ways his written work was the better for it. He was actually writing better
though writing less. He knew, even though no one else could, that it was
the throes of his loneliness and torment that were giving an edge to his
vision and a spicier pith to his thought. The result was leaner prose. He
became impatient with himself when he felt he was writing circuitously.

His style gradually became terse as a telegram. He permitted himself no trivia, no detours into conditional or subjunctive statements, no warm-ups or padded endings.

By the time he reaches the Israeli Embassy after his drive back from Annapolis, it is almost noon. A security officer with strained politeness leads him directly to the ambassador's office, where he is asked to wait for a moment, even though the ambassador, yes, is definitely expecting him but some unexpected official business is causing a slight delay. Gilchrist sits in one of the black leather chairs in the anteroom and picks up a current issue of *Time*, a magazine he assiduously avoids reading except at moments like this when he can reconfirm his convictions about how writing should not be written. He proceeds to peruse it, as is his usual practice, from back to front, and is halfway through when the door to the ambassador's office is opened, and the ambassador himself appears. Gilchrist feels that he is simply looking at another American official—the Brooks Brothers attire and stance, the definite "American" look in the eyes, the absence of any foreign hint in the man's demeanor. Then Gilchrist reminds himself that the man is (or was) an American, was educated at the University of Chicago, was even a captain in the US Army and subsequently carried out certain assignments for the Department of State. Gilchrist has seen the ambassador's photograph so many times in newspapers and magazines and on television that he feels a certain bored familiarity with the gray crew cut, the jut of the bearded jaw, the obvious purple wart under the man's right eye. He feels the same dislike for the ambassador in person that he felt when he saw him in photographs. There was something about him that suggested too much of a reliance on his rank, almost an identification with it, and Gilchrist knew from his own military experience that men who needed such an identification were not real leaders. He also knew that if they were in positions of power, they were dangerous because they lacked decisiveness. Flaunting rank was no substitute.

"Mr. Gilchrist," says the ambassador, "I hope you were not waiting long."

"Just arrived."

"Good," says the ambassador, shaking Gilchrist's hand. "Come in, please."

Gilchrist accompanies him into his office, where the ambassador pauses and with a gesture of his right hand indicates that Gilchrist should be seated. Gilchrist crosses in front of the ambassador to a chair when he stops so abruptly that the ambassador almost bumps into him.

"Sorry," says the ambassador.

Gilchrist is not listening. He is staring with some disbelief at the man beside the ambassador's desk. When Gilchrist entered the office, he noted only that the man was standing with his face averted. Now he can see him clearly.

"Gelb," says Gilchrist.

"How are you, Mr. Gilchrist?" says Gelb, turning away from the desk and approaching Gilchrist with his right hand extended.

"What brings you to Washington?" asks Gilchrist, not taking Gelb's hand. He sees that Gelb has lost a little weight but not much. The brown mustache seems a shade darker. Otherwise, the same man, the same plotter's eyes.

"An assignment change," answers Gelb.

"That's one of the reasons that I invited you to this luncheon, Mr. Gilchrist," interrupts the ambassador. "Mr. Gelb is to be my successor. The announcement will be made at the luncheon you'll be attending with us in . . ."—he looks at his watch—"ten minutes."

"Miss Levenson asked to be remembered to you," says Gelb.

"Ruby?"

"Yes, she came back to Washington with me. We are staying at her residence."

"Give her my best," says Gilchrist. Gilchrist can almost detect a new refinement in Gelb, as if the man is just beginning to try on the personality of a diplomat for size. Gilchrist has observed the metamorphosis so many times in the past in other men that he considers the change a kind of cliché. He can even list a few of the main examples by name—thugs or former terrorists or outright sycophants or liars suddenly transformed into statesmen, speaking tiredly in the generalities of office, visiting the sick or wounded and being photographed while doing so, kissing babies in public or laying wreaths at the tombs of dead heroes, wearing hand-tailored suits, moving from place to place with a retinue of assistants and assistants to the assistants, riding alone to evening receptions in what Gilchrist once described in a column as the "raven Cadillacs of death and governments." Then he wonders if Ruby had any inkling of Gelb's promotion when he saw her in Israel or if her continued relationship with Gelb was simply an appropriate way for her to get back to Washington and live at the level of her preference. She was always fascinated by ambassadorial parties. But no, Gilchrist reprimands himself, that was being too Byzantine about Ruby and her tactics. Or was this a carryover from what he saw in Holly in Annapolis and applying it to Ruby? If that was at the bottom of it, then he wasn't being fair to Ruby. There is a limit, Gilchrist tells himself, to female calculation. But still . . .

"Shall we go to lunch?" says the ambassador and indicates a door at the rear of his office. He escorts Gilchrist and Gelb into a table-centered dining room. The table has eight place settings. The five other attendees—four men and one woman—wait at their places as Gelb, Gilchrist, and the ambassador approach the table. Gilchrist knows from experience who they will be. Not personally, of course, since he has never seen any of the five before, but he knows the identity they will assume in these circumstances, and this will subsume their private selves as completely as if they were characters in a play. First, Gilchrist assumes, there will be Mr. Outspoken. After the amenities, Mr. Outspoken will, without warning or provocation or tact, declare his total fidelity to his cause, whatever that cause may be, field questions like a pugilist, and even provoke further questions as a way of keeping his psyche in the proper state of indignation. Then there will be Mr. Tactful, who will be no less an example of rank-and-file fidelity and no less pugilistic but will always manage to speak in the more intimate tones of a salesman of fine jewelry. Then there will be Mr. Servility, who will be more than deferential to all officials present and who will make his point, when pressed or confused, by taking refuge in the money or influence that his very presence brings to the cause. Then there will be Mr. Public Relations, whose primary consideration will be the "image aspects" of any and all problems and who will address himself exclusively to those, usually toward the end of the meeting. Finally, there will be Mr. Quiet. Mr. Quiet will invariably be the one who will volunteer little during the meeting but who will listen to everything as if every word spoken will be the first and last he will ever hear, who will have the deepest grasp of the political and strategic values implied, who may or may not be a person of wealth, who will regard public relations as so much frill and manipulate it as such, who will be listened to in private as if his words are the only words worth hearing, and who will possess, like a pope in a crisis, the authority, if not the vision, of last resort.

After Gilchrist and Gelb are introduced to the five guests, everyone in the party sits down and proceeds with lunch, during which only superficial matters are discussed—the weather, the congestion at the airport, the comparison of Washington hotel prices with those "back home" in Albany or Milwaukee or Pittsburgh. Gilchrist eats little. He wants to keep himself alert for whatever is to transpire, and, in an almost physical sense, he somehow does not want to share as a recipient in the hospitality of the occasion.

By the time the luncheon reaches the respite of coffee, the only woman present, Gilchrist observes, fetches a small cheroot from her purse and lights it with an electronic lighter. No one else is smoking.

Gilchrist waits for the opening remark, which, he guesses, should come at any time from Mr. Outspoken. He does not have to wait long. He knows that the real character of the man will turn into the caricature that his being on this particular committee will compel him to become. He has seen too many committees subsume the real characters of their participants to be shocked.

"I must say that I've been slightly outraged, Mr. Gilchrist, by the columns you've been writing lately. It made a lot of senators and congressmen have second thoughts about my government . . ."

"Your government?" asks Gilchrist.

"The Israeli government, the government I support and have been supporting for the past thirty years. I possess dual citizenship, Mr. Gilchrist, so my statement is accurate."

"Am I to assume that the Israeli government and the government of the United States are both your governments? Which one takes priority?"

"Don't patronize me, Gilchrist. In my considered judgment, you're doing my government and the government of the United States a great disservice by what you've been . . ."

"What Mel means, Mr. Gilchrist," intervenes Mr. Servility, "is that your columns don't seem to serve the common interests of the United States in that area of the world. I don't think we should make our disagreements just a matter of semantics, though. Perhaps we can define what we mean by the common interests of the United States and reach a consensus." He turns to Mr. Outspoken and asks, "Don't you agree, Mel?"

"Gilchrist knows what I mean," says Mr. Outspoken, "and he doesn't need a translation. He's just trying to cloud the issue, and you're helping him do it. Newspaper people are very good at that. He's been doing it in print for the past four or five months, and I've had it up to here. Somebody has to tell him."

"The media say what they want to say and print what they want to print," interrupts Mr. Public Relations. "We can't screw around with the First Amendment, Mel. All we're asking of Mr. Gilchrist is that he include stories from our side of the problem in addition to those he's already run. Surely, there must be some alternate stories, stories about social progress, medical programs, the Peace Now movement, things of that nature. Isn't it part of your ethical training as a journalist to print the whole truth and not just a selection of stories that enforce your bias?"

"I don't need to be reminded of my ethical responsibilities," says Gilchrist flatly.

"As far as I'm concerned," shouts Mr. Outspoken, "the First Amendment can go to hell!"

All the other guests as well as the ambassador and Gelb treat the remark as a joke and laugh it away. Gilchrist pays no attention to the remark or the laughter. He now knows the identities of Mr. Outspoken, Mr. Servility, and Mr. Public Relations, all of whom he considers irrelevant. This leaves only Mr. Tactful and Mr. Quiet, and one of the two will have to be the woman, who continues to smoke her cheroot with the rhythmic pleasure of someone who knows how and at what intervals to savor the taste of tobacco.

"I think we all know that a man with Mr. Gilchrist's credentials wrote only what he saw in the country," Mr. Public Relations is saying. "We simply think—in fact, we know—that there were other things he saw that he chose not to write about. Am I right, Mr. Gilchrist?"

"You do a pretty good job writing about your assets," Gilchrist answers. "I was just trying to bring a few other things to public attention. You apparently think that things like arrest without charges, imprisonment without trial, collective punishment, the closing of schools, and the separation of family members are minor matters. I just don't happen to share that view."

"That's a blood libel!" shouts Mr. Outspoken.

"But you do seem to concentrate on what gives Israel a bad name, Mr. Gilchrist," interjects the one man who has not yet spoken. He makes the statement with a smile, as if he wants to hide the sting of his words behind a spirit of shared goodwill. This is Mr. Tactful's way of saying things, and Gilchrist knows that the smile is only a zealot's way of disguising his zealotry. If he were to make a bet, Gilchrist would bet that the smile would disappear in thirty minutes, at which time Mr. Tactful and Mr. Outspoken would be indistinguishable.

"Not a bad name. I just deal in hard news. If that gives Israel a bad name, blame it on the news."

"But does your agenda compel you to focus only on what you call bad news, Mr. Gilchrist?" asks Mr. Tactful.

Gilchrist registers the question at a secondary level of his attention. He now knows that Mr. Quiet is the woman with the cheroot, and he is studying her as carefully as she is studying him through the blue-gray smoke that mists her like a private fog or cloud.

"Of course, we could not help but notice that one of your colleagues took vigorous exception to your reports," says Mr. Servility.

"Which one? Several took exception."

"Gregg F. Shilling, to be exact. And in my view Mr. Shilling is one of the country's most reliable journalists."

Gilchrist tries to hide a smile before Ms. Quiet can see it. Gilchrist has known for years that Shilling has been a crony of the ambassador and possibly of everyone else at the table. In fact, so close was Shilling's affinity with the ambassador and the powers represented by Messrs. Outspoken, Servility, Public Relations, Tactful, and Quiet that anyone desiring to know the Israeli party line in advance of its official proclamation had only to read it in Shilling's column. Quite a few of Gilchrist's fellow journalists often said that Shilling was a paid employee or freelancer for the government whose views he so predictably espoused, but the employee aspect of the charge did not interest Gilchrist. It was probably a slander anyway. When asked why he was giving Shilling the benefit of the doubt about a payoff, he said that investigating a journalist's background or motives was not another journalist's business. Only his published words were.

"I wasn't aware of Mr. Shilling's reservations about my columns regarding the Middle East," Gilchrist replies, straight-faced.

"He wrote that you were too negative about the Israeli occupation. According to his sources, many of the Palestinians are much better off financially than they were before."

"That may be, but it seems secondary to the oppression of the indigenous population. Their land is occupied, after all. And at last report, most people don't take to being occupied."

"What kind of oppression?" shouts Mr. Outspoken. "Those wogs never had it so good, and they know it."

"They want their political rights," says Gilchrist.

"We've given them more rights now than they've ever had," mutters Mr. Outspoken, thumping the table with the butt of his hand to emphasize his point.

"They don't seem to think so. They have no say in their own destiny, and for them that's what political life is all about. You can say that a man may have better economic opportunities and guarantee him better social services from the cradle to the grave, but if you don't respect his political rights, he's still a slave." Hearing an echo in his words, Gilchrist pauses, then immediately realizes that he is quoting Tabry and the mayor of Tabry's village almost verbatim. "The bottom line is that they don't want to be slaves. And that's what you and the Israeli government can't understand or accept."

"The government there has given them more rights than they've ever had in their history," contributes Mr. Tactful, whose tact is gradually disappearing. Gilchrist admits to himself that the disappearance he had anticipated has come slightly ahead of schedule. "Those people reproduce like gophers. In twenty years they'll outnumber us all. The government has to keep some leverage on them. Even you would admit, Mr. Gilchrist, that no government has an obligation to commit suicide."

"All I am sure of is that the people I met there would rather die than be occupied. They don't want to be slaves in the short run or the long run. This is the same view that I share with a group called Rabbis for Human Rights, and they say it in much stronger terms than I've used. Are you familiar with Rabbis for Human Rights?"

There is silence as Gilchrist's question lingers in the air as languidly as the smoke from Ms. Quiet's cheroot. A waiter enters the room with a tray of liqueurs. After everyone is served—while the silence persists like a fog that refuses to lift—the waiter leaves.

"Gentlemen," says the ambassador, "I'd like to take this occasion to propose a toast to my successor, Seth Gelb. In two weeks he officially becomes the new ambassador, and I wish him every success in his Washington assignment. I'm sure you all join me in that sentiment."

Gilchrist looks at Gelb but says nothing. He does not join the others in the toast to Gelb.

"It seems that I do not enjoy your good wishes and support, Mr. Gilchrist," says Gelb.

"It's hard for me to support you when we don't share the same point of view on a number of matters, but I'm sure you all knew that before you invited me here."

"Mr. Gilchrist," intervenes the ambassador, "We never had any intention of swaying you, believe me. We respect honest opponents. We only wanted to provide you with the opportunity of sharing our points of disagreement like civilized people. If that leaves us agreeing to disagree, then so be it. If we can't be good friends, we can at least be good enemies. Enemies across the table, you might say."

"Fair enough," says Gilchrist.

"I think you should know, however, that we will find it necessary in the weeks to come to challenge and attack you in the public arena with all the means we have at our disposal. This will all be done in the name and spirit of freedom of opinion. We have our opinions, just as you have yours. While we don't have access to the editorial page as you do . . ."

"But you have Gregg F. Shilling."

"Mr. Shilling is his own man, Mr. Gilchrist, just as you are yours."

"And you have the Israel lobby."

"Our lobby is fully credited to the US government, and you know it."

"So I can expect the usual tonnage of letters to the editor, endless e-mails, and . . ."

"I can assure you that your expectations will not be unfulfilled. You can be certain of that."

"Well, doesn't that prove what I've been saying for the past couple of years—that the real struggle for the Middle East is not where it exists on the map but right here in Washington, right here in the United States?"

Ms. Quiet tamps out her cheroot in the ashtray beside her liqueur glass. The gesture, Gilchrist senses, is meant to indicate to all those present that the luncheon is over.

"Mr. Ambassador," says Gilchrist, "I would like to thank you for the luncheon." He turns to Gelb. "It was a surprise to see you here. I'm sure our paths will cross again. Give my best to Ruby." He turns and walks erectly to the door, passing Ms. Quiet as he goes.

"I must say that you have excellent composure, Mr. Gilchrist," she says as he passes her.

"I'm glad you approve," says Gilchrist and smiles.

"Let's just say I was impressed."

"Thank you."

He enters the anteroom beside the ambassador's office. Sitting in one of the anteroom chairs is a man whom Gilchrist instantly recognizes. The man's inevitable bow tie, the carefully cultivated intellectual casualness of a midwesterner trying to assume a New England persona, the sense of privilege and rectitude that is as unignorable as the miniature American flag on his lapel.

"Shilling," says Gilchrist. "Should I be surprised to see you here?"

"It's not exactly the place where I would have expected to see you, Gilchrist."

"I would imagine that you're right at home."

"It's just one of my beats, Gilchrist."

"That's funny. I thought for a minute that you were here to visit old friends."

Shilling is on the verge of a retort, shrugs as if the effort is not worth the provocation, and busies himself with some papers on his lap.

"You don't find much that the Israelis do in any way objectionable, do you, Shilling?"

Shilling looks up from his papers and says, "The Palestinians are the real terrorists, Gilchrist."

"And what about the people in the South of Lebanon? The Israeli F-17s have been hitting them all week. Can you imagine the bravery it takes for a pilot to pick his targets at leisure without having to worry about antiaircraft fire or intercepting aircraft? He just goes in, blows the shit out of some house or school, and then flies back for lunch. Now that's what I call real valor."

"You have your pet causes, Gilchrist, and I have mine."

"But you know as well as I do what the Israelis are doing over there to a lot of defenseless people, and you don't have the journalistic balls to call them on it. Why is that?"

"I don't owe you an explanation."

"You owe your readers one. That's what journalism is about."

"I could ask you the same question."

"Why don't you ask me in print, and I'll answer you in print? That way we'll get the reading public interested. Is it a deal?"

Shilling looks down but says nothing. After a pause Gilchrist leaves the room and heads for his car. He realizes that he has an hour to drive to the airport for his flight to New York in order to cover the debate at the United Nations over the protest lodged by the Lebanese against the Israeli air strikes.

35

RETURNING TO HIS APARTMENT three days later, Gilchrist is fatigued. Several times on his drive from the airport, he almost nods asleep. Twice he shakes his head vigorously to keep his eyes open.

After parking the Mercedes in its slot, he lets habit alone lead him to the elevator and then to his apartment. He opens the door, shuts it behind him, and leans against it. He closes his eyes and relaxes as if the door might be his vertical bed. It is only then that he detects a scent in the room that does not belong there. Flowers? A specific flower? But which one? He looks at the porch windows, but they are closed. He turns to his desk. In the middle of the desk is a stack of eight-by-eleven sheets of paper. The stack is almost an inch and a half thick and is as concisely squared as an oversized deck of cards about to be shuffled and reshuffled. Concentrating on the stack, Gilchrist does not for a moment see the bouquet of lilacs in a vase beside the papers. When he finally does, he immediately remembers the lilacs that Raya left for him at Saranac. The sweetness as well as the poignancy of the memory make him smile, but it is a smile of regret and not of pleasure. Who could have put the lilacs there?

He sits in the desk chair and rakes his fingers through his hair. Then he turns the pages in the stack in front of him, page by page. He recognizes it immediately as the defiled issue of the journal, completely retyped. On several pages his editorial comments are included.

"Raya," Gilchrist whispers to himself.

He examines the rest of the manuscript and finds it in perfect ready-to-print order. When he finishes, he stands and walks to the porch windows. He half expects to hear the telephone ring or see Raya emerge from one of the rooms. Then he opens the sliding doors and steps out on the porch. Spring in Washington has always been for him worth the rest of the year. Azaleas, cherry blossoms, forsythias, lilacs, and tulips invariably manage to create their own two-week carnival. And just when the onlooker feels surfeited by so many bursts of lavender, red, yellow, pink, white, and all the other spectral variations, the carnival ends. Now in the very midst of the carnival with the knowledge that Raya or some messenger of hers has been in his apartment, Gilchrist feels more complete than he's felt in weeks. He leans on the porch railing and watches the facades of buildings across the street and beyond, and he is still leaning when he hears the apartment door being opened and closed. He turns and sees Raya walking to the kitchen with a bag of groceries in her hands. Gilchrist notices the bound leaves of a stalk of celery protruding from the top of the bag.

"Raya," Gilchrist says almost to himself.

Raya stops, looks at him with mild surprise, and smiles. Then she continues into the kitchen and begins unloading the groceries. Puzzled, Gilchrist follows her and stands in the kitchen doorway.

"Can you help me with some of these things, please, Dodge? I just picked up a few items for light housekeeping, but they should be enough for dinner. There was next to nothing in the refrigerator. Were you away?"

Gilchrist stands completely still for a moment. He is trying to comprehend what is happening. For weeks, nothing. Not a note. Not a telephone call. Then the sight of her with a bag of groceries. She speaks to him as if she has been gone for only an hour and not for week after week after week after week.

"I didn't know when to expect you," Raya says, selecting a skillet and a small pot that she evidently intends to use for dinner.

"Raya," says Gilchrist.

"I really had the menu planned. Now you have no choice but to watch me. It won't be a surprise."

"Raya, stop playing games. Look at me."

She puts the skillet she is holding on the stove and faces him. She is smiling, but her eyes have a slightly worried look.

"What's going on?" asks Gilchrist. "Why didn't you let me know you were coming? I thought . . ."

"Please, Dodge, don't ask me anything now. Not now. Please. Let me do what I planned to do, and then we can talk. I'll explain everything. Please do that for me."

Gilchrist sees that she really means what she is asking. He suppresses his desire to interrupt her. Then he remembers her plea to let her finish what she is planning to do. Stymied, he returns to his desk and rests his hand on the manuscript. He is still coming to terms with her actual presence when he hears the sizzle of butter melting in the skillet.

"I still remember how you like pepper steak," Raya calls to him from the kitchen. "I think I have all the ingredients. I did forget to buy mushrooms. I hope it doesn't make too much of a difference."

Gilchrist lifts the top pages from the stack and begins to read. He has not read more than five pages when Raya calls to him, "Dinner is served, Mr. Gilchrist."

Engrossed as he has been in his own thoughts and in his reading, Gilchrist has not heard Raya set the table in the annex. When he goes into the annex and sees the perfectly set table, he smiles. Everything about the scene has her touch—the exactly placed dishes, the flatware, the candles. There is an inch of red wine in each of the two wineglasses, and she has folded and festooned the napkins like flowers on each plate.

"I hope you like it," says Raya, serving the pepper steaks from an oval platter onto his plate and then onto her own.

Gilchrist holds her chair for her, and, after she places the empty platter on the edge of the table, he waits for her to sit down, edges her chair closer to the table after she is seated, and then seats himself. She looks across the table at him with a look of accomplishment in her eyes that tells him more than all the answers to all the questions he is preparing himself to ask. It is a look that tells him she is better now, much better, and her preparing this dinner by herself is the proof.

Midway through the dinner, Gilchrist puts his knife and fork aslant across his plate and sits back. Noticing this, Raya stops eating.

"Is anything wrong?" she asks.

"How are you?" Gilchrist asks bluntly. "Tell me exactly how you are, Raya."

Raya fidgets briefly with her napkin and looks down at her lap. Then she folds the napkin and places it beside her plate. "I'm trying to show you, Dodge. It's something that I want to prove to you this way—by doing what I'm doing."

"I can see that. But give me some details, some . . ."

"Dr. Voss," Raya begins. She reaches for the napkin as a prop, thinks better of it, and starts again. "Dr. Voss told me that he thinks I'm his miracle. That's the last thing he said to me after he drove me here this morning from Annapolis. Annapolis is where I've been. I've been staying with his sister. In the beginning it was very difficult. I thought I was doing well, and then I would run into a problem. Or I would say the wrong thing at the right time or the right thing at the wrong time. I had a hard time staying in focus. But the days went by, and little by little I could feel myself improving. And every day I noticed that I was starting to look like myself again. And that helped. It does help, Dodge, that kind of thing. But I've told you that. If you look well, you start to feel well. Then I started to type. I typed every day. And that helped me put my mind and my fingertips together, if you know what I mean."

"Is that why you typed all those pages that are on my desk?"

She nods yes. Then she says, "I knew the journal was spoiled, and the printer told me that the disc and the hard drive were ruined as well. The printer showed me where the only worthwhile copies were. There was dried paint all over them. But I finally put together a full set from a group of more than twenty of the still readable copies. Then I started typing them into the computer so that you could have the issue printed again if you wanted to. I've typed very carefully, and I've reread it twice. I don't think there are many mistakes I didn't find and correct. I even typed in as many of your editorial directions as I could remember."

"You amaze me. I'd really given up on the journal."

"The hardest thing was finding a set of pages I could work from. I had to go through copy after copy. The pages were glued together by the paint. But I was determined to do it."

They both finish eating without saying anything more. Gilchrist remains seated at the table while Raya removes the dishes and carries them into the kitchen. He listens to her working there. The moment takes on its own unreality. He has been alone for so long in the apartment that Raya's being with him seems more like a dream than a fact. He stands and walks back out on the porch. The entire city is bright with the late-afternoon wash of sun, and the steady basin air seems to be shimmering above the rooftops. Gilchrist is reminded of the summer torpor that is still months away, but his real thoughts are far from weather.

"Do you want more coffee?" Raya asks. She is standing between the sliding doors.

"No," says Gilchrist. "Do you remember this view?" He sweeps his hand over the cityrama.

Raya joins Gilchrist at the porch railing. They stand together, looking out at Washington.

"Raya?"

"Yes."

He opens his arms to her as she turns to him. It is as if she has only been waiting for this kind of gesture from him to permit her to respond. She draws next to him and lets him embrace her. She stays that way briefly, then joins her hands at the small of his back, and presses herself against him.

"It wasn't the therapy that was difficult for me," she says. "It was difficult, but I could deal with it. What I couldn't deal with was being away from you. The fact that I couldn't see you made your life more real to me than anything around me. And that tortured me. But I was determined that I would not come back until I was better." She pauses. "I made so many mistakes trying to get better. Sometimes I would decide to do something, and my hand or foot would refuse to do it or else do the exact opposite. Dr. Voss kept telling me to be patient. And his sister helped. She was so nice to me. They both were. I don't know how I can repay them. And that made me try all the harder to be well again."

"Does it help to talk about it now?"

"Oh, let me talk, Dodge, please. You don't know how many nights I wanted to call you, to talk to you. But I didn't permit myself. I wanted to wait until I was myself, until I was who I used to be. Can you understand?"

"I think so."

"And finally I reached the point where Dr. Voss thought I was all right. That was a little more than two weeks ago. But he told me to wait a little longer to make sure there was no relapse. So I waited. Those were the longest two weeks . . . But now I'm here. I'm with you."

Gilchrist tightens his arms around her, and she responds in the same way.

"Dodge," she whispers.

"Yes."

"I love you, Dodge. More now than before, more than ever."

Gilchrist's only response is to hold her more tightly, to let his arms do what his voice seems incapable of doing.

"Dodge," says Raya, "are you glad I'm back?"

"What do you think?"

"I wanted to surprise you."

"I don't think I had the time to be surprised. I looked up, and you were there with a bagful of groceries. It was as if you were never away."

"That's what I wanted you to feel." She looks up at him. "I never was away, Dodge. In my heart I was always here."

"It wasn't quite the same as right now."

"Did you miss me?"

"Very, very, very much."

What happens afterward seems to Gilchrist like a ballet. He walks slowly with Raya back into the apartment and into the bedroom where they sit down on opposite sides of the bed and unhurriedly remove their clothes. Neither looks at the other. When they are finished, they enter the bed.

Gilchrist lies on his back. Raya remains momentarily on her side of the bed before she turns and edges close to Gilchrist, her arm angling loosely across his chest, her cheek on his shoulder.

For Raya this is the first time in weeks that she does not have to be minutely aware of her body and how it responds to what she wants it to do. For each hour of each one of those weeks she had to wait for her arms or legs to disobey her, and such instances of disobedience, especially in the first week, were frequent. She recalls how she could not remember—or rather her hands would not remember—what she was supposed to pick up. Her fingers had a will of their own. She would try again. And again. Suddenly, her hands would rouse themselves from their amnesia and do what they were supposed to do. Now, lying next to Gilchrist, she feels that her body has regained its assurance. She feels a litheness in her limbs that was not there before. And she feels oddly tired as well, but it is a soothing tiredness that is not unlike the kind of tiredness she has known when her body was ready, truly ready, for sleep. Her arm across Gilchrist's chest is limp with its own peace. The very scent of his body soothes her, and she closes her eyes to lock out everything that might intrude upon this moment.

For Gilchrist, it is as if he has never been in bed with a woman before. In fact, he finds no parallel between any of his previous experiences in this very bed and his experience at the moment. The nude girl beside him seems as relaxed as he is. Once, when she was still in coma, he had tried to imagine his future without her, and he found it impossible. Now he finds the present moment too perfect to accept.

To have Raya beside him in his own bed in his own apartment—an apartment that for the previous months, except for the trip to Israel, he used only for sleep—is a reality bordering on illusion, but the small weight of her arm across his chest is no illusion, and the touch of her cheek-soft breast against his side and the matching smoothness of her thigh against his leg are no illusions. Yet Gilchrist cannot help but feel slightly at odds with his own desire for her, as if any sexual initiative at this time would destroy the fragile mood between them. It is almost as if he could be satisfied to let the moment go on interminably, to lie with her without moving or speaking, to let his body and hers become more accustomed to their own new and quiet symmetry. Nevertheless, he already feels the preliminary instinctive male response, and for once it disturbs rather than pleases him. If another woman were suddenly in Raya's place and if it were years earlier, he knows from his own history what the procedure would be—the usual fondling and stroking, the lips wandering wherever, the turning and coupling before the final tussle together, and, if necessary, the fingerings and easings if the woman needed help. Somehow it does not seem right to proceed with Raya this way. Something in him does not want to find out if she will respond as other women have, if her very scent will be the same as theirs, if her final pantings will remind him of different memories he has created with so many others in this same bed. Thinking in this way makes his arousal subside. He notices that Raya makes no movement of encouragement or discouragement. He detects an occasional tenseness in her body as it presses against his, but that is all.

"I saw you in Annapolis," he says.

"Saw me?" She raises her head and looks at him quizzically.

"I followed Dr. Voss there last Monday."

"Why didn't you let me see you?"

"I couldn't. I followed you down to the dock. You looked like yourself again, but I couldn't bring myself to go up to you, so I left before . . ."

"But all I was doing while I was sitting there was thinking of you. I wanted to see you more than anything in the world. It would have been so right if you would have just walked up to me, surprised me . . ."

"I guess I missed my chance, Raya," he says and smiles. "That's not unusual for me."

She places her head against his shoulder again. Gilchrist knows that she wants him to love her, to make love to her, to touch and kiss her, but he simply lies still. He can still taste the dregs of what his life was before he met her, and the taste rankles like acid on his tongue. It does not seem enough for him to know that his old self and his old ways are now repugnant to him. It's just that all this profligacy lies like another presence between them, paralyzing his desire and sledging him back to an identity he cannot quite discard. That and the full force of the devotion that he knows Raya feels for him fill him with such conflicting feelings of both regret and gratitude that he cannot bring himself to act.

Raya turns away from him, slides out of bed, and says, "I forgot to turn off the coffee."

He watches her hurry into the kitchen. It is the first time he has seen her nude. She seems slimmer and more delicately herself. Her black hair makes her skin seem lighter. He notices two skin dimples in the small of her back. When she walks back toward him, he sees her breasts lift and sway with her every step.

When she is again beside him in bed, she kisses him. Gilchrist senses the passion of the kiss and feels her arm tighten across his chest. Gilchrist feels his self-incrimination leave him like a broken fever, and he turns his head toward Raya just in time to see her raise herself on one elbow and smile down at him. He takes her head in both of his hands, his thumbs feeling a cool moistness (tears?) beneath each of her eyes. She closes her eyes before his stare as he draws her face toward him and kisses her on the forehead and then fully on the lips. Her reaction is to succumb to him, softening where he is tense, yielding where he is assertive, allowing herself to be held until Gilchrist feels that her will has passed out of her body into his.

For Gilchrist, the experience of love in this way is entirely new. The gymnastics of his previous assignations now seem like exercises in technique, nothing more. More athletic than amorous, these "couplings" (there was no other word) moved toward their peaks with the calculated and predictable inevitability of water coming to a boil. He recalls how he and his various lovers would often talk to one another during the act itself, each one prompting and coaching the other through a complete scale of pleasure, savoring each step even more than the end to which the whole progress was directed. At such moments Gilchrist thought he understood the "must" of animals, and he treated each affair as if it were little more than a mutually desired ritual in relief, a respite from a day of work that ended in a bankable pleasure, a barter of bodies.

Shifting on his side so that the total faces of their bodies touch, Gilchrist continues to kiss Raya on her face, her throat, her breasts, and the flat path of skin between them. Almost by reflex, his right leg, knee first, slides between her thighs and upward. She flexes her thighs around his leg.

Again the ghosts of his couplings with other women interpose themselves between him and Raya, and he realizes all at once that all his lovemaking prior to this moment was a matter of himself with someone else who always remained someone else from start to finish. The women he held in his arms in a multiplicity of positions and contortions were actually all the same woman, the obliging female with whom he shared an intimacy of organs, nothing more, nothing else.

With Raya he seems to be attending to another self. He feels her heart pulse against his chest as if it were his own, and each beat seems as important as a breath that may not be followed by another. And because his memories keep intruding and adulterating the intimacy of the moment, he curses inwardly the seven years of his life that he wasted, curses himself for using Holly and her rejection of him as a basis for a way of life that essentially amounted to nothing more than periodic spermatic entries into innumerable women he can now barely remember, curses the whole damn tradition that made him believe (or made him succeed in forcing himself to believe) that his pleasure and his personality were totally separate, that he could rut whenever he felt like it and then return to his computer on the following morning with a sense of physical relief and the taste of bitters in his mouth and convince himself that he was not the worse for the dalliance. His moment of truth makes him see himself as an aging Don Juan who had the means and the notoriety to finance his pleasures as ritualistically and as perfunctorily as he might fuel his expensive car. His old creed that he could somehow purify himself through his work was, he sees now, nothing but a deception, since it left unsatisfied a deeper part of himself in favor of a false life that had no Act 2. Tabry was right about him when he said he saw women as either "virgins or bitches." For Tabry, every man or woman was a person, and he never varied from that view. That was perhaps what Gilchrist admired most about Tabry—the fact that he was simple and pure at the core, pure as a vow that he never betrayed or compromised, pure because he had wedded himself to a purpose, had united himself with the apparently lost cause of his country despite the odds. He had refused to yield to the logic of history and made his own logic. This became his mission, and that in the end became his life and, after his death, his glory.

Now as he holds Raya in his arms, he feels that all the things he has done since Tabry's death—the newspaper column, the visit to Tabry's village, the decision to persist in what he now has made his mission, his disappointment in some whom he had considered friends—were but a small price to pay for the gift of this girl. But even this thought is tainted by his memory of Ruby's question. Has he embraced Tabry's cause for its own sake or because of Raya? Has he made the two one and the same in ways that would eventually subvert and confuse the identities of both or, in a reincarnation of his old self, idealize his desire to possess Raya in the name of a cause that now permits him to indulge that desire without guilt? How will he ever know? Or is he being scrupulous to the point of self-paralysis? Why is it, he asks himself, that he must always contend with undermining feelings and alternatives after he has made up his mind? And on the Palestinian issue he is positive, regardless of motive, that he has made up his mind. His evolving conviction about Tabry's mission and its rightness has given him the first true sense of purpose in his life. He knows that there is no going back even if he might choose to, and he has long since written off such a choice. By assuming Tabry's cause as his own, Gilchrist feels, again for the first time, a certain patriotism—not a foreign patriotism but one that somehow makes him feel more American. By placing himself as an American on the side of a people who have been desecrated and displaced and deracinated and by saying so in public, he feels he has discovered his true American identity. It's as if by fighting for someone else's rights, as he now reminds himself again and again, he is really fighting for his own. The fact that his is a minority position seems inconsequential to him.

He silences what is raging in his mind by tipping Raya's face to his and placing his palm under Raya's chin. He kisses her on the lips and holds the kiss until his lips and hers become more sensitive than fingertips touching fingertips. Raya's lips quiver slightly against his. The longer the kiss lasts, the more do Raya's lips yield to his. The kiss ends reluctantly, as if each of them must part to breathe, and Raya eases her head under Gilchrist's chin so that he can actually taste her hair.

Slowly, they let their bodies lead them now. Raya rolls on her back, and Gilchrist lets his palm coast down her flank to her waist, then her hips, then the inner skin of her thigh. Raya keeps her legs together, and Gilchrist is about to lift his hand when suddenly she eases her legs apart by inches, and Gilchrist is touching her. She pulls his face toward her and kisses him huskily on the cheek, the lips, the chin. Gilchrist removes his hand, then touches her taut breasts as he lifts himself on top of her. He burrows his hands around her between her back and the sheet. She raises her legs slightly against his sides as they probe for one another. Gilchrist does not thrust himself into her but penetrates carefully several times and waits for her response. Then when he is sure from her movements that she is ready for him, he lets himself enter further until he is fully extended within her.

For Raya, there is no discomfort. She had always heard that there would be discomfort, even pain, but as Gilchrist lies between her gripping thighs and inches himself gently into her, she feels nothing but the pleasure that this is giving her. Her forearms around him can detect the tension in his muscles just below the shoulder blades, and she locks her ankles behind his thighs and hugs him with her legs and arms simultaneously. She feels a mounting hunger in her entire body that makes her clench herself against him. She hears herself saying his name again and again.

Gilchrist can feel Raya's body rise and ride beneath him like a body on water. He moves slowly within her. When she tightens, he stops momentarily and then resumes. He hears her saying his name, hears her almost whimper in his arms, hears her breaths deepen as he continues. He realizes that this is the first time he has been with a woman when he is not at the mercy of his own mounting pleasure. His concern for Raya has somehow neutralized it, at least temporarily. He does not want anything spoiled for her, not because he wants a sense of momentary superiority by pleasuring her as his pleasure, but because he wants her climax to be complete. And even as he thinks this way, he can tell that her easing is happening to her. She breathes more quickly, says his name in quicker pants as if she is about to cry, then shudders and twists beneath him as if she is in the grip of a spasm whose pleasure she can no longer control. Finally, he feels the shudder at the height of her turning and thrusting and the final diminuendos in her entire body as her satisfaction racks her so that she holds onto him like someone who will otherwise drown. When at last she releases him, she lets her arms fall limply on the bed like useless wings. A moment later she embraces him again, holds him so that her entire strength is in the moment itself. She feels as if her body is plunging into darkness, then rising into a soothing fatigue she has never known before. She feels that her hands, her thighs, and her legs are no longer her own. It is not the helplessness she felt while she was recovering when her limbs would not do what she wanted them to do. Now it is as if they are independent of her. As her pleasure begins to diminish, there follows a quiet delicacy of feeling that ebbs and ebbs reluctantly into silence. She resists the silence. With Gilchrist still firmly within her, she wants the moment to rekindle itself and possess her again. She tenses her muscles, wanting it to happen.

Gilchrist, knowing that her moment has passed, seems to let go of himself. He moves less rhythmically as she relaxes, until finally her lessening movements, almost involuntary but somehow more intimate because of that, draw him to his own finale where he feels not merely the satisfaction of release but total freedom from all his old guilts and regrets.

Still inside of her and unwilling to separate himself from her, Gilchrist turns on his side and draws her with him. They hold one another until it is apparent to both of them that it is time to return to themselves again. Raya lies back, and her breasts beneath his forearm are slightly moist against his skin. He raises himself on one elbow and studies the face of a woman just loved. Raya does not open her eyes, and he peers at her as a sculptor might peer at a model at rest, memorizing all that he sees.

Still looking at Raya's face, Gilchrist does not hear the first ring of the telephone. When it rings for the third time, he reaches back to the nightstand and gropes for the receiver. Holding the receiver to his ear with the slightest lifting of his shoulder, he listens. He keeps listening before he frowns and says tonelessly, "Yes." Then he replaces the receiver on its mount. He is still frowning when he touches Raya's face, outlining it with his hand. She looks up at him. He says nothing. Then he shifts to the edge of the bed and stands, knowing that he has no alternative now but the one that the telephone call has just created for him.

VIII

The Time Remaining

36

"I'M BACK, RAYA," says Gilchrist, closing the apartment door behind him quietly.

Raya runs to him, embraces him while he keeps his arms at his sides, then steps back and looks at him.

"Are you all right?" she asks. Her hands are quivering.

"I'm all right."

"It was terrible here, just waiting. I waited all night and watched television."

"I'm sorry you had to go through that. I didn't know what I was getting into when I left."

"It was all on television. It's all that was on for hours. I couldn't turn away. Look. I'm still wearing my nightgown. I didn't know what to do. I thought I should get dressed. Then I thought it would be best to wait. I didn't know what to do."

"It's over now."

"I know."

"How?"

"Just now. There was a news bulletin on television. And then . . ."

Gilchrist walks past her and drops into a reading chair by the window. "And then what?" he asks.

"It's not important."

Gilchrist detects a certain evasiveness in her response. He looks at her, but she avoids his eyes, stations herself behind his chair, and coasts her fingers through his unkempt hair.

"What's not important?" asks Gilchrist.

"It doesn't matter, Dodge. No one would believe it anyway."

He looks at her skeptically and stands. "Tell me the whole story, Raya."

"Do you remember the man I spoke about to you, the man who interrogated me?"

"Yes."

"He's here. Gelb is here."

"I know."

Raya walks to the window and fidgets briefly with the sash of her (actually his) white bathrobe. "The report was that a Palestinian who had taken Gelb as a hostage in a house in McLean was shot. The report was that you had met with the man to negotiate and then came out with him. That's when the man was shot." She paused. "The report was that you made it possible for him to be shot."

"Who said that?"

"Gelb."

"Did they interview him?"

"Yes. He even identified the man. His name was Braheem Sabahi. I knew him. He was from our village."

"And Gelb said that I set him up to be shot?"

Raya nods.

"Do you believe that?"

She turns away from him and shakes her head no. "I wouldn't believe anything he said. I couldn't believe something like that of you. You know that."

Gilchrist sags into the chair again and puts his head in his hands.

"There's still some coffee, Dodge. Do you want a cup?"

While Raya busies herself in the kitchen, Gilchrist tries to assemble the events of the night in chronological order. He begins with the telephone call. The caller identified himself as the same Martin Cobb whom Gilchrist had met during the investigation of Tabry's death. Then he remembers being face-to-face with Cobb on the way to McLean, and Cobb is explaining the situation to him. Then Gilchrist's memory races to the single shot he hears as he leaves the house he had entered as Cobb's negotiator. Then back to Gelb. Then Cobb again.

Over coffee Gilchrist tells Raya what happened from the time he left the apartment after he received the telephone call until his return.

It was, he tells her, Cobb who had called him. It was the same Cobb who did not doubt that the death of Tabry had been anything other than an accident caused by a man who was drinking and smoking alone. Over the telephone, Gilchrist continues, Cobb explained that there was an "emergency situation" that had developed and that he was asking for his, Gilchrist's, help. When Gilchrist asked what kind of help Cobb wanted, he heard Cobb say that it would take too much valuable time to explain on the phone, but that he would appreciate it if he could come immediately in a squad car to pick him up at his apartment. Time was crucial.

"It seems," said Cobb when Gilchrist was seated beside him in the squad car returning to McLean, "that a single gunman has entered the home of a certain Ruby Levenson in McLean and is holding the newly appointed Israeli ambassador as a hostage there. We don't know how he got in. We've been in communication with him by phone. He says he's armed and has a bomb. So we've cleared the whole area, and everything's on hold. Ms. Levenson was in the house when this individual broke in, but he let her go. It was Gelb he wanted, and he's holding him in there."

"And?"

"Gelb's bodyguards and some Israeli security forces want to storm the house, but I've been able to persuade them to wait until I met with you."

"Why me?"

"Because the gunman asked for you. He said you had met his brother in Jerusalem."

"So you've actually talked to this man?"

"I had Ms. Levenson give me the telephone number. I called, and he answered. He sounded like he was expecting the call. I let him talk. He told me that he was from a town called Tabry on the West Bank. For some reason he wanted me to know that right off. Then I thought of you and that fire in Georgetown a while ago. I remembered that the man who died in that fire was named Tabry. Then this individual said he was armed and had explosives. He didn't give me any terms or conditions. He just asked to talk to you."

"What do you think I can do?"

"Find out what you can. See how well armed he is." Cobb paused. "This may just be a grievance matter. This individual told me on the phone that this new ambassador used to be the head of security over there. He said he practically wiped this individual's village off the map. He said he started at the top by exiling the mayor. Then he closed the roads in and out. Then one by one he began to bulldoze the houses until the people got the hint and started to leave. He told me that Gelb destroyed the town the way he destroyed the Tabry family."

"Did he say anything about himself?"

"He said he and his brother owned a taxi service. He said that you met his brother when you were in Israel. He told me that he was kicked out of the country for keeps, and this Gelb was behind it. That's why I think this could be a grievance case. But with cases like this, the outcome is in doubt until the very end. It's dicey. You have to be ultracareful. That's why I called you. I thought you might be the key to ending it. We've all had some training about how to handle incidents like this. I know you've written about assassins and the situation over there, but this case doesn't seem to be following the script. If murdering Gelb was in this guy's script, he'd have done it already."

"Is there anything that he's demanding?"

"He says he will tell you—just *you*—about that."

"Will tell *me* about it?"

"That's what he said."

"Did he say why?"

"He gave me the impression that he thinks you are one of the few who really understands what is really happening to the Palestinians. And he's a Palestinian." He studies Gilchrist for a reaction. "I don't like to put you in this situation, believe me, but I have a feeling that you might be able to resolve this before it gets ugly."

Cobb then told his driver to hurry, and the squad car, its top blue light revolving like an airport beacon, zoomed forward.

37

GILCHRIST SIPS the coffee that Raya has given to him.

"You must be exhausted," she says.

He picks up the cup again and drains the coffee left in it. He has the reassuring sense of almost total recall now, and he proceeds to tell her what happened after he and Cobb arrived at Ruby's house in McLean. He does not tell her that his study of assassins had given him all the grim alternatives he might be facing in this case. If the man holding Gelb was motivated by hatred—a hatred that could be explained through envy or even love—then there was a possibility of a resolution without violence. If revenge was the motive, the chances of resolution were smaller, since such assassins had little regard for their own survival. If the motive had something to do with justice or injustice, the hostage was not simply a potential victim but someone who could—through his position or influence—do what the assassin wanted. If the hostage refused, he was usually killed. If he cooperated, he still could be killed, but he might be spared. There was no way of knowing in advance what the outcome would be. It seemed to Gilchrist, based upon what Cobb told him as they were en route to McLean, that whoever was holding Gelb was an assassin-to-be of the last type. Gilchrist does not tell Cobb that this man, as Nadeem told him in Jerusalem, was also the brother of a woman who had been abused after her arrest by Gelb and had taken her own life in prison. That knowledge put a new and dangerous dimension on the situation.

Gilchrist looks across the kitchen table at Raya. She is sitting with her hands folded on her lap, and she is absorbing every word as if the events are happening before her very eyes.

"Cobb had set up a small command post about fifty yards from the house, and we went there to plan what we thought we should do. We called the house from there, and after just one ring the man answered the phone."

"I'm sure you remember my brother Nadeem from Jerusalem, Mr. Gilchrist," the man said. "And you also met my brother Samir in the hotel."

"I remember them," said Gilchrist.

"I am Braheem. I am the oldest."

"What is it you want, Braheem?"

"One thing. I want the world to know what kind of a man this Gelb is. I want him to admit to you what he has done to the Palestinians, and I want him to tell you this so you can remember and write about it so that the whole world will know."

"I'm afraid it's not that simple, Braheem. American journalism doesn't work like that."

"This man is a criminal, Mr. Gilchrist. He has committed many crimes against my people. The world must know what he is."

"You seem certain that he is guilty."

"He admitted it to me."

"Admitted it?"

"Admitted it, yes. He even admitted that he was the one who gave the order to kill Sharif Tabry and his brother, the poet."

The words hit Gilchrist like an electric shock. After a pause he said, "You mean he actually admitted that he had Sharif killed?"

"He gave the order."

"How did you get him to admit that?"

"It was not difficult, Mr. Gilchrist."

"Did you torture it out of him?"

"I did only what I had to do. It was not difficult."

"A forced confession won't stand up in an American court, Braheem." He waited for an answer, but there was only silence. "Would you let me come in and talk this over with you?"

"When?"

"Now." Gilchrist looked at Cobb, who was nodding yes. "I can come into the house now and talk this over while we still have time."

"But you must come alone."

Gilchrist saw Cobb nodding yes again. "Yes, Braheem. I will come alone."

"Do not deceive me, Mr. Gilchrist. I want to be able to trust you."

Gilchrist heard Braheem hang up. Gilchrist repeated what Braheem expected, and Cobb agreed. Gilchrist would go in alone and unarmed, and Cobb would wait for thirty minutes. If there was no change in the situation, Cobb would call the house for an update.

"Let me make sure that the Israeli security chief understands this. It's everything I can do to keep him from storming the whole place now," said Cobb and left to confer with the Israeli.

Gilchrist now explains to Raya that the Israeli security chief returned with Cobb and wanted to provide him with a small pistol, but he refused.

38

GILCHRIST WAITED while Cobb ordered the two spotlights that were trained on the house extinguished.

"You can go anytime now," Cobb said to Gilchrist. "I'll wait thirty minutes and call you."

Even though it was still evening, the moon was out early, and Gilchrist had no problem finding his way to the front door of the house. He put his hand on the doorknob and turned it a full twist. The door opened. Gilchrist paused for a moment and then entered. Then he waited, hoping that Braheem would announce himself.

"Braheem!" Gilchrist shouted. "It's Dodge Gilchrist. I just came into the house. I'm in the foyer beside the stairwell."

"Stop there, Mr. Gilchrist." It was Braheem's voice, and it came from the top of the stairwell. Gilchrist stood perfectly still before he heard Braheem say, "Come up the stairs, Mr. Gilchrist. Would you keep your hands high so I can see them, please?"

"Okay, but I might stumble. It's hard to see in the dark."

"I can see you. The stairs are beside you on your left."

Gilchrist located the stairs and, with his hands in the air, began his ascent, step by careful step. When he reached the top, he could see Braheem in the shadows at the end of the hall.

"I must ask if you came alone, Mr. Gilchrist."

"Yes. I told you I would."

"And I must ask if you are armed."

"No, I'm not armed."

"Do I have your word?"

"You have my word, but you can search me if you want."

"You may put your hands down, Mr. Gilchrist," Braheem answered and led Gilchrist into what looked like the master bedroom of the house.

The curtains and drapes were drawn, and the only illumination came from a small night-light near the bed. At first Gilchrist saw no one else in the room. Then to the right of the bed he saw Gelb. He was seated in a straight-back chair, and his hands looked as if they were tied behind his back, and it appeared that his legs were bound with cord around the ankles. Gelb's face showed intense strain, and his head was tilted slightly forward, as if he were holding something under his chin. Gilchrist took a step closer to Gelb, who looked up at him with a wild fear in his eyes. Actually, he did not look up by moving his head but only his eyes. It was only then that Gilchrist noticed what Gelb was holding under his chin. It was a grenade. It seemed to Gilchrist that it was a grenade of an earlier vintage, but it was definitely a grenade. Braheem had apparently lodged it against his larynx so that Gelb had no choice but to grip it with his chin against his upper chest to keep it from falling. Just when he was about to turn to Braheem again, Gilchrist detected the faint but unmistakable odor of human feces.

"Are you going to leave him like that?" Gilchrist asked Braheem.

"I think it's time for a pause," said Braheem, stepping forward and dislodging the grenade, clamping his hand on the firing pin as he did so.

"What if the grenade would have slipped while he was holding it there?" asked Gilchrist.

"Then Gelb would be no more. But I don't think this would have happened. This is the third time that Gelb and I have practiced this little exercise." Braheem tucked his pistol in his belt, and, still holding the grenade tightly in his right hand like a baseball, he crouched in front of Gelb so that his face and Gelb's were at the same level.

"Do you smell something, Mr. Gelb?" Braheem asked.

Gelb stared helplessly at Braheem. His mustache was sweated over his upper lip.

"What is it you smell, Mr. Gelb?" Braheem repeated.

Gelb remained silent.

"Can't you answer me, Mr. Gelb? Perhaps we can try our little exercise with the grenade for the fourth time. Perhaps that will help you answer my question."

"For God's sake, Gilchrist," muttered Gelb. "Can't you help me?"

Braheem seized Gelb by his hair and pulled his head back so that he was looking upward, his neck flesh beneath his chin stretched taut. Then Braheem stood up and, still holding Gelb's hair, made Gelb look directly at him. "Mr. Gilchrist is not here to help you, Mr. Gelb. He's here as a witness." He tightened his grip, and Gelb winced. "I asked you what it is that you smell. And the correct answer is that you smell yourself. You lost control of yourself the last time we played our little game with the grenade, remember? You soiled yourself. How does it feel to sit in your own shit, Mr. Gelb?" Braheem muttered something in Arabic, and for a moment it appeared to Gilchrist that Braheem was about to do something violent. Instead he released Gelb's hair and turned his back on him as a matador might turn his back on a bull, showing him the contempt of complete disregard.

"What do you want from him?" Gilchrist asked Braheem.

"Right now I only want him to feel what it is like to be tied the way he's tied. That's the way he tied us, all of us. He had our wrists tied together with plastic behind our backs and made us sit in the sun until he was ready to question us. We had to sit in our own smell for two days. We slept in it. I want him to know what that is like. My grenade was a good laxative for him."

"Gilchrist, for God's sake!" shouted Gelb.

"Nobody asked you to speak," said Braheem. "Nobody asked you to say a word." He came closer to Gelb so that there was no more than a hand's breadth between their faces. "Why don't you tell Mr. Gilchrist what you told me? Tell him that it was you who wanted to wipe my village from the face of Palestine. It was you who had Sharif and his brother killed. Tell him, or I'll put this little bomb under your chin again." He started to lodge the grenade again as Gelb began to retch.

"Yes, yes, yes," Gelb coughed, turning his head from side to side.

"That's enough, Braheem," said Gilchrist.

"Did you hear him, Mr. Gilchrist?"

"Yes, I heard."

Braheem took a step back and wiped his palm on the side of his trousers.

"I want you to write his confession, Mr. Gilchrist. I want the world to know him for what he is."

"That's something to talk about tomorrow, Braheem. Right now we have to decide what we're going to do before there's bloodshed. There's a Washington detective out there who trusts me to give this a peaceful ending, and he's going to call on that telephone in a few minutes to find out what's been decided. And Gelb's security force is out there too, and they'd like nothing better than to have a chance to make sure that you never live to see tomorrow. So we don't have much time."

"If they attack me, I will take Gelb with me."

"Is that what you want? Is that what you want me to say when the phone rings?"

"That is something between Gelb and what I feel for my country, Mr. Gilchrist."

"Listen, Braheem. Nobody's been injured yet, really injured. You've made your case against Gelb, and I'm a witness to that. You know you can trust me. You know that, don't you?"

Braheem waited and then nodded.

"Then I think you should let me tell Cobb when he calls that this standoff is over. I'll tell him that you've agreed to come out with me. Unarmed. You're going to face charges, but so far nobody's been killed. But we have to get out of this house. I'll make sure that your whole story, the true story, is out there for anyone who reads my column. That's really what you want, isn't it?"

Braheem listened carefully and nodded again.

"I promise that I'll do that for you, Braheem, but you have to listen to what I'm telling you now. We don't have much time."

"You promise that, Mr. Gilchrist?"

"I promise."

"If you write this Gelb's confession to me in your column, everybody in the world will understand. In the United States people listen to the truth, and everybody in the world listens to the United States."

Braheem's black-and-white view of what constituted a perception of justice in the United States and abroad almost brought a cynical smile to Gilchrist's lips, but he resisted it. He knew that the telephone would ring any minute, and he needed a plan.

39

AT THIS POINT in his retelling, Gilchrist pauses and looks across the table at Raya, who has not interrupted him and is reliving his story in her own present tense. He wants to tell her that he doesn't understand, even in retrospect, what more Braheem wanted except to confront Gelb and to have him for a time at his complete mercy. But the more he talked with Braheem, the more he realized that he was dealing with a total amateur and not a terrorist or assassin in any sense of either word. Braheem had really thought no further than gaining entry into Ruby's house and somehow capturing Gelb and making him admit his crimes. When Gilchrist asked him how he planned to escape, he heard Braheem tell him that this would take care of itself at the right time. Gilchrist did not ask the question again. On another track he tried, as a way of keeping Braheem rational and controlled, not to let Braheem's attention return to Gelb. Gilchrist knew it would be only a matter of time before Braheem's long-suppressed rage became a fury that would drive him to kill Gelb even as he sat bound in his chair. Braheem was like a cat toying with a mouse. But toying was by nature a temporary pleasure, and in the long run there could be only one outcome. Gilchrist now tells Raya that he did everything he could to convince Braheem to surrender while it was still possible. He does not tell her that at one point he almost wanted Braheem to complete the final act of his hatred so that Gelb could die as helplessly as Sharif Tabry died. The reciprocal justice of such an ending momentarily appealed to Gilchrist, but something in him counteracted this instinct. Whatever that something was told him that he would be an accomplice in Gelb's murder if he did not attempt to deter Braheem from committing it. If he failed and Braheem killed Gelb regardless, then at least he would not reproach himself for not having tried to intervene.

Slowly, he explains to Raya, his logic with Braheem became more persuasive. Finally, Braheem called Gilchrist aside so that Gelb could not overhear him and made Gilchrist swear that he would do what he promised he would do—that he would use his newspaper columns to expose Gelb for what Braheem knew him to be. Gilchrist promised to report the facts as he knew them to be. Satisfied, Braheem nodded and said he would give himself up and leave the house with him.

"What will we do with him?" asked Braheem, gesturing at Gelb as if he were now irrelevant.

"Are you just going to leave me here like this, Gilchrist?" Gelb asked.

At that moment the phone rang. Gilchrist answered it immediately and told Cobb that Braheem was willing to surrender. Cobb, after conferring with the Israeli security officer, said that the ambassador had to be released first. Then Gilchrist and Braheem should come out together.

"By rights," said Gilchrist to Gelb after putting the phone aside, "I should have let Braheem have his way with you. You deserve it." At that moment Gilchrist saw Gelb through Braheem's eyes, saw him as the man who killed or had ordered the killing of Sharif Tabry and humiliated and abused Raya. Facing Gelb, Gilchrist felt his anger harden like a fist in his chest. He waited until Gelb's eyes met his. "You killed my best friend, Gelb. You did it."

"There was nothing personal about it. He was simply one of the enemy. All I did was follow orders. The Tabry brothers and their village meant nothing to me. I was doing what I was ordered to do."

"Who gave the orders?"

"Orders are orders. Who cares who gave them?"

"You were following your own orders, you bastard. You made the policy. You had Tab killed, and it happened right here in Washington, right here. That what burns in my throat." Gilchrist was almost shouting. "Now that you're sitting in your own shit, your arrogance and your public relations and your stooges don't do you much good, do they?"

"I do whatever's needed to protect my country. I had to do what I did."

"You're a liar!"

"I did it for the good of my country, and I would do it again! Tabry was a dangerous man!"

Gilchrist started to reach for Gelb before he realized what he was doing. His hands were shaking, and he could feel the sweat running down his spine.

"Very brave of you, Gilchrist, to choke a defenseless man."

"You have got to be lucky, Gelb." He waited until he was calmer and said, "You're going to pay for the murder of Sharif Tabry."

Gilchrist felt just as he did when he had his tiff with Gregg F. Shilling. It was as if his momentary loss of control was a betrayal of himself, as if he had handed a kind of victory to Gelb that Gelb himself could not have gained in any other way. No, he told himself, that was not the way to fight. It could not be a victory of force or sarcasm or venom. It had to be, as Sharif Tabry had long ago realized and sought, a victory of intellect. Anything else was worthless.

"I'll save my best punches for the newspaper, Gelb. I'm going to lay out your whole record. I'll let that speak for itself and show what you really are." He turned to Braheem. "Untie him. Let's get him and ourselves out of here."

"There is such a thing as immunity, Gilchrist," said Gelb as Braheem freed him.

"For murder?"

"For whatever you accuse me of."

"We'll see."

Gelb preceded Gilchrist and Braheem down the stairway to the foyer.

"You go first, Gelb. That's the agreement."

Without another word Gelb left.

"If it weren't for you, Mr. Gilchrist," said Braheem, "I might have killed him."

"I know that."

"But I wanted you to hear what he admitted to me. You are a man that people listen to."

"I'll do my best." He noticed that Braheem still had the grenade in his hand. "What about that?"

"What?"

"The grenade."

"It is nothing. The man I work with kept it as a souvenir from his time in the war." He held the grenade up for Gilchrist to inspect it. "It is hollow. See?"

"You'd better give it to me. I don't want anyone out there to think the wrong thoughts. What about the handgun?"

"It is real. Fully loaded."

"You'd better give that to me too."

Braheem handed both the grenade and the handgun to Gilchrist and said, "I am your prisoner, Mr. Gilchrist."

Gilchrist slipped the handgun into his coat pocket and set the grenade on a reception table beside the front door.

"I never asked you how you found Gelb, Braheem. How did you know he was here in McLean?"

"I followed him from his embassy. He was with a woman. She brought him here."

40

WHAT HAPPENED after that remains a blur for Gilchrist. His retelling of it to Raya becomes almost haphazard, as if he is piecing the story together as he goes simply in order to convince himself that what happened happened. He tells Raya that he and Braheem waited for several moments after Gelb left the house and then started walking abreast toward Cobb and others waiting at the curb . . .

It was a single shot. When Gilchrist looked to his right, Braheem was no longer beside him but falling backward into a sprawl, his hands outspread. The bullet had struck him just above his right eye, and the force of it not only drove him back but almost turned him around.

Gilchrist stood paralyzed. He could see Cobb and several other policemen running up the path toward him, and he heard Cobb shouting, "My orders were that no one should fire, God damn it, no one! Who fired that shot?"

"It wasn't one of Cobb's men," Gilchrist tells Raya. "Cobb told me later that Gelb told one his security men, a sniper, that the Palestinian had to be killed. Cobb said he should have anticipated something like that. It never occurred to him that letting Gelb leave the house first would give him the opportunity to issue an order like that, but it did."

"Are you going to blame yourself for that?" asks Raya.

"I should have guessed. I'm not a babe in the woods. I should have known what Gelb was capable of." He pauses, shaking his head from side to side as if in disbelief. "Afterward Gelb's security team took him back into the house with Ruby, and Cobb and the DC police took charge of Braheem's body. The press was everywhere. I wasn't in the mood to answer anything, and I didn't. Cobb drove me later to his office, and we spent the rest of the night reliving what happened. Then he drove me back here. He's mad as hell at Gelb and his crowd. He thinks they used him and double-crossed him. He said it would be hard to prosecute anybody because of some kind of embassy exemptions and also because of politics. Then he thanked me for trying to save the situation. The last thing he did was to apologize to me, but I told him it wasn't his fault."

Raya stands. Her hands are still folded at lap level. "You did your best."

"Not good enough, I'm afraid. What did you hear on television? What did Gelb say?"

"They said they would broadcast it again at eight. I'll turn it on now. From what I remember, Gelb said just the opposite of what you told me."

"I'd like to hear it."

Raya switches on the television set. All that appears is a commercial for laundry soap. When it ends, the screen is filled with a wide-angle shot of Ruby's house with a brief voice-over account of what happened. The scene shifts abruptly to a full-face shot of Gelb. He speaks into a hand microphone being held in front of him by a reporter. Ruby is standing beside him. "I would like to thank the Washington police. They conducted themselves in the most professional manner possible under these dire circumstances. On behalf of my government I would like to express my deepest appreciation to them. But particular thanks are due to Mr. Dodge Gilchrist. Mr. Gilchrist, because of his adamant opposition to urban terrorism and because of his long-standing friendship with my host, Ms. Ruby Levenson, foiled this attack on my person, on the person of an Israeli official. He volunteered to serve as a negotiator. He successfully persuaded the terrorist who was holding me hostage to release me. Then when he emerged with the terrorist by his side, we were able to take action without endangering the life of Mr. Gilchrist or any others at the scene. At great risk to himself, Mr. Gilchrist created the opportunity for my embassy's security police to act. With terrorists, as you well know, there can be no negotiations and no quarter given. Sometimes these people wire their very bodies with bombs, explosives, or other devices. But Mr. Gilchrist's great courage in this situation is an example of how to bring terrorism to the end that it deserves. Mr. Gilchrist has proved himself a true friend of my country as well as a true American. This concludes my statement. Thank you."

"Turn it off," snaps Gilchrist.

"He made it sound as if all you wanted to do was to save him," says Raya as she turns the set off.

"Exactly."

"But that's not true."

"It's my version against his, Raya. And he was smart enough to get his story out first." Gilchrist stands and walks into the kitchen. "It's the perfect way to discredit me. Pretty ingenious, really."

"What will you do?"

"Something. I'll do something. I just have to think of what."

Gilchrist tries to mask his frustration and fury from Raya. What Gelb said on television strikes him as being almost flawless in its ingenuity. No matter how he tries to think his way out of the trap that Gelb has set for him, he can find no outlet, no way of squelching the implications of Gelb's public version of what happened in McLean and why, no refutation that would show instantly what was fact and what was fiction. No wonder Gelb wanted Braheem shot. Braheem's survival would have contradicted everything. Gilchrist sags into his reading chair. His elbow strikes something metallic in his right coat pocket, and his forearm zings with an instant numbness. He rubs the crazy-bone sting with his left palm until the numbness lessens. It is while he is doing this that he realizes that what his elbow hit was Braheem's handgun. He had completely forgotten about it.

"You should get some sleep, Dodge," says Raya.

They are both startled when the telephone rings. After the third ring, Raya asks Gilchrist with her eyes if she should answer it. Gilchrist shakes his head. After the eighth ring Raya picks up the receiver and offers it to Gilchrist, who rejects it. Raya then holds it to her ear. She says hello and listens. Then, placing her hand over the speaker's outlet, she hands it to Gilchrist and says, "It's a woman's voice. She is asking for you."

"Hello, this is Gilchrist."

"It's Ruby, Gil."

"Yes, Ruby."

"Gil, I just can't believe any of this. It's a total nightmare."

"I think that's as good a description as any."

"How are you?"

"I'm all right."

"I can't tell you how much I appreciate what you did. God only knows what would have happened if you hadn't gone in to meet with that man."

"Where's Gelb?"

"He's being checked out by the doctor just in case, but I'm sure he's grateful as well. He told me everything that happened, how you acted, what you said. I don't know if you heard his statement on television, but he gave you full credit for saving his life."

"I heard the statement."

"Seth meant every word of it."

"I didn't do it for him, Ruby."

"I don't know what you mean."

"I meant exactly what I said. I didn't do it for his sake."

"For whose sake then?"

"That's a private matter."

There is a long silence before Ruby says, "Don't you want to tell me, Gil?" Another silence. "You did it for me, didn't you? Is that what you mean?"

The question leaves Gilchrist speechless. Ruby's misinterpretation is one he never thought possible. Now he sees that her version of his motives has only compounded the distortion that Gelb's televised statement created for him.

"Good-bye, Ruby. There's nothing more to say."

"Good-bye, Gil." She waits and adds, "You'll never how much this means to me."

Gilchrist almost laughs as he replaces the phone. The absurdity of the entire turn of events becomes more and more preposterous yet more irrefutable.

"Please try to get some sleep, Dodge," says Raya. "If anybody else calls, I'll say you're not here."

"I'll try. If the phone rings, let it ring or just disconnect the damn thing."

Once he is lying down he thinks of Braheem and begins to understand how the man's history compelled him to do what he did, regardless of the consequences. Here was someone on the receiving end of repressive policies of which Gelb was the author, whose sister had been driven to suicide in prison, whose political leaders and fellow villagers had been either assassinated or evicted, and who had lived for years before his exile with grievances he had no way to redress. Vengeance had grown within him like a tumor, and then, when the opportunity arose that gave him a chance to do something, he acted. For those few hours when Gelb was his prisoner, he and Gelb were equals, and he had the lascivious pleasure of hearing Gelb confess and then saw his former oppressor so loosened by the fear of what the grenade might do to him that he lost control of his bowels. But it was not Braheem's amateurishness or ineptitude in controlling a position of sudden mastery that undid him. Gilchrist concludes that Braheem was not a trained tyrannizer in the way that Gelb was. Braheem was not an expert in anything except the art of endurance. When he confronted the very man who had forced him to become proficient on demand in the art of abuse, he found himself wanting. Having Gelb at his mercy seemed too inadequate a victory. Justice was really what Braheem wanted, justice for himself and for many just like him. At least, Gilchrist muses, Braheem did savor a brief taste of that. But he paid for the moment with his life.

Gilchrist cannot help but feel that continuing Braheem's and Tabry's struggle is now his duty. But how? He remembers Tabry's having once told him that he had all his life resisted what would turn him into a mere reactionary or bring him to the point of violence as a substitute for patient resistance. "A victory by force is no victory," Tabry had said to him. "But a victory of intellect, yes, that is a true victory."

That's the last thing he thinks about before he sleeps.

41

"DODGE," RAYA WHISPERS. "Are you asleep?"

Gilchrist opens his eyes. Raya is leaning over him.

"I didn't know if you were asleep or just resting. That detective is here. I told him that you were too tired to see him, but he said it was important."

"Cobb?"

"I don't know his name, but he said he was the same man you've seen before."

Gilchrist swings his legs to the floor, rubs his eyes, smoothes his hair, stands, and walks into the living room. Cobb is standing by the porch window.

"Sorry to bother you, Mr. Gilchrist."

"It's all right. I drifted off, but it wasn't a deep sleep. What's up?"

Cobb takes a few steps toward Gilchrist and asks, "I suppose you heard Gelb give you credit for saving his life."

"The television statement? Yes, I heard it." Gilchrist keeps looking into Cobb's eyes to see if he has an ally here or just a Washington detective who is curious.

"I heard it myself," says Cobb.

"And?"

Cobb nods his head in Raya's direction as if to suggest to her that he wants to speak to Gilchrist alone.

After Raya has returned to the bedroom and closed the door, Cobb says, "I heard everything that Gelb said, and it's a frigging lie."

Gilchrist is taken aback by Cobb's sudden frankness. He waits for something more, but Cobb simply repeats what he has just said.

"What makes you say that?" asks Gilchrist.

"Because I know differently."

"How do you know?"

"I heard differently."

"Heard?"

"The telephone. Remember the call I made to the house before you came out? I don't know if you did it on purpose or not, but you never ended the call, never cut the connection. I heard everything that was said by you and Gelb until the end. It's all recorded."

"I didn't leave the line open on purpose, Cobb. I guess I just forgot."

"Can we talk about it? I think it's really important."

"Have a seat."

They sit opposite one another.

"How much did you hear?" asks Gilchrist.

"The whole nine yards. I heard you talking to Gelb and to the man who was shot. I heard you mention your friend, Sharif Tabry. Wasn't that his name?"

"Sharif Tabry. That's right."

"When he died in that house fire in Georgetown, I gave you a bit of a hard time, Mr. Gilchrist."

"Call me Dodge."

Cobb smiles and nods. "Okay, call me Marty then." He pauses. "I went back over the files of that case this morning. Gelb's statement on television made me want to give it a second look. I was a Marine like you, Dodge. And one thing that the Marine Corps teaches you is how to spot a sea lawyer when you see one. And this Gelb is the sea lawyer of all sea lawyers. So I looked at the file. The doctor's statement was that the contusion on the side of Tabry's was probably caused by a blow because there was no sign that a falling beam or piece of plaster did it. In other words, nothing fell on him, and he didn't run into anything since he was still on the couch."

"How could you be sure?"

"A good coroner can tell, and my coroner is the best in the business. A blow from a club or the butt of an automatic creates a distinctive wound. It's not like anything else."

"What's your conclusion?"

"Someone hit him. The rest was a setup—the cigar, the booze. I checked it out with half the faculty at Georgetown and some of Tabry's students at the time. They all told me that they never saw Tabry smoke, and nobody ever saw him drink anything stronger than ginger ale."

"Where do we go from here?"

"I've already gone, but I have to say that the evidence is too flimsy for a case. It would make a good newspaper story, but we couldn't build a case on character witnesses alone. And we'd have no one specific to accuse. We could never pin it on Gelb. That's one clever son of a bitch."

"Sharif Tabry could have told you that a long time ago."

"A long time ago I wouldn't have paid any attention to the whole question. The goings on in Tabry's country could have been happening on the moon for all I cared. But now I think I'm starting to have a better grasp of the situation, and from what I see it seems that Uncle Sam is picking up the tab for what the Israelis are doing over there." Cobb puts a detective's emphasis on his statement as if to underline its importance to him. "What I'm getting at, Dodge, is that I'd like to work with you anytime you think I can help. I don't know how much help I would be, but it would let me feel that I was on the right side of things."

"It might make life a little difficult for you, Marty."

Cobb stands up, as does Gilchrist, and they walk to the door.

"By the way, Dodge, I think it might be a good idea if you gave me the handgun that you have in your coat pocket."

Gilchrist puts his hand in the pocket, lifts out the pistol, and hands it to Cobb. "How did you know?"

"I knew from what I overheard on the telephone that the deceased had one, but we didn't find the piece on him. But regardless of that, I've been around firearms long enough to recognize the outline of a handgun in a man's coat pocket when I see it."

Cobb examines the pistol, expertly removes the bullets, and tucks it inside his belt.

"What were you going to do with it?" asks Cobb. "Blow Gelb's head off? That would force me to book you on homicide, Dodge, and frankly you're not the type."

"To tell the truth, Marty, I don't know why I kept it. I wasn't thinking. Sometimes you reach a point where you're not thinking, where you don't want to think."

"I try to make it a practice never to reach that point, and you should do the same, regardless of your friendship with Tabry and regardless of what happened last night." He waits to see if his remarks have made an impression on Gilchrist before he goes on. "One thing that puzzles me is why you're so involved in this Palestine business. I've checked you out. You're from good old American stock back to the Pilgrims. Why did you get hooked up with Tabry and what his country's going through? You didn't have any reason, any blood reason, I mean."

"Through Tab at first. Then through his niece, the one who let you in. But the reasons go beyond that now."

"You married his niece a few weeks back. I checked that out too."

"That's only a part of it. I went to Tab's village on the West Bank a few weeks ago, and I saw what was happening to those people with my own eyes, and that's when I started to *feel* what was happening. It changed me."

"Do you think that's why Gelb tried to paint you as such a good friend of his and his country when he spoke on television? To make you look two-faced? To cut your balls off?"

"Exactly."

"He did a pretty good job. You and I know he's a liar, but all the people who heard him on TV don't know that. The phone call I've recorded will help, but he could discredit that. He could claim that he was forced to say what he said."

"He's already *discredited* me with what he said on television."

"You still have your column, Dodge. Use it. Let the facts speak for themselves. I'll even volunteer to let you quote me about what I heard on the phone."

"Would you really want to do that?"

"Why not? Gelb undercut me last night, too. He executed my prisoner. I've got some paying back to do." He pauses by the door. "Can I use your phone, Dodge, to call the station? I had my driver bring me here, but I told him not to wait. I didn't know how long we would be. Now I have to go back to McLean to do a follow-up with Gelb to complete my report."

"Would you like to use my car? It's parked in front downstairs."

Cobb weighs the offer for a moment, then says, "It would help. I want to leave this handgun at my office and do a few other things before I see Gelb."

"Go ahead, take it. Here's the key. It's the Benz coupe."

"I'll have my driver bring the car back this afternoon."

"You're a breath of fresh air, Marty. For a while nothing seemed to be turning out the way it was supposed to turn out."

"You can count on me, Dodge. Just call on me when you want to start. *Semper Fi.*"

42

RAYA HAS changed into a white blouse and navy-blue skirt. "Did he come with good or bad news, the detective?"

"Both. If I decide to write about this whole business, he said he would be willing to help me." He pauses. "I don't think he realizes what he is getting into. It's brave of him to volunteer, but I'm not going to put him in that position. He has too much to lose."

The sunlight inches into the apartment like a slowly encroaching tide on a beach. Gilchrist is studying the sunlight's patterns on the floor and does not hear the telephone ring.

Raya answers the phone. "Hello," she says and then is silent for several minutes, listening.

"Who is it, Raya?"

She continues to listen. Her expression changes from one of attention to one of apprehension and then one of fear. Slowly, she puts down the receiver.

"Who was it, Raya?"

"I don't know."

"What's wrong?"

"It was a man, Dodge. He spoke to me in Arabic."

"What did he say?"

"He said it was you who betrayed Braheem last night. He said it was you who made it possible for him to be shot. He said you would pay for it."

Gilchrist takes in every word but says nothing.

"Dodge," Raya pleads, "you have to find some way to prove that Gelb lied about you. You have to. You have enemies pretending to be your friends, and you have friends turning against you. It's not right."

Gilchrist remembers how Braheem's brother Nadeem laughed a single staccato laugh when they returned from their visit to Tabry's village.

It was a laugh that said that nothing was right but simply so, and there was no way to reverse that. That laugh now seems a perfect match for Gilchrist's mood, and he laughs as Nadeem laughed.

Raya watches him but says nothing.

"You know, Raya," says Gilchrist, "it's like a spectacular joke. The people I want to defend think I've sacrificed one of their own, and the government I oppose makes me out as their defender and ally. What am I left with?"

"The truth."

He looks at her and smiles, but it is a cynical smile.

"You know the truth, Dodge," Raya continues. "You know it, and there are people who will believe you."

"It won't be easy."

"But there is no other way."

"I wish I could promise you a rose garden, Raya."

"A rose garden?"

"It's a saying here. It has a good meaning."

He wants to tell her something reassuring, but nothing comes to him. Instead, he walks to her, embraces her, and kisses her. After they separate he has the feeling that he is standing at his full height, as if the floor of the apartment is the earth itself, as if the spirit of the ultimate justice that he has taken for granted all his life is alive within him like an Alamo of no further retreat.

"The only thing I'm afraid of, Raya, is that all this puts you in danger."

"As long as we're together, I don't care. I'm not afraid of whatever might happen."

"Every day will be a risk."

"Dodge," she says, "in my country there are men who go to work every day or go out on the sea in small boats to fish, and they don't know if they will be shot or beaten by settlers or if their boats will be taken from them, but they do what they must because it is their life. And their wives wait for them. I've watched them wait. And I know that it takes as much courage for those women to wait as it takes for the men to go out. If you have the courage to go out like that, then I'll find the courage to wait. But if I need to help, I'm ready. We can work together the way we did."

"I don't know if I can be as good as you make me out to be, Raya. It's been getting harder and harder for me to write. The words don't come so easily now. But the words that do come are better now. It's as if my whole life is in every word."

What he cannot tell her is that he is not unnerved by the challenges he now faces. He feels absolutely equal to whatever he must do. He remembers a time when he believed in ultimate victories, ultimate defeats. Now he sees that there is only the struggle for what must be struggled for, day after day after day. The life will be in the struggle, regardless of the consequences. He knows that the Gelbs of this world will not vanish, that the sufferers will go on suffering, and that he will suffer with them. He also knows that the drama of each day will be so consuming that he will never be distracted by nostalgia or presumption. He will just pit himself against what needs to be done and do it. But this conviction is tempered by the fact that something vicious or unintended or accidental could occur at any time, which tells him that his life with Raya can never be dearer or more dangerously and deeply theirs than it is right now.

"Do you see what's ahead of us, Raya?"

"Yes," she says and stands close to him. He puts his arms around her.

Gilchrist knows that the day to come may be, like the night he has just lived through, a permanent blend of life and death, of joy and danger, but this does not disturb him. Holding Raya in his arms, he understands as he has never before understood that his life and hers have reached the point of decision, and that this means wanting the present moment to go on forever while simultaneously knowing that it cannot.

It is a matter of hours before he will hear of Cobb's having been shot at the wheel of his Mercedes near Dupont Circle. It will be days before he will conclude that the identity of the murderer or murderers is less important than the certainty that he, Dodge Gilchrist, was the intended target. These things are part of a future that still awaits him. All he does know is that his life, despite the dangers and uncertainties, has become a life in full. His history now appears to have been nothing but a way of playing with life where he could choose whatever he wanted to do. Now there is only the ongoing present in a choice where any alternative would be a betrayal.

If Gilchrist himself were telling this story, he would, even though he knew it was impossible, stop here.